TIM

DEFENDER OF THE EARTH

D1434470

www.kidsatrandomhouse.co.uk

46070

www.**timdefenderoftheearth**.com

Also by Sam Enthoven:

THE BLACK TATTOO

'Sam Enthoven's clearly loving telling this story and his
energy creeps into the words on every page'
Philip Ardagh Guardian

www.**theblacktattoo**.com

T I M

DEFENDER OF THE EARTH

SAM ENTHOVEN

CORGI BOOKS

TIM, DEFENDER OF THE EARTH
A CORGI BOOK Paperback 978 0 552 55359 9
First Published in Great Britain by Doubleday,
an imprint of Random House Children's Books
A Random House Group Company

Doubleday edition published 2008
Corgi edition published 2009

1 3 5 7 9 10 8 6 4 2

The Random House Group Limited makes every effort to ensure that the
papers used in its books are made from trees that have been legally sourced
from well-managed and credibly certified forests. Our paper procurement policy
can be found at: www.randomhouse.co.uk/paper.htm

RANDOM HOUSE CHILDREN'S BOOKS
61–63 Uxbridge Road, London W5 5SA

www.**kids**at**randomhouse**.co.uk
www.**rbooks**.co.uk

Addresses for companies within The Random House Group Limited can be
found at: www.randomhouse.co.uk/offices.htm

THE RANDOM HOUSE GROUP Limited Reg. No. 954009

A CIP catalogue record for this book is available from the British Library.

Printed and bound in the UK by CPI Bookmarque,Croydon,CR0 4TD

To Gamera, Godzilla, Kong and the rest,
with love and bellowing.

SECRETS

London. Admiralty Arch. Within sight of Buckingham Palace. The black ministerial Mercedes turned out of Trafalgar Square and purred smoothly to a halt. The driver leapt out, opened the passenger door, and snapped to careful attention as his passenger emerged.

David Sinclair had been Britain's prime minister for less than twenty-four hours. Already he'd found something about the job that he didn't like.

'Why the hell don't I know about this already?' he asked, setting off for the Admiralty's entrance without waiting. 'Why wasn't I told about this before?'

'Because,' said Dr Alice McKinsey behind him, for what had to be the thirtieth time at least, 'it's *classified*. What you're about to see, Prime Minister,' she added, only just catching up, 'is the single most sensitive scientific project that the UK has ever been involved in. Only myself, my team, and a very select few others have the slightest idea of its existence. To keep it that way, it was decided early on that only the *most powerful person in the land* could ever be let in on the secret.'

She looked at the PM as she held the Admiralty's door for him, waiting for the flattery to work its magic. David Sinclair was the third prime minister to discover what she'd been working on all these years: she was getting used to the breed and the way they operated. Sure enough, this one seemed no different.

'I understand that, Dr McKinsey,' said Sinclair. 'There's not much you need to tell me about national security, believe me. But I was expecting . . . I don't know, key codes to our nuclear arsenal, access to special bunkers in case of attack, that sort of thing – not what you've been telling me. I mean,' he added, his voice rising again, 'it's fantastic! You couldn't make it up!'

'One moment, Prime Minister,' said Dr McKinsey. By now they had reached the life-size portrait of Winston Churchill that stood at the end of one of Admiralty Arch's echoing passageways. Long years of habit made her check her surroundings before she touched a certain spot on the picture's ornate gold frame.

'Identify yourself, please,' said a voice from Churchill's mouth, making Mr Sinclair flinch.

Dr McKinsey leaned towards the painting. 'Dr Alice McKinsey plus one. Password: Leviathan.'

'Voice pattern accepted,' Churchill announced. 'Password verified. Stand by . . .'

Titanium bolts slid back in their sheaths with a sound like distant thunder. The painting swung forward to reveal a small room behind it, luxuriantly upholstered in comfortable-looking old red leather with thick pile carpet underfoot.

'Shall we?' asked Dr McKinsey.

'After you,' said Mr Sinclair.

Dr McKinsey pressed a button on the brass panel on the wall. Churchill's portrait – now revealed as the front of a thirty-centimetre-thick door of what looked like solid steel – swung back into place. Then the lift began its descent.

'How long has this project of yours been going on?' asked

Mr Sinclair. The acceleration was smooth, but he could feel they were travelling at high speed.

'It was Stalin who gave Churchill the idea originally,' said Dr McKinsey, glad of the rare chance to explain the history of her life's work. 'In 1926 a group of Russia's top scientists were assigned to the task of producing a kind of "super-soldier", bred and trained from birth to be incredibly strong, insensitive to pain, indifferent to what they ate – in other words, *invincible*. Imagine it, Prime Minister,' she went on, her eyes lighting up as she warmed to her theme, 'an entire army capable of marching for days on only the most minimal of supplies. Soldiers who could fight tirelessly and unstoppably without pain or fatigue. That was the original basis for our programme.' She smiled.

'So . . . this creature,' said Mr Sinclair. 'Are you saying it was once . . . a man?'

'No, no,' said Dr McKinsey. 'Stalin's scientists experimented directly on living humans and animals, but since I came on board, we've never attempted anything like that here. What we've done instead is directly manipulate DNA – the building blocks of life – to create something completely new: a creature *based* on living, or once-living, things but that is in fact *entirely different*. Up until sixty-five million years ago, dinosaurs walked the earth. But while the superficial re-semblance is definitely there, nothing like what you're about to see has *ever existed before*.'

'Indeed,' said Mr Sinclair with a thin smile. He was perfectly certain that what Dr McKinsey was talking about couldn't be even a quarter as impressive as she was making it out to be. Whatever trick she'd managed to pull on previous

PMs to make them carry on providing such massive amounts of funding for her ludicrous scheme, it wasn't going to work on him.

But Dr McKinsey, for her part, had seen similar thoughts go through the minds of two of Mr Sinclair's predecessors. She knew that the prime minister's air of cynicism would vanish once he saw what she'd brought him here to see, so she wasn't worried – not yet.

Seventy storeys below the centre of London, the lift slowed smoothly to a halt. The door opened, and Dr McKinsey watched Mr Sinclair's expression carefully as he took in the scene beyond.

They were in a laboratory. It wasn't the biggest laboratory in the world, but it was a decent size – six rows of long worktops filled with computers and equipment. Eighteen technicians stopped what they were doing and stood up – white coats rustling – to look in the prime minister's direction.

But he wasn't looking at them.

Mr Sinclair's mouth had fallen open. Like a zombie, he shuffled forward straight past the lab and its contents while Dr McKinsey and her teams exchanged knowing smiles. When at last the prime minister reached the thirty-metre-long strip of reinforced glass that was the laboratory's far wall, he stopped and stood there, gaping at what lay outside it.

'It's . . .' he said finally, turning to Dr McKinsey and pointing at it. 'It's a monster. A *giant monster*. Here, under London.'

'That would be one way to describe him, yes,' Dr McKinsey answered. 'But we call him something else. Prime Minster,' she went on. 'allow me to present the Tyrannosaur: Improved Model. Tim for short.'

Mr Sinclair just stared. What he was seeing seemed to stop at his eyeballs and go no further: his brain simply couldn't take it in.

Beyond the glass lay a vast concrete chamber. The observation window where Dr McKinsey and the PM stood was about halfway up one of the smaller sides: the sheer drop into the colossal space outside the window was dizzying by itself. But the creature the chamber had been constructed to contain took up a full third of its volume.

It was a dinosaur – or it looked that way to Mr Sinclair's eyes. The creature's skin was grey-green and scaly; it had two hind legs, each one the size of a battleship, and a long and muscular tail. Its shoulders were surprisingly broad and powerful-looking; arms the girth of redwood trees led to huge hands with curving claws. The creature's head alone, with its elongated jaws full of stalagmite-like teeth, was bigger than any living thing the prime minister had seen before this moment. A ridge of short bony plates led up along the creature's tail and spine, culminating finally in a small lump on its bony forehead, a little above its eyes. The giant was lying on its side. Its eyes were closed. Its legs were drawn up; its arms were crossed on its chest; its sides heaved in and out colossally.

Dimly, the prime minister began to be aware of how closely Dr McKinsey was watching him. He turned.

Dr McKinsey was more than seventy years old, but at that moment you would never have guessed it. Her smile was like a young girl's as she savoured the prime minister's reaction.

Mr Sinclair cleared his throat. 'It . . .' he began.

'He,' Dr McKinsey corrected gently. Her smile widened.

Mr Sinclair blinked and frowned. 'He, then,' he said. 'He's . . . drugged? You keep . . . "him" – drugged like this? So he can't escape?'

'Oh no,' said Dr McKinsey. 'Tim's not drugged. He's just sleeping.'

She gestured out of the window – and just then, the enormous beast stirred. Leathery lips peeled apart, exposing more fangs. One huge clawed forelimb slashed listlessly at the air, and the sinuous tail lifted – curled – then slapped the floor. There was a distant rumble, and Mr Sinclair felt an impact tremor through the soles of his expensive shoes.

'Ah, look!' said Dr McKinsey. 'He's *dreaming* again. Isn't that sweet?'

Mr Sinclair did not reply.

'Tim first hatched back in 1995,' Dr McKinsey explained quickly, collecting herself. 'It had taken us well into the eighties to create a DNA chain that was stable enough, and to get him to the egg stage took even more work, as you can imagine – but that was the date he hatched: August 7th, 1995. And now' – she paused – 'Tim is reaching puberty.'

'Puberty,' the prime minister echoed.

'That's right,' said Dr McKinsey. 'Tim's a young teenager. He's growing extraordinarily fast: in fact, he's more than doubled in size in the last six months alone. It's not surprising that he needs a lot of rest.' She gazed fondly out of the window.

Mr Sinclair examined the face of the woman standing beside him. Dr McKinsey's smile was filled with pride. Not just pride in a job well done, either: her pride was more like . . . it wasn't, was it? It was! She looked like she felt almost *maternal* towards this creature, this leviathan slumbering below the streets of Britain's capital. And the beast had 'doubled in size in six months'! What (Mr Sinclair wondered with rising dismay) was supposed to happen in *another* six months? Or the six months after that? Was Dr McKinsey *insane*?

He swallowed. Time to get a grip on the situation.

'Am I right in thinking,' the prime minister began, 'that this . . . "Tim" is the only one of his kind?'

'That's . . . true,' said Dr McKinsey. She tried to keep her smile in place, but she could feel it slipping a little. She knew what was coming.

'So in all this time, only *one* of your . . . experiments has produced anything like the result you wanted, and this "Tim" is it. Am I correct?'

'We've never been able to replicate the original gene sequence,' Dr McKinsey answered. 'We've tried everything to simulate the exact conditions of the experiment, but . . . something's missing somehow. It's as if, that one time, something strange took place. Something extraordinary. Something *unique*. But . . .'

While Dr McKinsey was talking, Mr Sinclair turned his back to the window. The sight of the giant monster outside was putting him off, and he wanted no distractions while he made his next point. It was time to say what he'd come to say – what he'd wanted to say ever since one of his civil servants had taken him to one side and explained how, for the best part of a century, a full ten per cent of Britain's tax revenue had been siphoned off into a top secret military project.

'But all your other experiments in this direction have failed,' he put in.

'In that direction,' Dr McKinsey admitted, 'yes. We've tried thousands, possibly millions of different DNA combinations, but Tim is the only one that has resulted in a living creature.'

'I must say, Dr McKinsey,' Mr Sinclair continued, 'that's not a terribly high success rate for all these years of work – and funding,' he added with heavy emphasis.

'Tim may be the only living result of our work here, Prime Minister,' said Dr McKinsey carefully, 'but I think you'll agree, he's quite . . . impressive.'

'Indeed,' said Mr Sinclair. 'But impressive or not, in view of the costs involved, one could be forgiven for expecting something more by way of *benefits*.'

'Sir?'

'I mean, this creature of yours . . .' said Mr Sinclair. 'What does he actually *do*, apart from sleep?'

Dr McKinsey took a deep breath. 'In the course of this project we've made some staggering scientific advances, Prime Minister. Why, in the field of gene research alone, we're *far* in advance of anything the rest of the world has to offer, and—'

'Yes, yes,' the prime minister interrupted. 'But if I remember correctly, the original purpose of this programme was a *military* one. Am I right?'

'That's true, but—'

'Well?' asked the prime minister.

'We . . . haven't had a chance to test Tim in the field,' Dr McKinsey admitted. 'Frankly – as you can imagine – the security implications make that pretty difficult. It's not as if we can just take him out somewhere and put him through his paces. Not without the world noticing.'

'Quite,' said the prime minister.

'So for the last ten years – before we pursue that particular line of enquiry – we've been waiting for him to . . . mature,' said Dr McKinsey. 'At this point, we don't know what he's capable of. The potential, as you can see, is staggering. But . . .'

She took another deep breath.

'Well . . . as you may have noticed, he's beginning to out-grow our current facilities. To be honest,' she added, 'we're not sure how much longer we can keep him here. Like any youngster, Tim can sometimes become' – she paused – 'well, rather *exuberant*.'

The prime minister stared at her.

'So,' Dr McKinsey rushed on, 'if you'll only agree to the next bit of extra investment, then I think we'll be seeing some very real developments very soon. The next few years ought to be thrilling!' she added enthusiastically while wincing inwardly at the pleading in her voice.

'Dr McKinsey,' the prime minister began. 'Alice,' he added, striving for a little intimacy to soften the coming blow.

Her heart sank.

'I want to congratulate you – and the rest of your team – on everything you've achieved with this project. Really: I'm quite staggered by what you've done. It's a great shame in a way that your work has remained such a secret, because the whole of the scientific community owes you a huge amount of respect and admiration for your lifetime of selfless work.

'But I'm afraid I must be frank with you,' he went on. 'Britain can no longer afford to support you in your endeavours. I simply cannot,' Mr Sinclair said, 'in all good conscience, allow such a fantastic amount of this nation's taxpayers' money to be spent on . . . a *giant monster*. Especially,' he added darkly, 'a *teenage* one.

'I'm afraid this project can no longer be allowed to continue. I'm transferring your funding to an alternative programme. You are to close down your facility here and, naturally, ensure that all evidence of your activities is prevented from ever reaching the hands of anyone outside our shores.'

'What does that mean?' Dr McKinsey asked. 'What about Tim?'

'I'm afraid that means *destroy it*,' said the prime minister bluntly. 'Unless you can think of something else to do with your . . .' Words temporarily failed him. '*Pet*. Good night,' he added, and started walking back towards the lift.

'Wait!' said Dr McKinsey. 'Prime Minister! Wait!'

'Don't worry,' said Mr Sinclair, 'I'll show myself out.'

'But I have to ask . . .' she cried, 'what "alternative programme"? Who will our funding be going to?'

In the lift, Mr Sinclair turned. He smiled bleakly as he pressed the button on the brass panel. The doors began to slide shut.

'It's classified,' he said.

CHOSEN

The British Museum. The Great Court – the gigantic glass-roofed space at the museum's centre. On a summer's day it would have looked spectacular, with streaming shafts of sunshine making the marble floor gleam and the whole room seem to dance with light. But this was not a summer's day. The gloom from the leaden London sky above made the Great Court feel a bit like an oversized fish tank – and one that hadn't been cleaned properly at that.

'Now,' said Miss Appleby, 'has everyone got their partners? Has each pair got their clipboard? Great. I want you all to meet back here, without fail, in exactly an hour and a half's time. And *behave yourselves*. All right? See you later.'

The class scattered. In another moment, Chris Pitman and Anna Mallahide were the only ones left.

They looked at each other.

Chris Pitman was fourteen years and three months old. He was tall for his age, skinny, with black hair that had to be constantly and carefully tousled otherwise it would fall back into the neat side parting that his mum had imposed on him when he was four. His white shirt was carefully untucked, the tails sticking out under his school uniform blazer. He had two black wristbands on his right wrist and one on his left – not too many, he didn't want to look like he was trying too hard. He blinked, slowly moving his jaws in a chewing motion

11

even though he didn't actually have any chewing gum – and said nothing.

Anna Mallahide was fourteen years and one month old. Her pleated grey school skirt was regulation length – no rebellious shortening for her, she'd never seen the point. Her slightly lank mouse-brown hair was cut in a fringe across the front: deeply unstylish, but it kept it out of her glasses so what did she care?

Anna – as she'd expected – was the one holding the clipboard. She'd also expected to be the last person left as a partner: Anna was used to things like that. Chris, plainly, was not.

'So,' said Anna.

'So,' said Chris.

Chris was trying not to show it, but he felt awkward. He felt hurt – and surprised too. How come he was the one who was left to partner up with Anna Mallahide? He'd felt sure that one of the others, maybe Johnny Castle or Gwen Hadlock, would've picked him, but instead they'd just left him to be last. It had been embarrassing. He'd been made suddenly and uncomfortably aware that maybe he wasn't as much a part of the right crowd as he'd thought: maybe they didn't like him as much as he'd hoped they did. Worse yet, now with officially weird new girl Anna Mallahide as his partner, there'd be a reason for Gwen and Johnny to tease him. Chris had nothing against Anna personally, but there might be gossip; there might be speculation, no matter how little it was based on fact. Chris hated getting into any kind of situation that might make him a target like that.

The silence lengthened. Anna sighed.

'OK,' she said. 'Top of the list here' – she consulted the clipboard – 'is the Ancient Egypt section. The whole class'll be there right now, so I figure if we want to get ahead, we should answer some questions about another part of the museum – maybe the Etruscans. We deal with the Egyptians later, then we finish up early and go home.

'But first,' she added, 'before we do anything, *you're* going to have to make a choice.'

Chris just looked at her.

'Are you going to help me with this?' Anna asked. 'Or are you just going to go off and do whatever you "cool" people do and come back later to take the credit?'

Chris blinked.

'Frankly, I couldn't care less,' Anna added. 'I just want to know up front. Well?'

Chris pretended to chew gum some more while he considered this.

If he went off after Johnny and Gwen right now, he might catch up with them, dodge any possible bad associations from being partnered with Anna, and get to hang out with them instead of doing the quiz Miss Appleby had assigned.

But also – well . . . actually, he kind of liked the way Anna had said what she'd said. Maybe – just maybe – spending the next hour in her company wouldn't be as potentially embarrassing as he'd expected. He was looking at her, still considering how to answer, when—

'Fine,' Anna told him. 'See you later.' She turned on her heel and set off for the Etruscan room.

Chris found himself watching Anna's departing back. She didn't turn round – and he felt something he didn't want to admit, even to himself: he wanted to go with her. But that would mean chasing after her, and Chris didn't do things like that.

He watched Anna until she turned a corner, then, shrugging, he set off in the direction he'd last seen Johnny and Gwen heading.

Twenty minutes later he still hadn't found them. He was beginning to doubt whether he was going to.

The museum was very big, and it was filled with all kinds of *old stuff*. There were Egyptian mummies dating back seven thousand years. There were Stone Age spear points dating back *forty* thousand years – not that Chris cared about that. He gave up looking for Johnny and Gwen and started searching instead for somewhere he could sit down and listen to music until it was time to go back to the Great Court.

Chris was listless. It still smarted that he hadn't been picked for a partner – and he kept going over the conversation with Anna in his head.

Anna Mallahide had only joined the school about a month before. She was the new girl: she hadn't made any friends yet as far as he knew – people thought she was too clever, too weird. So, Chris wondered, why had she turned her back on him like that? She should have been *happy* to end up with him as a partner: that's what Chris told himself. Yet strangely, he didn't believe it.

Chris had been surprised by what Anna had said: surprised and kind of *impressed*. But before he'd even got as far as thinking about getting to know her better, he'd found he'd missed his chance. The person he'd thought he'd been stuck with had somehow managed to turn *him* down – just like everyone else had done. Alone, annoyed at everything around him, Chris kept walking without any idea of where he was going.

Then he found the strange room.

It was in the basement of the museum – he was reasonably certain of that much because he'd gone down a lot of stairs. The room was at the end of a long corridor, there was a faint smell of damp in the air, and the exhibits – from what he saw of them – all looked sort of . . . odd. There were earrings and necklaces and some very ugly little figurines: people with fins instead of arms and things like squids instead of heads, that kind of stuff – gross. The objects' labels, unlike those in the rest of the museum, were handwritten and almost impossible to read even if Chris had wanted to. But between two of the dusty glass cases was a chair. So Chris sat down, plugged in his headphones, and closed his eyes.

I don't care, he told himself.

He didn't care that nobody had picked him for a partner. He didn't care about Anna, or Johnny and Gwen, or anyone else in the school. In fact (Chris told himself), he didn't care about *anything*. Really: he was fine like this, fine by himself.

I don't care . . .

Almost immediately he felt a touch on his knee. Then someone prodded his shoulder. Startled but trying not to show it, Chris looked up.

A lady was standing over him. She was broad and thickset, with grey eyes and bristling crew-cut hair that was hennaed to an alarming colour. Her charcoal-grey uniform and badge marked her out as one of the museum guards, and – as Chris could tell from the way the loose flesh under her jaw was wobbling as she spoke – she was obviously very excited about something. But she wasn't angry. She was smiling.

Chris reached up and pulled his headphones from his ears. 'Sorry,' he said. 'What?'

'It's you!' said the lady, still grinning at him delightedly. 'I mean – you're it! After all these years! It's . . . amazing!'

'Er . . . what did you say?' asked Chris.

'Of course you don't understand,' said the lady, clasping her hands in front of her. 'How could you? You probably don't have the faintest idea what I'm talking about.'

'Well . . .' said Chris.

'But I've been waiting my *entire life* for you to come down here to me. And now . . . you're here! At last!' She beamed at him.

For a moment Chris looked up at her uncomfortably. 'Sorry,' he said again, 'I think there's been some kind of mis-understanding. I just came down here looking for a place to sit. I'm on a school trip, and I really don't think, you know, that you ought to be talking to me like this.'

'No, no,' said the lady with an impatient wave of one beefy hand. 'You're the one with the misunderstanding. The fact is, you're *exactly* the person I've been waiting for all these years. And I'm going to show you why.' She stepped smartly over to the room's doors, shut them, locked them, and put the key in her front pocket.

'Er . . . hang on,' said Chris, standing up.

'That display case beside you,' said the lady in a tone that showed she would take no argument: 'Look inside it.'

Chris looked at her and frowned.

'It's only the single most important artefact in the whole

museum,' said the lady impatiently. 'It's only going to make you realize the whole point of your life! And all I'm asking you to do right now is *look*. How hard can it be?'

'All right,' said Chris slowly. He shrugged, and turned, and gestured at the glass box to his left. 'What – this one? Why do you—?'

That was as far as he got.

When he'd first come in and sat down in the room, he'd only given the objects in the display cases a cursory glance: they were filled with more *old stuff*, just like the rest of the museum. But now, in the case beside him, something had changed.

The case was now filled with light – a glow strong enough to illuminate every speck of dust and fingerprint on the glass and cast Chris's shadow on the wall behind him: a strange, speckled, watery blue light that shivered and shone as he stood there staring at it. It was coming from one of the objects in the case – a small length of several wire-like metals plaited together into a loop: a wristband. The ends of the plaited-wire loop did not meet but ended instead in two weird cast-metal shapes: one end looked a little like the tip of a reptile's tail and the other like a long-jawed open mouth. The whole object was glimmering at him like it was electric.

He looked at the object's label, trying to make out the handwriting.

'*Found on the island of Krak*—' He tried again, squinting. '*Kraka*—'

'*Krakatoa*,' the lady finished from beside him. '*Possible remnant of a Melanesian sea cult. Estimated date of origin, 1000 BC.*' She clicked her tongue. 'Dr West always did believe in hedging his bets.'

Chris looked at her. 'Excuse me?'

'This object,' said the lady, her eyes shining with barely suppressed excitement, 'may have been *found* on Krakatoa. But that's not where it *comes from*. One second,' she added. 'I've just got to do something here.'

She reached into her pocket and pulled out another key, which she proceeded to fit into the narrow hole in the front of the display case. She twisted it until she heard a soft click. Then, to Chris's mounting surprise, she spread her strong hands with their thick fingers across the protective glass – and lifted it off!

'Hold on a second,' said Chris weakly as she set the glass cube on the floor. 'Are you sure you're really supposed to—?'

'Right,' said the lady, picking up the glowing bracelet. 'Give us your arm. Your left, please.'

Before he could stop her, she'd taken hold of his wrist. Chris felt a small shock of cold as the metal met his skin. He heard a soft but solid ratcheting *click*.

'There,' said the lady, eyes glowing with pride. 'I *knew* it.'

Chris stared at the lady. Then he stared at the extraordinary object that she'd just clamped onto his wrist.

'Look,' he said finally. 'I don't know what you're trying to tell me here. In fact, I honestly haven't understood a single thing you've said to me since you, uh, caught me in the chair there. But I should really be getting back to the rest of my class. *They'll all be looking for me*,' he added with heavy emphasis.

The lady took a deep breath and let it out again slowly. 'Fine,' she said. She walked over to the door, unlocked it and opened it, gesturing outside it at the passageway beyond. 'My work here is done. Off you go.'

'Great,' said Chris with huge relief. 'Great. Er, here: let me get this bracelet thing off for you.' With his right hand he attempted to unfasten it – without success. 'Um, could you give me a hand here? There's some kind of catch . . .'

The lady just looked at him and smiled. 'No,' she said.

'What?' said Chris distractedly. The mouth end of the bracelet thing seemed to have got hold of the tail end in an incredibly powerful grip. There didn't seem to be any way to separate them that he could see – in fact, looking at the object on his wrist, he was hard-pressed to see anything to indicate that the two ends of it ever *had* been separated.

'You have been chosen,' the red-crew-cut lady told him. 'The Earth needs her Defender once more, and you will be the channel of his power. It is your destiny: it is inescapable. And you will carry out your duty until you – or he – are dead.'

Chris had given up trying to take off the bracelet and was gaping at her openly now. The woman was clearly barking mad. He closed his mouth. It was time to take charge of the situation.

'So . . .' he said uncertainly, 'you just want to . . . give me this thing?'

The lady smiled. 'That's right.'

'You're not going to turn round and say, I don't know, like I *stole it* or something?'

'No.'

'But isn't it . . . like, *valuable*?' There. This was her last chance. After this, Chris reckoned he'd done his best.

'Young man,' said the lady, 'you may be the chosen one, but you're obviously not very bright. What you've got there' – she pointed at the bracelet on Chris's wrist (which had now stopped glowing and was rapidly becoming dull and dusty-looking again) – 'is more "valuable" than you could understand. But it's yours. It's been waiting for you – alone – to claim it, and now it belongs to you.' She paused. 'My advice to you is to get back to your class. If the time of the Defender is at hand, you've got bigger problems coming, believe me, but' – she smiled – 'there's no sense getting in trouble with your teacher if you can avoid it. All right?'

'Uh . . . sure,' said Chris weakly.

'See you around,' said the lady.

'Uh, right,' said Chris.

But the doors had slammed shut and locked again. He was standing out in the passageway alone.

THE MALLAHIDES AT HOME

Chris Pitman was an idiot. Or that's what Anna kept telling herself on her way home.

What had he been thinking, arriving last at the Great Court like that and obviously from a different direction to her? There'd been no less than five announcements made on the British Museum's PA system; the museum staff were looking apprehensive, and Miss Appleby had started talking about calling Chris's parents. Even perennial troublemakers Johnny Castle and Gwen Hadlock had arrived a good ten minutes before Chris finally showed up – and when at last he *did* actually shuffle into view, he was incredibly dim-witted about saying where he'd been. Anna had practically had to force-feed the words into his mouth about 'checking the last few answers for the quiz' – which was doubly infuriating since (as she also told herself) Anna shouldn't have cared whether Chris got into trouble or not.

Still, she thought as she turned the corner into her street, if he hadn't been with Johnny and Gwen, where had he been? And why had he kept tugging at the left sleeve of his blazer in that weird and nervous manner?

It's not your problem, Anna thought firmly, reaching for the buzzer of the discreet government-owned block of flats where she currently lived with her father. Unconsciously she smoothed her hair down at the sides before looking at the camera over the door.

'Hey, Anna,' said the voice from the speaker.

She heard a buzz, the soft *thunk* of thick bolts drawing automatically back in their sockets, and then the door swung smoothly open.

'Hi, George,' she said to the burly military man who was standing guard behind the foyer's deceptively plain pine-effect desk.

'How was school?' George asked.

'Oh, you know,' said Anna.

'Not that bad, surely!' said George.

Anna gave him a wan smile. The lift doors slid open and, still smiling politely, she was about to step inside when—

'Sorry, Anna,' said George. 'We've got to do the thing again, I'm afraid. Silly, I know, but orders are orders.'

Anna shrugged and came back to the desk. George had pressed the button. The retinal scanner had already emerged from its secret compartment on the counter, so without needing to be prompted, she bent slightly and put her right eye to the eyepiece.

'Ready?' said George. 'And . . . there. All done.'

Anna stood up straight, blinking from the sudden flash. 'Well, George?' she asked, smiling at him politely. 'Am I who I say I am?'

'Go on with you, cheeky monkey,' said George.

Trying not to show how little she liked being called that, Anna got into the lift.

Anna had lived in places like this all her life. The geographical locations varied – her father's work had taken them to all sorts of countries all over the world – but their accommodation didn't, not really. Government-run buildings

– impersonal blocks of flats built for the secure housing of important personnel and their families – were pretty much the same everywhere. Because of the nature of what her father did, he and Anna had always had to live with special security arrangements of one kind or another. It was just the way things were. Anna didn't know anything else.

Sometimes she imagined what it was like for other people – growing up with the same surroundings all the time, making friends with the expectation that you'd know them for a while rather than being constantly aware of the fact that at any moment you might have to cut yourself off again and move to another country. She thought about people like Chris Pitman and what it must be like for them. Chris was an idiot in a school full of other idiots. But at least he managed to *fit in*.

Anna grimaced: she was certainly thinking about Chris a lot, it seemed, idiot or not.

She felt bad about dismissing him in the way she had: that was the problem. She'd got so used to being the new girl in places, so used to being shunned or ignored, that the old defences had gone up and she'd sent Chris packing before she'd even given him the chance to disgrace himself. That, Anna knew, had been a bad step: she'd crossed a line there. How was she ever going to make any friends if she never gave people a chance?

Anna pursed her lips. The lift doors were opening.

Feeling in the bag for her keys, she crossed the landing to the door of their latest apartment. Some of her and her dad's stuff was still in boxes: she was most of the way through the unpacking, but even though they'd been there a couple of months already, she hadn't had time to finish it yet – and of course, her dad had been no help. He was going to be no help tonight, either. She knew exactly what she'd find when she opened the door: there would be a light winking on the answering machine with just one message showing – a message from one of the assistants telling her that her father was very sorry, but he was going to be home late again. As she'd done countless times in countless other places, Anna would put her school bag down, change out of her school uniform, then steam some vegetables in the microwave before starting her homework and another evening in, alone.

But she was wrong. The door was unlocked.

She pushed on it uncertainly. Her mind flashed on security briefings she'd received over the years about espionage, kidnapping and the other potential threats facing top-secret military scientists and their dependants. Then she told herself not to be so dramatic. There was no way that anyone could have got up here without George or someone else knowing. But the alternative was just too weird to imagine. It couldn't be . . . could it?

'Dad?' she asked.

'Anna!' said Professor Mallahide. 'You're home! Come here, let me give you a hug.'

Obediently, if a little warily, Anna did as he asked. She couldn't remember the last time he'd been home when she'd got back.

'Hey, Dad,' she said once he'd let go. 'What's going on? And what's that *smell*?' she added, wrinkling her nose.

'Oh no! The pizza!' Wildly Professor Mallahide lunged for the oven: the whole room began to fill with choking smoke when he opened the door to reveal its charred contents. 'Oh, *hell*,' he said. 'What is it with me and cooking?'

Anna sighed.

Professor Edward Mallahide was fifty-seven years old. The lines around his glittering grey-blue eyes had deepened over the years, but with his narrow shoulders, his nervous energy and the sense that his arms and legs were somehow too long for him, he seemed much younger than his age implied. Anna had come to think of him not as a proper grown-up but as something else, some strange creature that didn't operate on the same wavelength as other human beings, a high-powered mutant of some kind. He was her dad, the one person she had in the world, but he could be totally exasperating at times.

'Pizza's your favourite,' he pronounced glumly. 'And now look at it – ruined.'

Anna hadn't felt like eating pizza for a year at least, but she wasn't going to tell him that. 'I'll order in for us,' she said. 'Honestly, Dad, don't worry.'

'Fantastic idea!' said the professor, brightening instantly. 'Now – where'd that bottle go? Ah! Here we are.' Grimacing slightly, he twisted the cork free of the bottle of champagne he'd just produced from a plastic bag: *phut!* He started to pour. The glasses didn't match, and the champagne was warm because he'd failed to put it in the fridge. But Anna didn't mention these things either.

'There!' Mallahide announced triumphantly. 'A toast!'

'To what?' Anna asked.

'How about "to my darling little girl and her staggeringly talented father"?'

Again Anna tried not to grimace: she didn't like being

called what *he'd* called her either and hadn't for some time now. But they clinked glasses.

'Dad . . .' said Anna once she'd taken a polite sip. 'What's this all about?'

'What d'you mean?' he asked back. 'Can't a man drink champagne and burn his daughter's dinner once in a while?'

'It's not my birthday,' Anna pointed out. 'And it's not yours either. So—'

'Anna . . .' the professor interrupted. He took a deep breath and said: '*I've done it.*'

Anna's smile vanished, and cold fear opened a sluice in her stomach.

'Done what, Dad?' she asked as casually as she could.

'I've got permission to allow the swarm to self-replicate! At last!'

Her father beamed at her. Anna didn't beam back.

'It's all off the record, of course,' he went on, tapping his nose with one finger. 'Very hush-hush. Wouldn't want the rest of the world finding out Britain's about to break the Nanotech Non-Proliferation Treaty, eh? But I've got the nod from the prime minister himself: he's found the funding from I don't know where – some other project – and we're all set to start working towards the main experiment *tomorrow*. Isn't that great?'

He took another large swig from his glass. Anna pursed her lips.

'What did you tell them?' she asked. 'Not the *truth*, presumably?'

Mallahide paused and looked guilty. 'Well . . . no,' he

admitted. 'I did have to spin them a bit of a yarn; they'd never've agreed otherwise. Remember China?'

Anna didn't need reminding. When her father had unwisely told a colleague the full extent of where his experiments were heading, their stay there had ended very suddenly. If it wasn't for the top-secret nature of his work, he would have been all but laughed out of the country.

'Well,' said Mallahide quickly, 'that's not going to happen this time. I'm *close*, Anna.' His eyes shone with an enthusiasm Anna loved but had grown wary of. 'I'm really close; I can *feel it*.'

Anna sipped the warm champagne. 'Mmm,' she lied. 'Delicious.' Then she too took a deep breath.

'Dad,' she said, 'you do remember what you promised me – right?'

Mallahide blinked, surprised. He smiled at her once more, but the smile was less warm than before. 'Anna, really, we've been through all that—'

'*No testing on yourself*,' she reminded him firmly. 'Not until you're certain it's safe.'

'All right! All right!' Mallahide threw his hands up in mock surrender. 'But Anna . . .' He sighed. 'You know how important my work is to me.'

Anna did – all too well. It was the reason she hardly ever saw him. It was the reason she'd spent her life moving from place to place, never staying anywhere long enough to make real friends or be accepted. But she said nothing.

'If this succeeds, it's going to change the entire human race. Do you see?' Without waiting for her to answer, the professor plunged on. 'Poverty, famine and war will be things of the past. There'll be no more disease. No more pain – and no more *death*. If my nanobots can do what I believe they can do, then no one ever again will have to go through . . . what we went through.' His expression darkened. 'Nobody will have their loved ones taken away from them just because their frail human bodies gave up on them. Families will never again be split apart by stupid things like accidents, or age – or . . . or *cancer*.'

He looked up at Anna pleadingly.

'Think about it,' he said. 'If the kind of technology I can develop had been available when your mum was—'

'Don't bring Mum into it,' said Anna quietly.

'How can I not?' Mallahide asked. 'She's the whole reason I'm doing this! Not a day goes by when—'

'I know,' said Anna, annoyed. 'You don't have to tell *me*.'

'Well, now it's in my grasp,' said the professor. 'The whole human race is on the brink of the biggest single change it's ever faced. *It's really going to happen!*' he added. 'Isn't that exciting?'

Anna just took another sip of her champagne.

TIM

To a person, the cube of blue plastic was about the size of a bungalow. To Tim, it was a building block to play with: it fitted comfortably between his two front paws, and the colour made it his favourite.

He sat there in his room, with his gigantic hind legs sticking out in front of him and his tail curled up behind. For a while now the room had been too small for him to stand up straight in, so he often just sat like this for hours, gazing at the block, letting his head fill up with slow, blue thoughts. Tim stared until the colour swam in his vision and he felt like he was drifting away inside it, a cool blue world rushing past him as he sank into his trance, deeper and deeper.

What did it remind him of? Tim didn't know. He'd lived in this room his whole life. Nothing in his experience should have caused him to feel anything from the blue but a straightforward reaction to a colour he liked. But as he sat there, gazing, his head seemed to fill with something else. There at the bottom, in the blue's dark heart, something was waiting. It was calling to him.

This here is not for you, it said.
This place is not your place.
Your time is coming.
You are needed elsewhere.
Break out of your prison and—

Tim blinked and scowled. He picked up the block and hurled it away with great force: it bounced, leaving two large gouges in the concrete walls of his room, which had never happened before, so it upset Tim even further. He bared his fangs and made a noise in the back of his throat.

He'd been daydreaming again.

It had been happening more and more often lately – and Tim didn't like it. What Tim liked (he told himself) were the simple things in life. He liked eating. He liked sleeping. And the rest of the time – up until recently, at least – he'd been content to sit or lie where he was, waiting for the tiny people to bring him whatever he needed.

But now . . .

Now it was different. Suddenly, to Tim's dismay, it *wasn't enough*.

He kept having these daydreams: not just the long blue sinking dreams but others, too. Dreams of destruction and combat. Dreams that made him want to flex his new muscles, thrash his tail and stamp his great feet through the floor. The strange feelings they brought (*trample crush bite rend smash*) were disturbing enough, but where had they come from? Why wouldn't they leave him alone? What was it stirring in his blood like this when all he'd always thought he wanted was to sit and lie in peace?

His mood was broken by a sudden hiss from the ducts in the walls and ceiling of his enclosure. Agitated – fretful – Tim sniffed the air . . .

Up in the laboratory, Dr McKinsey took her finger off the release button. Her hand shook slightly and her eyes were tearing up. But she'd done what she'd been told to do. Her life's work was coming to an end. Now her beautiful monster was going to die.

Killing Tim was never going to be easy. After all, the whole object of the project had been to create an animal that was as physically tough as possible. To this end, Dr McKinsey and her technicians had worked tirelessly, using genetic material in the same way an artist might use a palette of paints, mixing and combining to get the effect they wanted. They had looked to the world around them for their source materials, learning what they could not just from reptiles but from plants, insects, marine life, mammals, birds, anything that might be combined into something that would give the military an edge. And what hybrids they had made! Had they only succeeded, the results would have been spectacular – but all had failed. All had either failed to stabilize before birth or had died soon afterwards. All but Tim.

What had happened that day when Tim had been created? Why had that particular combination worked where all the others had failed? And why had it resulted in the gigantic and magnificent beast that she saw before her now? To be honest, even after all these years, Dr McKinsey still didn't know. She felt a tremendous sense of pride whenever she looked at Tim. He was her one success in life – a single being of fantastic size and strength that she herself had created out of almost nothing. But sometimes, in her darker moments, she had doubts in her own ability. Sometimes it seemed to her that something . . . almost *mystical* had occurred.

Dr McKinsey bit her lip. Well, it didn't matter now. At that moment, Tim's enclosure was being flooded with cyanide gas. The gas was being delivered through the enclosure's air-conditioning system: it was the only way to hurt him now since nothing with less than the drilling power of an oil rig could possibly penetrate Tim's scaly hide. Supplying the poison in sufficient quantity had been a serious challenge. Dr McKinsey had seen the tankers arriving: it had taken a week for the whole shipment to be delivered, and still she was worried it wouldn't be enough.

She wiped her eyes on the sleeve of her lab coat – and watched.

Wary now, Tim sniffed again, huffing great gusts into his nostrils, then waiting as his brain slowly sifted the information. Yes: something was definitely wrong. The air had a strange kind of tang to it. It was making his insides feel weird – a tickling sensation at first, which rapidly (as he thought about it) began to turn into a biting, itching, stinging sort of feeling that Tim didn't like one bit. Tim's eyes, too, were starting to smart. He ground his scaly knuckles against the outsides of his eyelids, but that only made things worse, and when he opened his eyes again, a sort of haze seemed somehow to have filled the enclosure.

Grunting, Tim got to his feet. From force of habit, he ducked his head forward so he was standing in a kind of hunched crouch. His clawed toes tapped nervously at the concrete. His tail walloped listlessly from side to side. For another long moment he just waited in increasing discomfort, wondering what would happen next.

Then suddenly, he found he couldn't breathe.

Tim panicked. The air had stuck in his chest like a knife, as if something enormous was lodged in his throat and nothing could pass around it. Now his colossal heart was beating frantically and great shaky shivers were running down his arms and legs as if all the nerves in his body were firing instantaneously. *What was going on?* Tim didn't know. *What could he do?* Tim didn't know. The ceiling suddenly seemed to be pressing down on him with a crushing weight, and beyond the thickening haze in the air the walls looked like they were closing in. Tim wanted to scream and shout and roar, but it just wouldn't come out. He had to get away! He had to make it stop! He had to do something!

In a blind ecstasy of panic, Tim began to beat his arms at the ceiling.

CRASH! Cracks starred out in the concrete around each blow. CRASH! The whole laboratory complex shivered. The ground trembled under Dr McKinsey's shoes, and out in the enclosure great chunks of masonry fell to the floor. But Tim was oblivious. He kept on pounding again and again, the pain and breathlessness making a thin red gauze of blood seem to descend over everything he could see.

'Yes,' murmured Dr McKinsey around the knuckle she'd been biting as she watched Tim's struggle. 'Yes!' she said louder, surprised at herself. She hadn't wanted Tim to die, but she especially hadn't want him to suffer. 'Yes, Tim!' she yelled now. 'Yes! Go on, you can do it! *Go on, Tim! Get free!*'

Suddenly, shockingly, the ceiling collapsed. There was an instant of chaos, of noise and choking dust and boiling smoke.

Then nothing.

First Incursion

It had been dark now for several hours, but Trafalgar Square always had visitors. At that moment there were exactly ninety-seven people crossing the square itself: for an instant, when the first impact tremor struck, every single one just froze.

Was it an earthquake? Nobody knew.

The great paving slabs reverberated under a second great blow. This second was quickly followed by a third and then a fourth, each one seemingly more powerful than the one before. Abruptly Trafalgar Square's denizens decided they didn't need any further prompting: they fled, and within moments the square was empty. But then, as everyone realized that (bizarrely) the ground tremors seemed to be confined exclusively to the area of the square itself, people stopped. Clogging the streets, they waited to see what was going on.

Nelson's Column – the fifty-six-metre-high pillar of stone with a statue on top that stood at Trafalgar Square's centre – began to tremble. It wobbled, drifted first one way, then the other – then shattered. Several tons of granite crashed to the ground. Splashes of water from the fountains rose high into the night sky: their stone sides split, the pools emptied out over the bare paving. There were a few screams from the onlookers, but as if in answer to the echoing crash of the falling column, the shuddering blows from below ground seemed to pause, and a hush descended on the waiting crowd once more.

Suddenly, with a great *heave*, the ground seemed to bulge upwards. It stayed that way for a whole two seconds – then fell back as the crowd watched, breathless. Another great *heave* and the ground lifted again, higher this time, as paving slabs that had lain next to each other for two centuries suddenly parted to reveal black London clay beneath.

Then something emerged.

It was about the size of a large car – a limo, say. Illuminated by the square's remaining streetlights, the object's colour was dark green, almost black. It consisted of five long appendages attached to a wider plate of thick matter. The object's size made it unfamiliar: the watching crowd didn't identify it at first, not until the earth split open again and the object was joined by a second one, its counterpart. Both objects began scrabbling for purchase on the lip of the enormous hole that had now appeared at the centre of what had been one of Britain's most famous landmarks. Tim's claws found their grip. He heaved himself up . . .

Then the screaming really started.

Commander Geoffrey Draper of the British Grenadiers, currently standing guard in full dress uniform in a box just inside the gates of Buckingham Palace, had heard the noise. The echoing *booms* from the ground had travelled right up The Mall and under his boots. His heavy, hairy busby hat, worn ceremonially by grenadiers while guarding the palace, had been making his neck feel very stiff. But now he'd stopped thinking about that and reached for his radio.

'Sarge?' he asked. 'Sarge? Come in please, over.'

The radio crackled. 'What the hell d'you want, Draper? Over.'

'Sarge . . .' Draper gulped. He hadn't been a grenadier for long, and he was nervous. 'Sarge, I think we've got a problem.'

'What sort of problem?'

'There's some kind of disturbance over at Trafalgar Square,' said Draper, doing his best. He stared as hard as he could down the long avenue of trees that led to Admiralty Arch. He could hear the thin, oddly inhuman sound of distant screaming, but he couldn't see what was causing it, not yet.

'Sarge,' he said, 'I think you'd better come 'n' 'ave a look. There's . . . wait.' He paused. 'I can see something! Something's coming into view over the top of Admiralty Arch. Some sort of . . .' He paused again and gaped.

'What's that, Draper?' barked the radio. 'What did you say? Come in, Draper! Over!'

Draper could see Tim now. The great silhouette of him seemed to be growing as the monster got to his feet – getting taller and taller until it reached an impossible size, standing black against the violet of the London night sky. For a whole ten seconds the young grenadier's jaw worked up and down uselessly while the words simply failed to come out. *There's a giant monster standing in Trafalgar Square*, he wanted to say. But he couldn't. Even now, the thought of what his superior officer's reply might be stopped the words at his lips.

'Send backup,' he spluttered finally.

'What's that, Draper? You're breaking up!'

'*Send everything you've got!*' said Draper. 'NOW!'

For a long time Tim just stood there, experiencing an emotion he had never felt before. The tiny people far below him were staring up at him in terror, aghast at the simple size of him. Tim, as it happened, was feeling something similar.

All his life he had lived in a box. To Tim, the box had become something akin to the warmth and security and enclosedness that he still dimly remembered from his egg, but now – as if he'd hatched again – he was free. He was out in the open, outside in the world for the very first time. The night sky gaped around him, impossibly, immeasurably vast. He looked up at it, looked everywhere, searching for where the walls were, but he *couldn't find them*.

Tim felt the London night air on his reptilian skin and saw the horizon and how far away it was, even for him. There was a swelling sensation inside his chest; his tail began to thrash the air, and his claws opened and closed on nothing, helplessly. For a wild second he wanted to climb back underground again, back to his enclosure, but there was no going back, only this huge cold emptiness that seemed to expand around him the further he looked.

For the first time in his life Tim, huge as he was, felt small. He felt exposed, and alone, and horribly, horribly *scared*. It was scary, he decided. The whole situation was scary! Alone, helpless, he opened his mouth . . .

And he screamed.

It was an astonishing sound. It was louder than aeroplanes taking off. It was as if the hole Tim had come out of was a great mouth in the Earth and the whole planet was bellowing in terror. Some who heard it just collapsed on the spot, their legs turning to jelly underneath them. Some turned tail and fled, and were tens of metres away before they'd even realized they were running – crying and screaming themselves as the hideous sound continued on and on.

Tim screamed. The people far below him screamed. For a

long moment they stayed like that, a stalemate of fright . . .

And that was when the first helicopters arrived.

The airwaves crackled with radio transmissions. 'Dear God, look at the size of that thing! What the hell is—?'

'Cut the chatter, Eagle Two. Control, this is Eagle Leader. Target sighted. Permission to engage?'

'You can't leave a thing like that running round the centre of London, for Christ's sake! I say we drop him where he stands.'

'I'm with you, Eagle Six. Eagle Four? Eagle Three? Cover me, I'm going in!'

'Negative!' barked their leader. 'Wait for orders! Do not, repeat, do not engage until we are authorized to—'

'Target locked. FIRE!'

'FIRE!'

'FIRE AT WILL!'

ZOOSH! A volley of missiles split the night sky with their trails. The squadron of attack choppers peeled outwards as the missiles found their target and detonated to flashes and thunder.

Tim staggered. The missiles had struck him on his side, in his ribs. For a moment, the combined weight of the impacts and the explosions threatened to knock him off balance – but he wasn't wounded; mostly he was just surprised. When the onslaught finally paused, Tim turned to face the direction the attack had come from. Six rattling, clattering objects were hovering around him, all keeping a cautious distance.

ZOOSH! More missiles flew at him.

FOOM! Their explosions flowered briefly, then vanished.

But Tim was ready that time. Experimentally, he swiped at the nearest one with his right forepaw, oblivious to –

'EVASIVE! EVASIVE!'

– the screams and panic that this caused in the cockpits. The rattling thing he'd tried to grab just danced back in the air out of his reach – and the rest of them . . .

ZOOSH! FOOM! FOOM!

. . . just shot at him again with more of their irritating weapons. More rattling things were coming to join them. Tim could hear them coming from all around. Well, Tim thought, there was no other choice. He had to try to get away from them. He had to move. Almost swatting a couple of them just by accident with the resulting swing of his tail, Tim turned . . . and set off.

He leaned forward, trying to get himself up to the loping trot that was his top speed. For a moment Tim felt almost like he should have been enjoying himself: because of his fast growth this was the first chance he'd had to flex his muscles and really move in more than a year. But he was constricted. The streets were too narrow and too full of things. His giant hips barely fit between the buildings. The outer walls of Whitehall offices buckled and shattered as he passed. With each step cars were squashed flat; streetlamps were knocked to the ground; windows and concrete shivered into powder at the slightest touch of his thrashing tail. And still the clattering things kept shooting their little missiles into Tim's back.

With rising annoyance, Tim did his best to walk faster. As ever, he had no clear idea where he was going or what he was doing. But the shape of the street was forcing him in one direction: the Houses of Parliament.

NEWS FLASH

The BBC's nightly *News at Ten* broadcast was drawing to a close: apart from one tense moment when Colin McLenahan (one of its presenters) had fluffed the pronunciation of the name of an important visiting Russian dignitary, the programme had been an uneventful one. So far . . .

On set, Mr McLenahan suddenly put a hand up to his earpiece. 'And . . . I'm sorry,' he said, 'we're going to have to interrupt that item as reports are coming in of dramatic events taking place while we've been on the air. Right now, in the centre of London, it seems that . . .' He paused and frowned.

As an experienced newscaster, Mr McLenahan was used to having to maintain a calm front while chaos reigned backstage. What he was hearing in his earpiece now, however, was testing his professionalism to the limit. His face turned red. 'Look,' he said, glaring off camera, 'is this some kind of joke? What sort of idiot do you take me for? I'm not reading out *that*!'

'Er . . . *thank you*, Colin,' said Fiona Pilkington, his co-presenter, taking over smoothly. 'News is breaking as we speak of dramatic scenes in the centre of London tonight. The military has been mobilized. The West End is being evacuated, and the use of live ammunition has been authorized. Approximately fifteen minutes ago . . .' She too paused and gulped: her throat seemed to have gone suddenly dry. But the pictures were up on her monitor now. What was happening *was*, it seemed, really happening.

'Eyewitness reports all confirm that approximately fifteen

minutes ago, London came under attack from a *giant monster*. No, ladies and gentlemen: this is not a hoax. A giant monster is on the rampage in the centre of London. First sighted in Trafalgar Square, the monster is estimated to be about one hundred metres tall and similar in build to a . . .' She paused again and blinked. 'A *tyrannosaur*. The monster left Trafalgar Square in ruins and appears to be heading towards the Thames. Our BBC helicopter was scrambled as soon as the news came in.' She waited, one hand to her own earpiece. 'And . . . yes: we can now go live to our correspondent in the helicopter, Nelson Akubwe. Nelson, what's going on?'

The camera shuddered yet kept its focus on the incredible events unfolding below. Even under the heavy *whup-whup-whupp*ing of the BBC chopper's rotor blades, the excitement in the young reporter's voice was obvious.

'Thank you, Fiona. As you can see, the military have swung straight into action – in fact, we're having trouble getting any closer because they're warning us to keep back. But such is the scale of this extraordinary scene that you can easily make out what's going on even from here. Ladies and gentlemen, what you are watching is not a film: it may look like something from Hollywood or Japan, but I can definitely confirm that this *is* really happening, right now, in the heart of Britain's capital. A gigantic monster has emerged from under Trafalgar Square and is now, as I'm talking to you, making its way down Whitehall . . .'

In minutes, reports of Tim's appearance had flashed right around the globe. All over the world, via the Internet, satellites, television and radio, the news was spreading, creating astonishment wherever it went.

Watching the scene on monitors in his bunker, deep underground in an undisclosed location, Mr Sinclair was less than happy. With supreme efficiency the men and women of the Secret Service had spirited him and his family away from their home at 10 Downing Street and out to safety. So great had been their efficiency, however, that the prime minister had yet to have time to change out of his pyjamas, and the air in the Crisis Room (the top-secret nerve centre from which Britain could be run in the event of catastrophe) was, he found, decidedly chilly. From where he sat, Mr Sinclair could access most of the country's significant computer systems and all of the world's media. But nobody – neither his minions nor himself – seemed able to find the switch that controlled the air-conditioning.

'So,' said the prime minister, in a voice as cold as the room, 'it seems the good Dr McKinsey's "little secret" is now out.' He eyed his aides. 'Well? What are we going to do about it?'

Field Marshal Clement 'Clem' Thompson, commander in chief of the British army, cleared his throat. He disliked the prime minister's disrespectful tone and, frankly, he disapproved of his choice of dressing gown. But as a military man he appreciated that this probably wasn't the time to mention these things.

'Two battalions of tanks are at present en route to the area,' he said. 'Our plan, sir, is to force the creature out into the Thames, where it can do the minimum amount of damage. Then, in a combined effort with my colleagues in the navy and air force' – he nodded to the Admiral of the Fleet and the Marshal of the RAF, who were standing beside him – 'we shall drive it as far as the Thames barrier, where we are setting up a barrage of our heaviest artillery as we speak.'

'Will that work?' asked Mr Sinclair.

'It's the best chance we have,' Thompson replied. 'While air-to-air missiles and cannon fire have failed to penetrate the creature's hide so far, it's still pretty clear that he . . . er . . . doesn't like it when we shoot at him.'

'But the *big guns*,' said the prime minister, annoyed: 'are they going to be enough to kill the monster? That's what I'm asking you.'

The field marshal, the admiral, and the air marshal exchanged a look.

'We . . . don't know, sir,' Thompson admitted.

'What do you mean, you don't know?'

'Our tech boys are attempting to retrieve Dr McKinsey's data from the lab complex now,' said Thompson. 'But all the indications so far are that . . .' He paused again. 'Well, we think the monster may be immune to conventional weapons.'

'*What?*' asked Mr Sinclair with some emphasis.

'We'll, ah, see how the tank battalions get on,' said Thompson. 'But I'm afraid it . . . doesn't look good.'

The prime minister stared at him. 'Oh, brilliant,' he said slowly. 'That's absolutely brilliant. I can really see why the tax-payers spend so much money on you. All right, let me ask you something else.'

He gave his advisers a long look.

'Did it never occur to anyone else to think *before* about what might happen if this creature ever escaped?'

The silence in the Crisis Room lengthened.

'God help us!' said Mr Sinclair, throwing his hands in the air. 'God help London. God help us all.'

Meet the Monster

So far that evening Chris had managed to keep the bracelet a secret. This had mostly been achieved by wearing his longest-sleeved top and constantly pulling at the left cuff as if from some kind of nervous tic. But it had worked: all through dinner and his family's trip to the theatre his parents hadn't noticed, and now they were on their way home. They were in the car. His mum was driving. Chris's dad was safely wittering about the play they'd just seen. They were about to cross the Thames via Westminster Bridge when it all began to go horribly wrong.

First, the bracelet suddenly started glowing again, even more brightly than before at the museum. Instantly Chris stuck his hand behind his back – but not instantly enough, apparently.

'What was that?' said his father.

'What was what?' Chris tried.

'That glowing thing. The one on your wrist. The one you're trying to hide behind your back,' said his dad infuriatingly.

'What . . . this?' Chris asked as casually as he could. The bracelet's eerie greenish light seemed to glitter all around him, reflected in the windows of the car. 'It's . . . er . . .'

'I don't think you've shown me that before,' said his dad with a frown. 'It's new, isn't it?'

'Oh . . . yeah,' said Chris weakly. 'It's, ah . . . the latest thing. Everyone's got them at school.'

'It's really bright,' said Chris's dad. 'How's it work? Batteries? Let's have a look—'

But then the car screeched to a halt.

'Ah . . . *what*?' said Chris's mother. 'What on Earth's going on *now*?'

In front of them was a motorcycle policeman: he was waving frantically.

'I think he wants us to turn round,' said Chris's dad.

'Why?' asked Chris.

'How should I know?' Chris's mum replied. 'Maybe the bridge is closed.'

The three members of the Pitman family peered out of the windscreen. By the orange light of the streetlamps, they could see that the bridge did indeed seem to be empty. Apart from the solitary motorcycle cop, nothing stood between their car and (on the far side of the bridge) the Houses of Parliament, rearing up out of the darkness.

Chris's mum rolled down the window.

'I'm sorry, ma'am,' said the policeman, 'but I'm afraid this whole area is being evacuated.'

Chris noticed that the bracelet was glowing brighter and brighter with every second that passed. He sat on his hand.

'What's going on?' asked Chris's mum.

'You wouldn't believe me if I told you,' said the policeman. 'But take it from me, it's really best that you just get out of here *right now*. For your own good,' he added. 'OK?'

'Not really,' Chris's mum announced. 'No. I'm not going anywhere until you tell me what's happening.'

'Ma'am—'

'No, really. Either you tell me or I'm just going to stay here.'

The bracelet's glow was now searingly bright. It was filling the car with its yellow-green glow – even from under Chris's bottom.

The policeman sighed. 'All right, have it your way. I'll tell you. It's—'

BOOM! A sudden tremor rattled the car, and the rest of the policeman's words were lost.

'What was that?' asked Chris's dad.

BOOM! The noise came again, louder this time.

'Oh God,' said the policeman, turning white with fear. 'It's coming this way!'

'Now, come on,' said Chris's mum kindly. 'I'm sure that there's no need to panic. What is it? An earthquake?'

BOOM!

'Is it terrorists?' asked Chris's dad. 'I bet it's terrorists! I—'

BOOM! *BOOM!*

'Look,' said the policeman, quite firmly now. 'For heaven's sake, will you please just do as I say and *leave the area*! Run for your lives! While you still can!'

And at that moment something rather surprising happened on the other side of the river. One of the buildings on the opposite bank of the Thames – not the Houses of Parliament but another block, uncomfortably close to it – suddenly *vanished*.

Its facade exploded: hunks of jagged masonry flew out and splashed into the Thames. The rest of the building sagged in the middle before finally losing its battle with gravity and toppling in on itself entirely, making dust and debris fountain into the night sky in a cloud that, for the moment, was impenetrable. At the same instant, the air seemed to come alive with the thunderous chatter of helicopters, flying so low that Chris felt the wash from their blades through the window even from where he was sitting. The choppers shuddered to a halt in the air around the wreckage of the building. Lines of smoke sizzled out from all of them as their terrified pilots unleashed their missiles, and the night was set alight by a shattering bloom of explosions.

An unfamiliar tingling sensation travelling up his arm briefly reminded Chris of the bracelet. Its light was almost unbearable now. The inside of the car was awash with it: a brightness brighter than day. But still, as what had destroyed the building finally stepped into view, Chris simply could not spare the mysterious artefact anything more than a cursory glance.

Tim ploughed through the wreckage of the office block he'd just flattened – and paused.

'Good heavens,' said Chris's mother. 'What on Earth's *that*?'

'What do you think it is, woman?' Chris's dad snapped back. 'It's a monster!'

'I can see that, dear. But what's it doing *here*? In London?'

'What do we care?' asked Chris's dad, not unreasonably. 'Come on! Let's get the car turned round and get out of here!'

'No,' said Chris. 'Let's not.'

It was the first time he'd spoken for a while. For a moment his parents were so surprised that all they did was look at him.

Chris was feeling very strange.

He was scared. That was part of it. And in a way that wasn't surprising: there was, after all, a giant monster standing on the other side of the bridge. But the thing was, as soon as he examined the feeling, he knew that this wasn't the reason. He was scared, he realized, in a different way: his whole body – radiating from the bracelet at his wrist – was positively shivering with adrenaline. His blood hammered in his ears. His stomach sluiced inside him like it was filled with icy water. But what he was feeling, he realized, *wasn't coming from him*.

'. . . Frightened,' he said aloud.

'What's that, dear?' whispered Chris's mum. 'Are you scared?'

'Not me,' said Chris, shaking his head and not really believing that he was about to say it. But he gestured out of the window. 'Him.'

Chris's parents stared at him, then—

Suddenly the gigantic beast was on the move. Thighs bunching colossally for a moment, Tim tensed his hind legs and sprang forward into the Thames.

The river gouted up around him. With a crash, a long barge moored upriver at the embankment was simply washed upside down onto the bank by the tidal wave of displaced water. Slowly, but with gathering speed, Tim began to wade across.

The engine of the Pitmans' car coughed twice, then fell silent.

'You've stalled it!' Chris's dad pointed out.

'Yes, dear,' said Chris's mum.

'We need to get it started!'

'Yes, dear,' said Chris's mum.

'Turn the key! Get the engine going! Now!'

'Yes, dear,' said Chris's mum through gritted teeth as the desperate whinnying of the ignition was drowned out by the sound of the approaching giant. But the engine failed to catch.

'Oh God!' said Chris's dad. 'It's coming to get us! We're doomed!'

'No,' said Chris again, with a strange and sudden certainty, 'we're not.'

He was right. Tim had stopped.

From where Tim was standing, the Thames came halfway up his shins. The car was up on the river's embankment. If Tim bent over far enough, his eyes were almost level with the small metal box and its occupants. He laid his head with its long jaws almost flat on the high ground at the other side of the river and brought one of his eyes right up beside the car.

Tim, too, was feeling strange. For the first time since leaving his home and coming up into the world, he felt oddly . . . calm. His fear and confusion had receded a little, to be replaced by a kind of peace. It was something to do with the light: the strange greenish yellow light that seemed to be coming from the arm of one of the tiny people. Tim was curious.

By now, Chris's mum had given up trying to restart the engine. Silence had fallen inside the car. No one said anything: there was nothing to be said. Chris and his parents just waited, stock-still, while Tim's gigantic eye continued to examine them. From where they were sitting, his eye was so

big that its pupil filled the whole windscreen. The eye's iris –
around the vertical slit of the pupil – was an extraordinary
warm green colour with flecks of orange in it. They could
hear the great snort of Tim's breath like the chugging of some
colossal generator and the thick drip of his spittle as it fell
from his fangs. Chris's mum was rigid with terror. Chris's dad
was whimpering quietly. But Chris . . .

Not knowing why he did it but unable to help himself,
Chris took his arm with its glowing bracelet and held it up
for the monster's eye to see.

The pupil shrank instantly, reacting to the light.

Tim blinked.

For a long, slow moment Chris and Tim looked at each
other . . .

. . . then a fusillade of explosions took them both from
each other's sight.

While Tim had been distracted, the two battalions of tanks
had arrived. They had formed up on the far side of the river,
just next to the Houses of Parliament.

'Target acquired, sir,' Field Marshal Thompson had said to
the prime minister. 'Permission to fire?'

'Yes! Shoot it with everything!'

'Permission granted. Fire at will.'

Knocked sideways by the sheer pummelling weight of so
many large-calibre shells, Tim straightened up. Confused for a
moment by all the smoke and noise – but no more hurt than
he had been by the helicopters' missiles – he turned, looking
around for where this latest attack had come from. It took
him a while to make out its origin, but he found them soon
enough: those long, flat, box-like objects on the other side

of the river, the ones with the barrel things pointing at him.

Tim bared his fangs. Now he was getting annoyed. He was doing his best not to break things, he really was, but he was having a very unhappy and confusing evening, and the tiny people trying to hurt him were not helping matters. While more explosions pounded off his chest and abdomen, his eyes narrowed. He took a purposeful wading step back towards the Houses of Parliament, and another one.

Chris's mum and dad were cowering, their heads between their knees. Chris was still upright: mesmerized, he watched what happened next.

Tim had reached the tanks now. One by one, they'd stopped firing as their occupants – seeing Tim's approach and how little effect the shelling was having – had simply opened the hatches and *fled*. It was lucky they had, because at that moment Tim picked up two of the tanks in his claws. He stood there for a second, hefting them as if weighing them, then with a short, easy movement he brought his great hands together, flattening the tanks against each other in one blow.

'Hell's teeth!' roared the prime minister, sitting forward on his chair, all thoughts of how cold he was momentarily forgotten. 'Did you see that?' He jabbed at the monitors with one finger. '*Did you see that?*'

'This is Thompson to all ground units,' said Thompson, who had, in fact, 'seen that'. 'All remaining ground units, abort. I repeat: abort. Pull back out of range until further instructions. Air units, provide cover and continue to engage with the enemy. Drive the monster downstream as best you can.'

'What are you doing?' asked Mr Sinclair.

'I'm pulling my men out,' said Thompson as patiently as he could. 'I can't ask them to go up against *that*. And I hope you don't expect me to go against my judgement on this, *sir*.'

Surprised at the sudden venom in the field marshal's voice, Mr Sinclair blinked. 'But . . . what do you propose to do?' he asked.

'A direct assault is too risky,' said Thompson, searching the faces of his colleagues from the navy and air force. 'Agreed?'

They nodded.

'Very well: then our only chance lies in attempting to drive the creature down the Thames and out of the city as quickly as possible.'

'Drive it where, though?' asked the prime minister.

'Frankly, sir,' said Thompson, 'I don't know. The *sea* would seem to be the most sensible option. But for the time being our first responsibility must be to London's civilians. If we can persuade Tim to stick to the river, then the damage to buildings and property should be kept to a minimum.'

'But the bridges . . . !'

'London's bridges are a small price to pay compared to what other damage this creature might cause. Sir . . .' added Thompson, 'we can't fight this thing, not now and certainly not *here*.'

'Very well,' said Mr Sinclair, pouting.

A fresh volley of missiles struck Tim in the side. He stopped playing with the tanks and stood up straight.

Tim wasn't bright, but he wasn't entirely stupid either. With all the explosions and everything, he was beginning to get the hint that the tiny people didn't like him being there very much. Well, that was fine by Tim: he didn't like it there either.

He looked down at the dark water, feeling the way the current surged around his scaly legs. There were fewer things to break or get in his way out here in the river. And walking would be less effort if he followed the flow, so that suggested a direction.

Ignoring the helicopters, Tim turned and set off down the river. Chris watched him go.

After a time, Tim noticed, the tiny people gradually stopped trying to shoot him so much. They hung back, watching him from their clattering flying vehicles, and – apart from the occasional distracting shattering of the bridges across his legs – things gradually became quieter and less dramatic.

Now, at last, Tim had a little more time to think.

Where was he going? Tim didn't know. What was he going to do? Tim didn't know. Right now all he was doing was walking . . . and seeing what he could see.

The world, he decided presently, certainly was very *big*. The further Tim walked, the more the possibility began to occur to him that this place might not actually have *any limits at all*. Was that possible? Could he keep walking and never reach the end of it? The idea of this was very frightening. Above him, the open sky loomed down: pitilessly infinite. Ahead of him, the furthest point Tim could see had now developed an infuriating habit of just . . . changing into something else whenever he thought he was getting closer to it. Big as he was, Tim felt small and alone. The only thing that kept this feeling under any kind of control was if he just kept walking. So he walked.

The world watched him. All over the globe they stared, awestruck, at their screens, seeing his huge silhouette against the sky. To either side of the river people trembled in their beds at the surging thunder of Tim's watery footsteps – hardly believing that this gigantic creature still wasn't going to choose that moment to start causing more havoc. But Tim didn't: apart from the bridges (and Tim couldn't help that) he didn't appear to be attacking anything. He just walked on, endlessly, through the night.

The river was widening. The water was getting higher too, reaching slowly up past his knees and as far as his scaly belly, but Tim kept walking. As he walked, he sniffed the air, huffing in great gulps of it through his cavernous nostrils, tasting what it contained. The hot metal taint, the sickly machine stink of the tiny people, was gradually beginning to recede. At the same time, the pinkish tinge to the air from the lights of their city was fading, revealing more of the stars. Still pursued by the rattling, clattering machines, Tim kept walking, and soon the water was up to his chest. Before much longer it was up to his neck, then covering his face. And soon after that, following the memory of his daydream and a strange dark urge to keep walking like this until a better idea occurred to him, he vanished under the water.

'We've done it, sir! He's heading out to sea!' one of Field Marshal Thompson's aides confirmed delightedly.

'Thank you, Jenkins,' Thompson replied. 'That will do.'

'Well?' asked the prime minister, still wearing his pyjamas and dressing gown. 'Is it over?'

'Frankly, Prime Minister,' Thompson answered, 'there's just no way of knowing.'

Field Marshal Thompson knew that the monster's departure had little to do with anything he or his chief-of-staff colleagues had done. Clearly, a creature like that only went somewhere if it *wanted* to. But Tim had left London, with a minimum amount of collateral damage.

For now.

THE GOD OF SMALL THINGS

'So, Professor . . .' said Mr Sinclair the following morning, 'we've agreed to the funding you wanted, and we're prepared to let you break a treaty ratified by the United Nations. As I'm sure you know, we currently have a *rather large problem* on our hands, so tell us: what exactly are we going to get from you in return?'

Professor Mallahide looked from the prime minister to the rest of the party. Among the small but highly select crowd visiting his laboratory at such short notice (and on a Saturday, too!), he recognized the head of MI6 as well as various commanders in chief from the British army, navy and air force: an impressive audience, even if they did all currently look a bit anxious. He took a deep breath.

'Ladies and gentlemen, I have one word for you.' He smiled at them. 'GRIN.'

'I'm sorry?' said the prime minister.

'GRIN,' Mallahide repeated. 'It stands for Genetics, Robotics, Information and Nanotech – the four cornerstones of the current scientific revolution. And although the first three all have their parts to play in this project of mine, my particular area of specialization lies in the *N*: *nanotechnology*. Now, can any of you tell me what *nanotech* actually means?'

There was a pause. The assembled VIPs exchanged awkward glances. They'd been expecting a straight demonstration, not a school lesson.

'Anyone?' asked Professor Mallahide delightedly, enjoying their discomfort.

'Isn't it . . . the science of making things that are very small?' asked Sarah Flitwick, the head of MI6.

'How small?' Mallahide shot back.

'Tiny,' Ms Flitwick replied. 'Particle size. So small you can barely see them under a microscope.'

'Correct!' said Mallahide. 'The name *nanotech* comes from nanometre, the unit of measurement that I – and others like me – most commonly work in. One nanometre is one millionth of a millimetre. The results of most of my efforts take place around the one-hundred-nanometre mark: that's a thousand times smaller than the thickness of the average human hair. And in that realm, ladies and gentlemen – in that magical dimension, so far beneath the limits of everyday human perception as to seem, to the untrained mind, completely insignificant – in that realm, I do not flatter myself when I say that I am the undisputed leader of the world: the God of Small Things, to quote the title of the well-known novel.'

Mallahide beamed. The VIPs were frowning. But he was just hitting his stride.

'I make machines,' he said. 'That's the shortest way of saying it. Tiny machines, capable of operating at a cellular level. And what do my machines do?' He paused, sweeping his audience with another dazzling grin. 'My machines – my *nanobots*, I call them – can quite literally do *anything*.'

'Anything?' the prime minister echoed, raising an eyebrow.

'That's right,' said Mallahide. 'The first and most important thing that they can do – now that we have your permission' – he nodded graciously at Mr Sinclair – 'is replicate themselves: make more nanobots. They can also work together to manufacture other things, depending on how I instruct them: larger or more complex items, increasingly powerful and complicated machines – whatever I tell them to do! Each individual nanobot is networked with the rest: they can share information; they can work as a team; they can move in a swarm as one.'

'Professor Mallahide,' said the prime minister. 'That's all' – he coughed – 'absolutely fascinating. But is there any way we can skip any further preamble about your work and cut straight to its military applications? Those are what we're here to see, after all.'

Mallahide's gaze went cold, but his smile didn't change in the slightest. 'Of course,' he said easily. 'Please, step this way.'

He led the party over to the large picture window that dominated one side of the room.

'Through there, as you see,' said Professor Mallahide, 'is the central area of my laboratory. For obvious reasons, my work requires an environment that is as sterile as it is within our powers to make it – so this will be as close as you'll be coming for today, I'm afraid. Nonetheless, with the kind help of my assistant, Dr Belforth, I've taken the liberty of preparing a little demonstration that should be of some interest to you.'

He reached for the intercom that was on the wall beside him and pressed a button.

'Belforth? Bring the test subject in now, please.'

In the glittering icy-white lab space beyond the triple-layered glass screen, a figure shuffled into view. The figure was wearing a thick white protective suit that covered its whole body from head to toe: you couldn't even make out if it was a man or a woman under there, and the suit was thick enough to make the figure's movements quite ungainly. A cart with a rectangular object on top of it was wheeled into position in front of the window; with a flourish, the figure drew off the white sheet that had been covering the object to reveal . . .

'Ladies and gentlemen,' said Professor Mallahide, 'I give you the star of this afternoon's show: *Sciurus carolinensis*.'

'A *squirrel*,' said the prime minister, eyeing the bushy-tailed creature in the box before the window with an expression of distaste.

'An American *grey* squirrel,' Mallahide corrected. He put his mouth to the intercom again. 'Thank you, Belforth. You can begin connecting the box to the hive now, please.' As the white-suited figure in the lab shambled to do his bidding, Mallahide turned again to face his audience.

'As my *daughter* first told me,' he said proudly, 'there's actually a rather interesting story attached to these fellows. Common as they are in this country's parks and wild spaces nowadays, the grey squirrel isn't actually a native of the British Isles. As his name implies, he was brought here from the United States and introduced into the wild – for, I believe, *ornamental* purposes originally – in Cheshire, in 1876. In the short time since then,' the professor went on, 'our friend here and the rest of his species have utterly taken over from *Sciurus vulgaris* – our own red squirrel – to the extent that grey squirrels now outnumber red ones by a factor of no less that *sixty-six to one*. Due in part to a type of smallpox the greys carry but to which they are immune, the British – or *Eurasian*

– red squirrel, to give it its proper classification, is now being considered as a candidate for the international list of *endangered species*. And all because someone once decided they preferred the colour of this chap's fur. Extraordinary, isn't it? There's a lesson for us all in there somewhere, I think.'

The squirrel in the box didn't appear to care: it was too busy nibbling at the nut it had grasped between its powerful front paws. It sat there, its tail arched up behind it, staring at the party behind the glass with something like suspicion in its beady black eyes. The prime minister, too, was less than impressed.

'Professor, at the risk of repeating myself,' he began, 'we are all rather busy people. Do you think you could hurry this along, please?'

Professor Mallahide blinked but said, 'With pleasure.' He pressed the button on the intercom again. 'All set, Belforth?'

The white-suited figure stood upright from behind the squirrel's box and gave a clumsy thumbs-up.

'Splendid.' Professor Mallahide reached into one of the pockets of his lab coat and produced a small black disc of plastic with a red button mounted in its centre. 'Ladies and gentlemen, I must ask you to watch what happens now very carefully. Everybody ready? Then let's go.'

He pressed the button.

'There,' he said. 'I've just allowed some of my machines to be released. At this moment, a swarm of nanobots so small as to be almost invisible to the naked eye are making their way into our furry friend here's container. Look carefully: there's a couple of billion nanobots in the swarm; it's possible you may just catch a glimpse of it.'

And it was true. The members of the assembled top brass who were prepared to strain their eyes hard enough found that they could indeed make out something that had appeared in the case besides the squirrel. Something wavered in the pitiless light from the fluorescent bulbs on the lab ceiling: a haze, shimmering in the air around the animal.

The squirrel suddenly stopped nibbling on its nut, and froze.

'By now, my machines have penetrated the squirrel's skin and are moving freely through the creature's bloodstream,' said Professor Mallahide. 'Our friend here doesn't know it yet, but something rather extraordinary is about to happen. Again, I must ask you to watch very carefully. *Now.*'

The squirrel in the box twitched its nose. Behind it, the great curve of its tail arched and thrashed the air in an expression of mounting nervousness. But it wasn't panicking or in any obvious pain. And what was happening had already started to happen.

The dirty grey colour of its fur was starting to change. At the same time, imperceptibly at first – the squirrel was beginning to *shrink*, becoming physically smaller before the eyes of its audience as the strange haze around its body continued to do its work. Now the fur had taken on an unmistakable russet-brown hue: the colour was spreading all over the squirrel's shrinking body.

'And . . . there,' said Professor Mallahide with satisfaction.

He pointed through the glass at the creature that now stood in the container.

'Ladies and gentlemen, I present to you my own little attempt to redress the balance in the squirrel population.

Sciurus vulgaris, the Eurasian *red* squirrel. As a species, he's a little smaller than his grey counterpart. But with the help of my machines, he's now immune to the smallpox virus. I think he should get along just fine.'

There was a short silence in the room. The prime minister, the military chiefs of staff and the other bigwigs all exchanged another look. It was the prime minister who spoke first.

'That's it?' he asked.

Mallahide raised his eyebrows. 'I beg your pardon?'

'That's what you wanted to show us?'

'Well . . . yes,' said Mallahide, his smile becoming uncertain. 'That's my demonstration.'

'I'm sorry, Professor,' said the prime minister, 'perhaps I'm missing the significance of what I've seen here. But it seems to me that all you've managed to come up with for us is a way to . . . change a squirrel's hair colour.'

He smirked. Some of the other bigwigs – anxious to show they appreciated the prime minister's little joke – smirked too.

'You mentioned military applications for your work,' Mr Sinclair went on. 'Those are what we're here to see. Not . . . cosmetic care for rodents.'

Professor Mallahide gave him another smile, but it was thinner than before. 'I assure you, Prime Minister,' he said, 'what I and my machines have achieved just now is rather more than *cosmetic*. Look at that animal out there,' he added, gesturing again at the squirrel, which had gone back to eating its nut. 'I appreciate you'll have to take my word on this, but if you were to take a sample of his blood and perform tests on it, you would realize that in real terms, he bears no relation whatever to the creature that was standing on that spot a few moments ago. My machines have just rebuilt his whole body structure, changing it – cell by cell – into a different animal entirely. Imagine for a moment, if you can, what that change involved. Almost every single molecule in that creature's body has been subtly altered. It happened very fast. It caused the creature no pain, as you saw – but that squirrel now belongs to a *different species*. I did that: I and my machines. Truly,' he said, and paused, 'the power that this technology offers is nothing less than God-like!'

The prime minister shook his head. 'Professor, let me put this as simply as I can,' he said. 'We're talking about war. You're talking about squirrels. I'm sorry, but I'm not really seeing the connection. Show us something we can *use*, please,' he said very slowly and deliberately. 'I'm afraid that your funding depends on it.'

For a long moment Professor Mallahide and Mr Sinclair looked at each other.

'Very well,' said Mallahide. He turned and looked past the glass at the hapless creature that stood in the box in front of them, still obliviously working on its nut. *All right*, he thought. *Time to show these people something they can understand.*

'Compared to changing a creature's species,' he said, 'applications of a more . . . *aggressive* nature for this technology are absolute child's play. If instructed, my machines can act in exactly the same way as diseases such as botulism, Ebola, anthrax, or AIDS. They can take on the properties of cancer cells, generating random and debilitating mutations in the body that can progress towards their fatal results at any speed

I see fit. And those are just conditions that already exist today: if I choose, my machines can even *invent new ones*. New diseases, specially designed. Ones for which the treatments don't exist.'

He sighed. *I'm sorry*, he mouthed at the squirrel – then he gave the order. He didn't bother to use the button this time: he just signalled the swarm wirelessly through the tiny chip he'd installed in his own brain. He could have done this at any point, of course, but it didn't do to let on too early to these people just how far he had already progressed with his own side of the project.

Invisibly, his billions of tiny machines began to do his bidding . . .

'The *simplest* course of action, however,' Mallahide went on, 'is to allow the nanobots to do what they do most naturally: make use of whatever raw material is to hand to *reproduce* and make more of themselves.'

He turned his back to the window. He knew what was about to happen, but he had no wish to see it for himself.

'Imagine it,' he said. 'With only a relatively small initial quantity of nanobots, no army on Earth would be safe. Effectively invulnerable to conventional attack, the nanobots' numbers would multiply at an exponential rate. Even a small swarm would become an unstoppable *tide* of machines, consuming everything in its path. Buildings. Armour.'

He paused significantly.

'. . . And *flesh*.'

The assembled bigwigs weren't looking at him any more. They were staring past him, expressions of horror already taking over their faces. Behind him, out in the glass case beyond the window, the process was now well under way.

The squirrel's fur was the first thing to go: the soft russet-brown hairs on the creature's tail and body were vanishing as quickly as they'd come. In moments, the squirrel was completely bald, the delicate grey-blue of its veins showing clearly in patches through the suddenly denuded skin. All this while, Mallahide's millions of machines danced around the animal in a strange and shimmering haze.

Abruptly the squirrel's skin vanished too. The whole process was happening so quickly that it was only at this point that the animal seemed to wake up to the danger it was in. Its small dark eyes suddenly widening in panic, the squirrel finally dropped the nut and began scratching and clawing at itself all over. By this point, of course, it was already too late: all it was doing was hurting itself, its sharp claws digging great bleeding furrows in its own lacerated and diminishing flesh. Yellow-pink layers of glistening subcutaneous fat seemed to evaporate as Mallahide's machines went about their work. The squirrel fell on its back, convulsing, exposing the small pale-grey knot of its intestines – then it froze, helpless, as its bones appeared, open to the air for all to see. For another half-second its bare skeleton lay in a rictus of death on the floor of its glass cage. Then the bones vanished too.

The squirrel was gone. Nothing remained in the box to give any indication of what had occupied it. For all intents and purposes, the squirrel had ceased to exist. All that was left was the same strange glittering haze – fractionally darker, fractionally thicker than before, but still so close to invisible as to appear to be nothing more than a trick of the eye.

The entire process had taken just over six seconds.

Professor Mallahide was not a cruel man: six seconds was longer than he would have liked, but it was the compromise he had settled on between sparing the squirrel as much pain as he could and giving his audience something to satisfy their bloodlust.

He, in turn, watched them, gauging their reactions.

Ms Flitwick had her hand to her mouth. Field Marshal Thompson was biting his lip. The rest of the party all also looked more than a little sick. The prime minister's mouth was open. Mallahide just watched them and waited.

'That . . .' said Sinclair finally. 'That's . . .'

Field Marshal Thompson cleared his throat. 'The – the swarm,' he said: 'would it be vulnerable to things like wind or rain?'

'Not especially,' said Mallahide. 'The nanobots are self-propelling: they move by themselves, and they're capable of overcoming most practical obstacles. You might lose some of them, but sheer weight of numbers will more than make up for any casualties.'

'What about delivery?' Thompson asked.

Mallahide shrugged. 'Whatever you like. Once released, they'll go wherever I tell them.'

'And how do you "tell them"?' asked Ms Flitwick. 'How do you control them, exactly?'

Mallahide smiled. 'I'm afraid that's going to have to remain my little secret for the time being. As I'm sure you'll understand, an invention like this carries with it certain . . . *responsibilities*. I won't allow my work to be used without my permission or involvement. But you may rest assured that the swarm is entirely and completely at my own exclusive command.'

At this, the prime minister seemed to snap out of his trance. He exchanged another look with the rest of the top brass: this last bit of news was, Mallahide knew, something they hadn't wanted to hear. Mallahide didn't care. He had them now.

'Well, Prime Minister?' he asked. 'What do you think?'

'Impressive, Professor,' the prime minister admitted. 'Very impressive. You have this government's full permission to carry on with your research. Thank you for your time.'

'Thank *you*, Prime Minister,' said Mallahide. 'Would you mind terribly if I didn't see you out?'

'Not at all. Good day to you.'

'Goodbye, everyone. Thank you for coming.'

Mallahide watched them all filing out of the room. The door closed. Then he waited. When he was absolutely sure they'd all gone, he turned back towards the window.

'Morons,' he said. Then he signalled his machines again.

Instantly the swarm reacted, the shimmering haze condensing momentarily into a ball of darkness as it rushed to do his bidding. Newly created nanobots sacrificed themselves willingly, allowing themselves to be broken back down again into their source material. Each molecule, teased into being with unimaginable delicacy, was reconstructed exactly according to the information that the swarm had stored. The bones came first, knitted into shape and extended: blood, flesh, muscles, skin and then fur all followed – *grey* again this time. Then the squirrel was standing there in its glass box once more.

It blinked. It shook its tail. Then it picked up the nut it had dropped.

'Good as new,' said Professor Mallahide.

Morons, he said again, without speaking this time. No doubt about it: he was working for morons.

But not for much longer.

BIGGER FISH

Tim liked the water. He liked the feel of it all over his scaly skin and the effortless way that it supported his weight. In fact, his long body and powerful tail seemed ideally suited to this new environment. Undulating easily onward, paddling with his limbs, Tim found that he didn't even need to breathe.

How long had he been swimming? Tim didn't know. Where was he going? He didn't know. All he knew as he sank into the welcoming deep, lashing the dark with his tail and feeling the water surging around him, was that for the first time since leaving his old enclosure, he was something close to being happy.

Then suddenly a voice said, 'At last. Took your time, didn't you?'

Tim stopped swimming. He was so surprised, he didn't know what to do. Nobody had ever spoken to him like this before, and the way the words had arrived in his head meant he had no way of knowing where they'd come from. For a long second he just hung there, suspended in the watery dark. Then the thing that had spoken to him showed itself.

All around him, the sea began to take on a strange kind of glimmer. What Tim had thought of as empty water suddenly erupted into an incredible tracery of neon-bright patterned. multi-colours, shimmering and fizzing. And while Tim kept staring, dazzled and fascinated—

Abruptly he was seized about the waist by a thing like an

electric-pink snake covered in rubbery suckers: it wrapped around him no less than three times and effortlessly yanked him deeper into the water.

At the same time, the pulsating colours around him resolved themselves into a sizable acreage of body: the patterns, Tim realized, weren't actually appearing by themselves but were instead just displaying on something's skin. Something big: many times bigger than Tim. Something strong: immeasurably, impossibly strong. Something – Tim realized as the tentacle held him before a vast eye for further examination – that was *looking at him*.

'No!' said the voice in his head. '*You're* the one who's going to replace me? HEE HEE HEE *HEE!*'

The water around Tim eddied and boiled with glee: the whole ocean seemed to shake with the monster's laughter, and the tentacle that held him quivered.

'Come on,' said the voice, getting itself back under control. 'You've got to be kidding! You're . . . tiny!'

Tim looked back at the eye. Big as he was, he was barely the size of the eye's pupil. Still not really knowing what to do, he just froze and stared back at it.

'You can speak to me, you know,' said the voice. 'I can understand you; in fact, I'm the only one who can. You know why that is? Because you're the only thing in the world that can understand *me!*'

Tim said nothing.

'Hmm,' said the voice. 'Or maybe not.' Its owner sighed. 'Just because it's all I've done for the last million years or so doesn't mean I actually *like* talking to myself. All right, little one: time to give me a sign here.'

Tim blinked. Then he opened his mouth. A lot of water came in.

'Not like that,' said the voice quickly. 'With your *mind*.'

'Oh,' said Tim, surprised at himself. 'Like this?'

'That's it. Like that.'

'Um . . . hello.'

'Hi,' the voice replied.

There was a pause.

'I am *the Kraken*,' said the voice. 'And you are . . . ?'

There was a word his tiny keepers had used the most whenever they'd tried to speak to him in their language: 'They call me . . . Tim,' said Tim.

'Well, it's a name, I suppose,' said the Kraken. 'I've been waiting a long time to meet you . . . Tim. It's a pleasure.'

Tim didn't really know what to say to this, so he didn't reply.

'I guess you're wondering why I brought you here.'

'*Brought me?*'

'That's right,' said the Kraken. 'You remember: anytime you got curious about what the world was like outside that little egg they kept you in . . . anytime you felt like breaking out of it, right up until now when you came out here to meet me? Well, that was me, giving you a little nudge.' The Kraken paused. 'You're a little *lazy*, if you don't mind me saying so. I don't think you'd ever have done it otherwise.'

'But . . . how? How did you do that? How did you get in my head? Who are you? How are we talking now? *What's going on?*'

'Easy there!' said the voice. 'No need to panic: the answers are coming in good time.'

'But—!'

'You're here with me now. I'll protect you for the time being and prepare you for what's coming as best I can. You see . . . that's my job. My *last* job.' The voice fell silent.

In the long moment that followed, Tim felt very strange. He was realizing something: he wasn't as scared as he'd thought he was. A part of him was still frightened by this enormous creature that held him in its tentacle as if he was a toy; a big part of him was still tremendously confused by what was happening and, indeed, by pretty much everything that had happened to him ever since he'd left his home behind. But another part of him felt . . . calm.

It was the same sort of calm that he'd experienced when he'd seen the strange light before that came from that tiny person's arm. Something inside him was responding to what was happening – responding to it all as if he'd known it was coming. He felt peaceful, as if it was all familiar somehow; as if . . .

As if he'd found what he was looking for.

'That's right,' said the voice in his head, while all around him the incredible patterns in the larger creature's skin dimmed down to a soothing and gentle display. 'You know what this is all about, don't you? You feel it.'

Tim said nothing.

'We're two of a kind, Tim,' said the voice. 'That's how we can talk to each other like this. In all the time I've lived, this has only happened once before: once, when I met *my* predecessor. We lead lonely lives, the likes of you and I.'

'What do you mean?' Tim asked. 'What *are* you and I? Predecessor to *what*?'

'Follow me,' said the Kraken. 'I'm going to show you.'

'How do I take this off?' asked Chris, holding his arm out.

'I'm sorry?' asked the security guard, surprised.

Going back to the British Museum wasn't exactly Chris's ideal way to spend a Saturday. It had taken him a long time to find the weird lady again, and he was in no mood to mess around.

'This bracelet thing you put on me,' he said. He thought about mentioning the previous evening's incident with the giant monster but decided to settle instead with repeating his main point: '*How do I take it off?*'

The security guard lady gave Chris a long look. Then she stood up and closed the double doors. 'What's your name?' she asked.

'Chris,' said Chris, still holding his arm out.

'I'm Eunice Plimpton.' She took Chris's extended hand and shook it, making him blink. 'How do you do? Call me Eunice if you like.'

'Charmed, I'm sure,' said Chris, gritting his teeth. 'Listen, I'm not here to make friends, you know? You've done something to me, and I want to know what.'

Ms Plimpton sighed. 'Oh, dear. This is obviously going to be even harder than I expected.'

Chris frowned at her. 'Huh?'

'Please,' she snapped, 'just *sit down*, will you?'

Surprised, Chris did as she'd asked.

Ms Plimpton ran a hand through her henna-red crew-cut.

'The first thing you should know,' she said, 'is that "I" haven't done anything to you. My job – my sacred task – was to guard the talisman until it gave the sign it had found the right person.' She paused. 'Think about it: you saw it yourself. You saw the way it glowed when you sat down next to it. I didn't choose you. The *bracelet* chose you. That's the first thing.'

Chris opened his mouth to say something to this, but—

'The second thing is, now that it's chosen you I'm afraid there's no going back.' Ms Plimpton smiled thinly. 'You've probably tried to take it off – right? Even though it's the single greatest gift a person could have, the highest honour our planet could bestow upon one of its inhabitants?'

'Well . . . yeah, as it happens,' said Chris. 'But—'

'Human tools won't help you,' said Ms Plimpton, shaking her head. 'Nothing will. The only thing that will make the bracelet let go of you is if it's time for another bearer. And it'll only be time for another bearer,' she finished, 'when you're *dead*.'

Chris gaped at her.

'Now,' she went on, 'believe it or not, I truly want to help you in any way I can. So I want you to listen to what I tell you next *very carefully indeed*. Which means,' she added, 'don't ask me any damn fool questions until I'm good and ready. All right?'

'But—' Chris began again.

'*All right?*'

'I guess . . .' Chris grumbled.

Ms Plimpton closed her eyes for a moment, gathering her thoughts.

'All life on this Earth,' she said, 'gives off a kind of *energy*. Simply by being alive, all living things give off waves of power. You and I sitting here may not be able to see it, but we're surrounded by it, a mantle of life force, flowing all around us always. In times of great danger, when our planet is under threat, this power can be . . . harnessed.

'You,' she went on, 'have been chosen to be the channel for that power. That bracelet now connects you to all life on this planet. Through it – through *you* – all living things will focus their life force so that it can be called upon when the Defender needs it. OK,' she added graciously, 'now you may speak.'

'But . . . *why me?*' Chris asked, his voice rising in a whine. 'I mean, never mind all that crap you just said – why me? Why was *I* chosen?'

Ms Plimpton gave Chris an appraising look – one that (Chris was offended to discover) clearly did not end in any great approval of the look's object.

'Frankly, Chris,' she told him, 'I don't know. Right now that's as much of a mystery to me as it is to you' – she grimaced – 'especially now that I'm getting to know you. But chosen you were. The bracelet reacted to something in you that makes you the right person to do this. What that quality of yours actually *is* . . .' She shrugged. 'Well, you tell me.'

Chris opened his mouth, then closed it again.

When he was younger, Chris had always dreamed of something like this: a staggering secret that nobody had ever suspected about him, even himself; a secret that – once discovered – would make everyone realize how powerful and important and special he was. He'd imagined magic, super-powers, being the lost heir to a hidden kingdom . . .

But then Chris had *grown up.*

Chris was nothing special. And in his view, that was a good thing.

At school, being special just made you a target. At school, you were either normal or you were a freak. It wasn't something Chris cared to talk about, but at one of his earlier schools he'd experienced first-hand what happened to people who got themselves labelled the wrong way. Since then Chris had made it his business never to risk doing or saying *anything* that might make him stick out from the pack. In short, he'd learned to keep his head down.

Sometimes it was difficult. Sometimes he didn't like it: being careful never to show too much enthusiasm for anything and keeping any strong feelings he had to himself. Sometimes he felt that it meant he couldn't talk to anyone, not really. *But* (he told himself) *better that than the alternative*.

Chris thought about what Ms Plimpton had said. He thought about the weird moment the evening before, not just the giant monster (though that had certainly been weird enough) but about the emotional connection he'd suddenly felt.

He held out the bracelet. 'Take this thing off me,' he said.

Ms Plimpton blinked. 'Chris,' she said, 'I told you, I can't. But even if I could,' she added, puzzled, 'can't you see how important this is? You've been chosen to represent all life on Earth! And if the bracelet has activated, if the Defender's been called, then something truly terrible must be coming.' She shook her head. 'It'll all come down to you. You must unite Earth's population behind the Defender so our power can be there for him when he needs it. You, Chris, must *join the world*. If you don't, then—'

'You *can't* take this thing off me?' Chris clarified. 'That's what you're saying?'

Ms Plimpton pursed her lips. 'That's right.'

'Fine,' said Chris. 'I'll find someone who can.'

He turned his back and left the room.

TRANSFIGURATION

Everything was ready. Mallahide looked at the box where his transformation was going to take place and licked his lips.

He had a right to be nervous, he told himself. Who wouldn't be? When he, Mallahide, stepped into the box, humanity was going to make an evolutionary leap. He stood there, looking through the box's open door and into its blindingly bright ceramic interior.

Once again, he wondered if he should call Anna.

He frowned. What would he say? 'Hi, honey. I know I promised I wouldn't, but I'm about to have my body broken down into its component atoms while my mind is transferred into a cloud of machines: don't wait up.' Ridiculous. Of course not.

But what if it went wrong? What if the box turned out to be his coffin? Didn't he owe her some form of explanation in advance? Some reason for what he was about to do?

No, he told himself. He was being foolish. He would not tell Anna anything, for one simple reason: *it would not go wrong*.

The tests had all been successful. The squirrel had shown no signs of being affected by being broken down and then re-constructed: its body processes were completely identical. More significantly, its *consciousness* had been unaffected too: the entire contents of the squirrel's brain had been temporarily stored as information by the swarm, which had then used that information to recreate it perfectly. The only outward sign the squirrel had given of the process having taken place was an understandable dissatisfaction with still being cooped up in its box without any trees to climb. There was no reason why what he was planning would not work. So why was he hesitating?

Taking a deep breath, Mallahide walked across the lab towards the box.

From the outside, the box looked a little like a shower cubicle. The floor of the box's interior was a metre square, and it was a little over two metres high. Its ceiling, floor and walls were lined with the same ceramic tiles as the squirrel's box had been, and were completely smooth except for the small grille high on one wall through which the nanobots would enter.

Without letting himself pause to think about it too much, Professor Mallahide got into the box, turned, and closed the door.

The six titanium-steel dead bolts slid into place. The door was now locked: it could not be opened again until detectors in the box indicated that what was about to take place was over. There was no handle on the inside. There was no going back. Mallahide pressed the button to open the connecting pipe to the hive. Concentrating, he gave the swarm their orders. Then he waited.

The overhead light was very bright, reflecting off the tiles. The small, hot, white, antiseptic little cubicle made Mallahide uncomfortably conscious of himself physically. He felt moist, gross, sweaty – animal. Still, even anxious to be rid of his body as he was, he felt another twinge of nerves: he ran his tongue over his lips, but his mouth had gone suddenly dry. Not for the first time, he wondered what it was going to feel like.

Would he know when it had started? Were the machines in the room with him already? *There*. Something flickered at the corner of his eye. He turned but of course saw nothing. Perhaps it had been a trick of the light.

He knew in his heart that it wasn't. It had begun.

He looked down at his hands and saw they were glistening with sweat. Despite his best efforts to calm himself, his heart was speeding up. But he forced himself to stare at his hands, to keep staring at them – until, at last, he saw them begin to change.

Under his instructions, his little machines began to work with their usual efficiency. Mallahide's clothes vanished first, even his shoes: for a second the tiles were cool under his suddenly bare feet.

Then they started to work on his skin. All over his body his flesh seemed to turn suddenly dark as the layers dissolved to reveal the glossy blood and meat beneath. In moments the muscle structures were revealed in all their glory, as neat and clean as any anatomical model. All the blood, the goo and the gore, was being broken down – held in its place by the work of the machines.

It didn't hurt in the least – which was exactly as Mallahide expected. This was for the simple reason that his machines were already hard at work in his brain: some of the nanobots travelled the neural pathways, neutralizing any messages of pain and shock that his dissolving body was able to send. Meanwhile, other members of the swarm were addressing more important matters.

From the outside in, they had begun to take his mind

apart. Cell by cell they worked, examining each atom, recording its every detail in the minutest possible accuracy before destroying it.

Panic struck Mallahide in a sudden ugly rush.

There was a hot itching behind his eyes. He could feel them, the machines, like insects inside him – a seething multitude of tiny prying mechanical fingers, pushing their way through the soft delicate tissues, opening his thoughts and exposing them to the air. At the same time he felt a tremendous *drifting* sensation, a head-rush like when you stand up too fast, as the machines stripped his mind back to nothing. The world was falling away from him: his mind scrabbled for a grip on the edge of annihilation but was slipping . . . slipping . . . He tried to move, but there was nothing to move with. He tried to think, but there was nothing to think with. All there was in his mind was a face – Anna's face – and for a rushing, spinning fraction of a second Mallahide regretted his decision.

The lights – the room – a roaring in his ears –

Then all sensation ceased.

THE FIRST VISIT

Anna made dinner, then threw it in the bin. Anna did her homework – or tried to, anyway: she wrote a paragraph of her history essay then gave up on that, too, and went back to pacing around the flat. Her dad hadn't called. She had a bad feeling. And at 11:37 p.m., as soon as she heard the voice of the person who rang her from the lab, she knew her bad feeling was right.

'Some kind of accident . . .'

'An experiment gone wrong . . .'

'We're sending someone over to be with you right now . . .'

'We'll help you with all the arrangements . . .'

'Deepest sympathy . . .'

The wave of words washed past her. Anna didn't even reply because all she could think of, underneath it all, was how she was feeling. And it wasn't how these people were expecting her to feel.

Anna was *angry*. That was how she felt. Not grief-stricken, just angry: really, *really* angry.

How could he *do* this? she asked herself. How could he get himself killed and *leave* her like this? What – had he *forgotten* that without him she was alone in the world? *No*, she corrected herself, that was the point: of course he hadn't forgotten – he'd just believed he knew better, believed in his machines instead of in her, and now he had gone and done exactly the stupid, stupid thing that they'd talked over and fought over all through the preceding few years.

She'd lost count of how often they'd argued about it. She'd lost count of how many times she'd made him promise not to take his work to its conclusion. And all this time – as if she couldn't have guessed – he hadn't been listening. He'd been making his own plans, he'd been intent on carrying them out, just the same as if Anna had said nothing. She might as well not have bothered.

The doorbell rang.

It was a lady counsellor, provided by the government – just like Anna's home and everything in it. Anna let the lady in. Anna let the nice lady say the words she'd been paid to say, all the 'so, so sorry's and the 'you're not alone's. She accepted them without comment, without the slightest outward sign of how angry she was. But when she went to bed, she was still fuming.

It was simple, she realized: her father's work had just been more important to him than she was. She'd always known that, really: she might have wanted to believe his attempts to prove he felt otherwise, but she hadn't been fooled, not really.

His machines were his life, not her. And now they'd been his death.

Finally, exhausted by her own anger, she slept.

'Anna,' said a voice.

She stirred in her bed.

'Anna . . .' the voice repeated. It was her father's.

'Piss off,' said Anna, assuming she was dreaming. 'I've got nothing to say to you.'

'Anna, listen to me—'

'No!' said Anna. 'You never listened to *me*, so why should I—?'

Then she sat up. She blinked.

Her father was standing in the room with her.

'Hi,' he said.

Anna looked at him. She didn't move. She didn't try to turn on her bedside light. She just sat there, still unsure if she was awake or not.

He looked exactly the same as he had the previous night, when she'd last seen him. He was wearing the same clothes. His tie was rumpled and his hair was a mess. He was smiling.

'It's me,' he said.

'OK,' said Anna, 'now I'm really confused.' She took a deep breath, feeling her heart lurch in her chest.

'Someone called me from your lab,' she told him, taking it as slowly as she could. 'They said there'd been an accident with the nanobots. They said you were dead: they sent a lady to look after me, and she's downstairs staying over right now; in fact, I had to use a dirty sheet for the sofa bed because you didn't do the laundry – *again*. What's going on?' she asked. '*What are you doing here?*'

'Shh!' said her father. 'Shhh – quiet. She's sleeping; you might wake her up.' Then he went back to smiling again.

'Anna . . .' he said, taking a step towards her, '*it worked*.'

Anna frowned. 'What?'

'The experiment. The nanobots. Even getting out of the lab! It's *worked*, Anna. I'm *free*!'

'OK, stop,' said Anna. 'What do you mean, you're *free*? You're . . .' She gulped. 'You're *not* dead?'

He shook his head. 'Nope.'

'Then it was some kind of trick?'

'Nope!' he repeated, grinning. 'Anna, it's *real*.'

'You released the nanobots . . .' said Anna.

'Yep.'

'They took you to pieces . . .'

'Go on.'

'And now you're . . .' Anna stopped.

'I'm part of them, Anna,' said Professor Mallahide. 'And they're part of me. I've joined with them, merged with them. Anna, it's *amazing*!'

But then behind him, beyond the bedroom door, Anna heard footsteps.

Professor Mallahide had forgotten his own warning: he'd spoken too loud, and now the counsellor – woken by the noise – was coming to see what was going on. There was a knock at the door.

'Anna?' said a voice from outside. 'Anna? Are you all right in there?'

'I'm fine!' Anna called.

'It's not a dream, Anna,' her father whispered. 'But until I'm ready, it has to be a secret. Don't worry.' He smiled at her. 'You'll see me again.' Then his face lost focus. He burst apart into nothingness. He vanished.

The door opened.

'Are you OK, Anna?' said the counsellor, oblivious to the strange patch of cloudiness in the air that briefly shimmered, then disappeared from sight. 'I heard voices. Are you having trouble sleeping?'

'I'm fine,' said Anna after a moment. 'Really. I'm fine.'

But she wasn't fine. Not really. Not at all.

THE GATHERING SWARM

'Who is it?' the voice from the intercom squawked. 'Who's there? What do you want?'

'I'm from the council,' Geoff Snedley replied. 'I'm here about your pest problem?'

'All right, all right,' said Mrs de Winter, opening the door. 'No need to tell the whole block about it. Come in before somebody sees you!'

Dutifully doing his best not to wrinkle his nose at the smell, Geoff followed the old lady in.

Mrs de Winter didn't get out much. Also, and rather importantly, she had lost her sense of smell after a bad head cold some years before. Her flat stank – of bad air, stale food and loneliness. But she didn't know. And Geoff, who had been to plenty of places just like this before, saw no reason to tell her.

'So,' he said. 'What exactly is the problem again?'

'Cockroaches,' Mrs de Winter stated bluntly. 'Little 'orrors are everywhere. The bathroom. The lounge. I woke to one waving its nasty long feelers at me over the top of the *duvet* the other day: must've been an inch long at least! And as for the kitchen, *well . . .*'

'The kitchen,' said Geoff. 'That's where you see them most?'

'I'm a *very clean person*,' said Mrs de Winter with great emphasis. 'Just like I told that young lass on the phone yesterday. I'm very careful, me. Very . . . *hygienic*.'

'I'm sure,' said Geoff, still managing not to wrinkle his nose. 'Through this way, was it?' Unstrapping the tank of insecticide from his back, he followed her into the tiny room. Again, Geoff had seen hundreds of places just like it. Crater-like holes in the plaster on the wall. A damp patch in one corner. Carpet tiles sticky underfoot.

'Very nice place you've got here,' he lied. 'Would you mind standing over there by the door, Mrs de Winter? I'm just going to shift this cooker of yours and see what we find.'

'You'll see!' crowed the old woman. 'It'll be crawling with them. *Crawling!* Nasty brown bodies. Wriggling little legs!'

'Well, if it is, we'll be ready,' said Geoff, patting his tank of insecticide with what enthusiasm he could muster. 'Won't we?'

Switching on his torch and angling it to get a good view, he took a deep breath, pulled the grease-covered cooker a few centimetres from the kitchen wall – and looked.

Nothing.

He'd taken Mrs de Winter at her word: if she'd seen cockroaches, then the place was probably riddled with them. But nothing was there. Nothing in the cupboards, either.

'Hmmm,' he said. 'Shall we try the bathroom?'

While the old woman prattled on around him, he care-fully pulled back one of the panels on the side of the bath. Another prime spot – but the same non-result.

The bedroom? Nothing. The lounge? Filthy like the rest of the flat, but still nothing.

'*Well*,' said Mrs de Winter in fury, 'if that isn't just bloody *typical*. I wait in all week for one of you lot to come by. And what happens when you get here? They're *hiding*. Yes! They heard you coming and hid! That's what they're doing, the little beasts!'

Leaning down, Geoff ran one gloved finger along a patch of the baseboard. The finger came away coated in dust, old hair and – he noticed – the tiny black dots of cockroach droppings. He frowned.

They'd been here. No doubt about that. And once roaches were in a place, they didn't leave unless you *made* them: he'd been an exterminator for six years; he knew that much. Stranger still, this was the third false alarm he'd encountered that morning. All over the place, it seemed, people were finding their cockroach problems had miraculously cleared up before he'd arrived. Much more of this and he'd be out of a job.

Where were they? Where had all London's cockroaches gone? *What was going on?*

In Finsbury Park, in North London, Mr Pinkerton sat on a bench with his bag of bread clutched in his hand. He'd been waiting there for nearly an hour already, but the pigeons hadn't come. He'd been told often enough that they were vermin, that he shouldn't feed them, but since his wife had passed away he had nobody else to talk to, and now listening to the delighted bubbling noise the pigeons made when he threw them the bread had become the highlight of his whole day.

But they weren't there. They didn't come, even when he waited. In fact, there was no sign of them anywhere. The reason for this was simple: there were no longer any pigeons left in the park.

Mr Pinkerton could sit there all day if he chose: there were no pigeons left in London. There were no squirrels either, of course. There were no mice and no rats: under London's surface, in the miles of sewers built more than a hundred years before, the only sound was the movement of the water.

Imperceptibly – for now – London was starting to change.

Professor Mallahide needed to grow. He needed to increase himself – increase the size of the swarm of machines he had become. Until he did so, he could be confined in one place and was therefore vulnerable to attack or capture: his whole beautiful, transcendent experiment could be strangled at birth. This was not a possibility he was prepared to tolerate: hence the need to lie low and not reveal himself – except to Anna, of course – until he was strong enough.

He needed source material, raw ingredients for the nanobots to build more of themselves. He needed *mass*. It didn't much matter where he got it. So to start with, he decided to take a few things that – he thought – wouldn't be missed.

It wasn't exactly like stealing or killing, he told himself. Each creature he took – each tiny life he claimed and each small body he converted into more of himself – was only *borrowed*, after all, not destroyed. On the contrary, he told himself: every single detail of his victims – every cell, every atom – was meticulously stored. His memory was now vastly expanded: its storage capacity had been multiplied by his transformation and was growing exponentially all the time, as the swarm did. So these weren't 'victims' at all. They could be returned to life and their original form at any time he chose – and he would do so, he told himself, just as soon as there was enough of him to spare the mass. Of course he would. He wasn't a killer. *And* (he told himself) *it was worth it*.

Exulting, letting the wind currents play all the way through himself, Mallahide hung in the air over London.

For the last ten years of his life he'd been waiting to take this step – waiting to abandon the constrictions of his physical body at last. It was even better than he'd dreamed! He didn't need to eat, or sleep, or go to the toilet; he felt no pain and he never got tired. But wonderful as it was, the thrill of being released at long last from everyday human weaknesses . . . well, that was only a part of it.

All the information, all the memory and sensation and feeling from every creature he'd taken, was all his to access when he wished. He knew what it was to fly like a bird. He knew the sensations of mice: the quivering, shivering, hyper-awareness that came with their speeded-up nervous system. And he now knew more about *cockroaches* than cockroaches did themselves: their movements, the exact consistency and construction of their armoured brown bodies – *what it felt like to be one*. Cockroaches, the professor had decided, were *particularly* fascinating . . .

Humans always went on about 'the real world'. When Mallahide told them what he could offer them, he anticipated that many of them wouldn't understand at first: they would be scared of leaving their bodies behind, scared of becoming like him because they'd think that things wouldn't feel the same.

But that, of course, was where they were wrong. Of

course they could make things feel the same for themselves – if they chose to. Mallahide's own original body could be remade if he ever missed it: that was how he had managed to pay Anna his visit. His machines could replicate any of the body's sensory mechanisms: taste, sight, hearing, even touch. But as well as the human senses, his machines could make *better ones*.

Already Mallahide was building on the knowledge he'd taken from the creatures he'd absorbed. Already his capabilities had developed far beyond those of ordinary humans. He could see in spectra beyond human comprehension, in colours that human beings didn't even have names for. He could taste the world like a gourmet, his machines instantaneously registering not just exact chemical composition but the sensations of the chemicals interacting. He could hear everything in the city, switching through the frequencies at will, from the heartbeat of its smallest insects to the individual explosions of the petrol that powered the thunder of its traffic.

By leaving his human body behind, Mallahide hadn't made himself artificial. He had made himself *more real*. The world was more real to him than it was for anybody else: he could sense more, feel more, touch more than anyone else alive.

But not for long. Soon, he hoped, there would be others . . .

'And finally,' said the announcer, 'scientists are baffled by the thin grey haze that seems to have appeared over the London skyline. Just your typical overcast London weather, you say?

Apparently not: meteorologists claim that according to their best information, the skies should be completely clear! Environmental campaigners are blaming the cloud squarely on one thing: pollution. More on this item after the break.'

'That's what we're telling them?' asked the prime minister.

'It's easy enough to believe, sir,' said his press officer. 'I think people will be convinced.'

'They'd better be,' said Mr Sinclair. 'I mean, if the world actually found out the *truth* . . .' He shuddered. Then he turned to face Professor Mallahide's ex-assistant. 'Right, Dr Belforth: I want you to tell me everything again, once more, slowly, from the top.'

Belforth, a slightly overweight twenty-five-year-old man whose prominent eyes and habit of talking out of one side of his mouth gave him an unfortunately goofy expression, took a deep breath.

'It's the machines,' he said. 'Mallahide's nanobots. Somehow they must have escaped from the lab.'

'*Somehow*,' Mr Sinclair echoed, with heavy emphasis.

'I don't understand it, sir,' said Belforth unhappily. 'We took every precaution. The security systems were designed by Professor Mallahide himself—'

'And we all know how well that worked out for *him*, don't we?' the prime minister replied.

Belforth bit his lip. 'The news gets worse, I'm afraid,' he said. 'The swarm is expanding at an exponential rate, exactly as it was programmed to do. We're tracking the nanobots as best we can, but—'

'All right,' said the prime minister again, waving his hand. 'Enough details: how do we stop this?'

'That's just it, sir,' said Belforth – and bit his lip again.

'Let me guess,' said Mr Sinclair. '*You don't know.*'

SENSITIVITY

A gap in Chris's bedroom curtains had let through a beam of daylight that crossed the room and hit his pillow. Chris opened his eyes a crack, and it was just as if someone was hammering pokers into his skull.

Chris felt horrendous. His throat was dry, and there was a strange kind of throbbing in his head. At first he thought it was tinnitus, like he'd been listening to his headphones too loud. But there was another note to it, something darker and uglier, between a grind and a screech, on and on. He felt weird in his mind too: twitchy and stressed, for no reason he could see or understand.

The bracelet, of course, was still attached to his arm. The night before, Chris had actually broken one of his dad's pairs of wire cutters on the damn thing . . .

There was a knock on the door. Chris burrowed himself under his duvet and groaned. It was his mother.

'Morning!' she said brightly. 'Come on, you, it's time to get up.'

'Mum,' he said from under his duvet, 'I . . . don't know. I think I'm sick with something.'

He heard her hesitate at the door. He knew what she was thinking: it was a weekday after all – she probably thought he was trying to get out of going to school. But she came over and felt his forehead.

'Well, you don't have a temperature,' she told him. She

94

gave him a long look. 'Chris . . . you know, Mr Cunningham called this morning.'

'Yeah? What did he want?' Maybe he was saved. Maybe his headteacher had rung to say the school had been squashed flat by the monster the other night. Then he could stay in bed and—

'He said that the school is open as normal today.' His mother grinned as she saw Chris's disappointment. 'Kiddo,' she announced, 'if a giant monster appearing in the middle of London hasn't stopped the world going about its business, then I think you can cope with a little headache. Come on, get yourself together.'

So that was how Chris had found himself back at school again. He still felt rotten, but that wasn't going to save him from the school morning's opening event, a brutal double dose of biology. Chris hated biology. Without lifting his eyes from the ground, he shuffled over to a desk. His bout of self-pity was abruptly interrupted when a shadow appeared in front of him. He looked up. To his surprise, he saw Anna Mallahide.

The counsellor had wanted to call the school to tell them Anna wasn't coming and why, but Anna had refused. She didn't want to stay in the apartment; she didn't want special treatment. What Anna wanted was a friend.

'You look kind of rough,' she told Chris.

'Weird weekend,' he muttered back. If he'd asked Anna about hers, he might have got a surprise, but he didn't. 'What?' he asked instead when she kept standing there in front of him.

'Listen, I'm . . . sorry about the other day,' Anna

announced quickly. 'I walked off without giving you a chance. That was rude of me. I apologize.' She bit her lip.

Chris stared at her.

'Ms Lucas said for today she'd want us all to get in pairs,' Anna reminded him. 'So . . . how about you and I forget last week and try the whole *partner* thing again?'

Chris blinked, then shrugged. 'All right.'

'All right,' said Anna.

'Today we're going to start something new,' Ms Lucas announced once the class had settled. 'We're going to do an experiment on *live creatures*. Naturally this means you've got to treat the subjects of the experiment with a bit of respect. These are *living things*, helping us to learn about the world – and if I see anyone being mean or cruel to them, there's going to be trouble. Understood? Now, has everyone paired up?'

Chris and Anna exchanged a look. The fact that they were together again had not escaped the notice of other people in the room. At the desk beside them, Johnny Castle made a sort of contemptuous snorking noise through his nose. Gwen Hadlock – the other person Chris had, until recently, been trying hardest to impress – just smirked.

Chris sighed.

'Everyone got their gloves on? All right,' said Ms Lucas. 'It's time to introduce you to the animals we'll be working with for the next two weeks. Boys and girls?' She paused, grinned, and whipped the cloth off the rectangular glass tank on her desk. 'Meet your new friends, the *earthworms*.'

There was a groan of disgust from the class as they caught sight of the glass tank's wriggling pink contents. Still grinning, Ms Lucas picked up the tank and began to take it around the desks.

'Each pair gets to pick their own worm,' she announced. 'Pick 'em up gently. Come on, they're not going to bite you!' Ignoring the exaggerated cries of horror, she started going around the room, dispensing her charges.

When the tank got to Chris and Anna's desk, Chris stared at the worms: their slithering segmented bodies, the livid pink of their saddles, the crumbs of black soil, and the way the worms tangled around each other. He gulped.

Letting out a short sigh, Anna – beside him – picked a worm out of the tank and deposited it on the small plate in front of them.

Johnny Castle, watching this, sniggered.

'Now,' said Ms Lucas, 'what I want you all to do with your worms is very simple: I want you to take your rulers and *measure them*. I warn you, the worms aren't going to stay still, so while one partner measures, the other partner is going to nudge the worm so that it lines up as straight as possible alongside the ruler. *Gently*, now,' she repeated. 'Try not to hurt them. In a moment I'm going to ask you all to give me your measurements, and we're going to work out an average length over the whole class. Then I'll take the worms back to their worm bin. We'll keep measuring them every so often over the rest of the term and see how they're progressing . . .'

While Ms Lucas continued to talk, Anna and Chris looked at each other.

'You want to measure or nudge?' asked Anna politely – almost as if she didn't already know the answer.

'I'll, er, measure,' said Chris – hoping that nobody overheard him.

'*Wuss*,' said Johnny delightedly.

Anna sucked her teeth but said nothing – just started gently encouraging the slithering, wriggling worm to lie alongside Chris's ruler.

'Any lengths yet, class?'

'They keep *changing*, miss!'

'Earthworms can expand and contract to an incredible degree,' said Ms Lucas. 'It's how they move around underground. You don't have to be super-accurate; just a rough idea will do fine. Anna and Chris, have you got anything yet?'

'Eleven centimetres,' said Chris, with effort. Suddenly he was feeling strange again.

It was a little like the way he'd felt when he'd first woken up – only now, in the last second or two, it had become much, *much* worse. The throbbing in his head had returned with reinforcements: angry purple splashes passed in front of his eyes, and a dreadful kind of *racking* feeling seemed to travel all through him.

It was coming from somewhere. *It wasn't . . . was it?* Chris glanced at the bracelet on his wrist. He touched it. It was warm – much warmer than it could have become from his own body heat. It was almost . . . *hot*.

'Johnny and Gwen, do you have an answer yet?' asked Ms Lucas.

Watching Johnny and what he was doing at that moment, Gwen stifled a giggle.

'Wow!' said Johnny with a hard edge to his voice. '*Twenty-one* centimetres, miss – so far. Now it's twenty-*two* . . . !'

To Gwen's delight, Johnny had taken hold of the hapless worm at each end and was *stretching it*.

Pain flooded Chris's body. His head rang with a dreadful inhuman noise, a screaming like brakes, like agony. It hurt so much he could hardly speak, and the bracelet now felt hot enough to burn him. He turned to Johnny and Gwen, saw what was happening to their worm, and the word came out before he could stop it:

'Don't . . .'

Johnny looked up from what he was doing. Stretched between his fingers, the hapless earthworm quivered like a pink guitar string. 'What?' he asked.

'Don't,' Chris repeated. 'You're – hurting.' The word came out without him thinking about it. The pain vibrated through him like an electric shock: welling out from the bracelet, echoing in his head, making his whole body shudder with it like each nerve was on fire, and all the time the terrible inhuman screech in his head went on and on and on.

'Stop it!' said Chris, standing up, not realizing that he was yelling, oblivious to the stares of his teacher and classmates. 'Stop it! *Stop it! STOP IT!*'

For a moment there was a stunned silence in the classroom.

'Johnny Castle, you let go of that worm *at once*!' said Ms Lucas.

Grinning broadly, Johnny did as he was told.

'Leave this class and report to the headteacher right now,' Ms Lucas hissed in fury. 'You too, Gwen Hadlock. *Shame* on you, the pair of you, torturing a helpless creature like that.'

But Chris didn't hear her.

On the desk Johnny's worm twitched once, then lay still. And now something else was happening.

For Chris, the pain was gone. The agony had left him. In its place was a kind of howling black freezing emptiness. It opened up beneath him like a mine shaft, swallowing the classroom, the world, everything.

The bracelet's metal went ice-cold on his wrist.

Chris swayed on his feet; then, with a crash, he collapsed to the floor.

'Euuuuugh,' said Chris presently – and sat up.

He felt like his entire body had been stepped on, very slowly and carefully, all over. He sat there, blinking, because the daylight through the orange curtains on the other side of the room stabbed mercilessly into his skull every time he opened his eyes. As soon as he could manage it – which took a while – he looked around.

He was lying on a bed in the school sick bay. On the wall over his bed was a small red box-shaped object with a glass panel: he was so groggy it took him a second to figure out it was the fire alarm.

Anna was sitting on a chair beside him.

'Hey,' she said, 'you're awake.'

'Er . . . hey,' said Chris. He looked at her. 'Um, what just happened?'

'You fainted,' said Anna, the barest hint of a smile playing at the corner of her ordinarily so serious-looking mouth. 'Right in the middle of a science class?'

'Oh,' said Chris. Then he remembered. 'Oh *no*!'

'It was kind of spectacular, actually,' said Anna, pursuing

Chris's obvious embarrassment mercilessly. 'Really, Chris, I'd never have guessed you felt that strongly about cruelty to poor defenceless little creatures. I mean,' she added, 'the way you pleaded with Johnny Castle to spare that worm's life – that was almost . . . *noble* of you, I'd say.'

'No,' Chris repeated to himself. 'Oh no, no, no . . .'

'Then, of course,' Anna carried on blithely, 'you crashed out right there on the floor. Made quite a racket, I can tell you.'

That's it, Chris was thinking. *My life is over.* What could have possibly happened to make him behave like that in front of everybody? And just because of a *worm*! He would never live this down. He might as well go and throw himself off the top of a tall building or something, because physical death seemed better to him just then than the social kind he'd just condemned himself to. Doom, doom, doom, doom, doom, doom, *doom*.

'It took two people to carry you up here to the sick bay,' Anna was saying. 'I had to come too to answer questions from Nurse Hatchard about what happened. She's gone off to call your parents right now.

'By the way,' she added, looking towards the sick-bay door for a moment to make sure they weren't being overheard, 'I just told Nurse Hatchard that as far as I know, you hadn't taken any medication or *drugs* of any kind.' She leaned a little closer towards Chris. 'That's right, isn't it?'

'Sorry?' said Chris.

'You're not on drugs at all – right?' said Anna. 'Only, I'd hate to have been anything less than completely helpful. I mean, who *knows* what you' – she sniffed delicately – '*cool* people get up to on school time, eh?'

Chris looked at her bleakly.

'I'm the one who stands up for the rights of earthworms, remember?' he said finally. 'I don't think I really qualify as a "cool person" any more.'

'Seems more like you *fall over* for them, not stand up,' Anna pointed out, 'and yes, from the way Johnny and Gwen were looking at you, I'd say your cool rating has taken a bit of a knock.' She looked at him carefully. 'Does that bother you, by the way?'

'Does what bother me?' Chris shot back. 'The fact that everyone in the school now thinks I'm some kind of weird freak? What do *you* think?'

'I don't know,' said Anna mildly – surprising him. 'I know how *I* feel about it. I'm used to it.'

Chris stared at her. But then he heard the door open: presumably Nurse Hatchard had returned. He looked over at the door – and got another surprise.

It wasn't Nurse Hatchard; it was someone else: three people, in fact. They were men: big men with big shoulders, in black suits with white shirts and narrow black ties. The nearest one had just taken off his sunglasses, but the other two were still wearing theirs.

'Anna Mallahide?' said the first man.

Chris looked at her.

Anna sighed. 'Yes. That's me. And what do you gentlemen want, as if I didn't know?'

'We're from MI6,' said the first man, making Chris boggle even further. 'We'd like you to come with us, please.'

'Why?' asked Anna – still sitting down.

'Come on, miss,' said the first man, not unkindly. 'You

know how it is. We'd rather not discuss it with . . . *civilians* present, if it's all the same to you.'

'Civilians?' asked Chris. 'Who? Me?' He looked at her: 'Anna, who *are* these people? What's this all about?'

'If it's about my father,' said Anna with dignity, ignoring him, 'then I don't think it'll matter much if Chris here hears whatever you have to say. If what I think has happened has actually happened, then *everyone's* going to have to be told the truth soon enough.'

'So you know, then?' said the second man.

'I . . . can guess,' said Anna carefully.

'Anna,' Chris repeated, '*what's going on?*'

'Chris,' Anna replied, 'yesterday these men told me that my father was dead.'

Chris was gaping now. Even when the men arrived, he'd still been thinking about how much of an idiot he'd made of himself in class earlier. Now, strangely, that didn't seem to be the most important thing in the world any more.

'But what's bothering them now, I think,' Anna went on, looking up at the men again, 'is that he actually *isn't* dead. Am I right?'

The three men exchanged a look.

'Very well,' said the nearest. He snapped his fingers, and the one guarding the door unzipped a small cloth case from which he produced a laptop computer. 'You'd better take a look at this, then – both of you, if you like. It's a live satellite feed.'

'Of what?' Anna asked.

'There's . . . a situation going on at the BT Tower. It's on all the news.'

'Is it him?' said Anna.

'It's him,' said the man. 'But brace yourself. It's worse than you think.'

'Show me,' said Anna.

ANNUNCIATION

Sir Reginald Sheridan paused, wineglass in hand, to savour his most recent fragrant forkful of Dover sole and admire the view. *Yes*, he thought: this was, most definitely, the life.

He was sitting in a restaurant on the thirty-fourth floor of the BT Tower – one of the most famous buildings in London. Beyond the floor-to-ceiling glass in front of Sir Reginald's table, as if set out specifically to complement his meal, was a panoramic view across almost the whole of the city. Better yet, since the BT Tower was cylindrical in shape, the restaurant had been built to *revolve*. Sir Reginald's view, spectacular as it was, was therefore also constantly changing: the restaurant took exactly twenty-two minutes to perform a complete revolution, so Sir Reginald never got bored. Finally – and best of all – thanks to some silly business with a terrorist leaving a bomb in the toilets back in the early 1980s, the restaurant was no longer open to the public. Sir Reginald and certain other select individuals were therefore free to dine there in utmost luxury without any danger of having to mix with . . . *ordinary* people at all. Sir Reginald was in his heaven and, as far as he was concerned, all was right with the world.

The BT Tower had been built in 1964 as a tele-communications hub. Constructed from over 13,000 tons of concrete, it stood a full 189 metres tall – the tallest structure in London at the time it was built. It was also incredibly strong, having been designed so that the floors and floors of broadcasting and communications equipment that made up the vast majority of the tower's contents could remain protected and continue to function even (supposedly) in the event of a nuclear attack. And Sir Reginald was sitting on top of it.

Sometimes Sir Reginald liked to imagine the floors of humming machines and equipment, vibrating just faintly below him with the terrific speed of their secret calculations. Sometimes he liked to imagine that it was all happening just for him – those sorts of thoughts tended to make Sir Reginald very happy. But now, washing the sole down with a flinty sip of white wine, Sir Reginald touched his napkin to his lips – and frowned.

Annoyingly, the view suddenly didn't seem to be quite as spectacular as usual.

It was this confounded *haze* that had started appearing lately. The skies over the whole of London seemed full of it now, casting its sludgy orange pall over everything. Still, Sir Reginald consoled himself, if the view was disappointing today, the food certainly wasn't. The fish was *sensational*. Sir Reginald's latest mouthful of Dover sole was about to follow its predecessors when he froze in mid-chew. A shadow seemed to have fallen across his table.

The sky was darkening outside the restaurant's windows: not just the sky, Sir Reginald noticed, but *everything* seemed to be darkening, the light leeching away as if the sun was setting. He checked his watch. It was two in the afternoon! How could it possibly be—?

Abruptly – shockingly – the window went blank.

Still with a mouth full of fish, Sir Reginald gaped. *What was going on?* The outside of the windows – the outside of the whole building – seemed to have been suddenly coated in something, as if giant hands had wrapped the tower up in a blanket. It was dark orange-brown in colour, like a dust storm of some kind, only the dust was boiling, *seething* outside, almost as if . . .

Well, as if it was alive.

At the corner of Sir Reginald's eye, something flickered for a moment. He turned.

Someone was standing beside him. There had been no footsteps, no signs of anyone approaching, but a tallish man with unkempt hair and a strange twinkle in his eye was standing at Sir Reginald's elbow, looking down at him.

'How do you do?' asked the apparition. 'I'm Professor Mallahide.'

Sir Reginald remembered to swallow his fish, but no suitable reply occurred to him.

'I'm sorry to have to disturb your meal like this,' said the man who'd just appeared out of nowhere. 'But I'm afraid I'm going to have to ask you to leave. You see, I'm taking over this building. In a moment or two I'm going to use the equipment it contains to broadcast a quick address to the nation, and then the whole of this structure – and everything in it – is shortly going to *vanish*.'

'Are – are you some sort of *terrorist*?' stammered Sir Reginald, finding his voice at last.

'Oh no,' said Mallahide. He grinned. 'No, not in the least – rather the opposite, if anything. Still,' he added, 'for your own sake, I'd advise you to take what I say very seriously. This place is no longer safe for you. In a few minutes, my machines' – he gestured at the boiling orange-brown mass waiting patiently just beyond the glass – 'are going to go to work, and everything in this building will be . . . *changed*. If I was you,' Mallahide went on politely, 'I'd make sure I was safely back at ground level before that happened.'

Sir Reginald looked up at the man and, frowning, touched his napkin to his lips. 'What absolute balderdash,' he replied. 'This restaurant is private: I don't know how you managed to get in here, but I think it's *you* who should be leaving. In fact, I wouldn't be at all surprised if the men in white coats were on their way right now to take you back to whatever mental ward you've obviously just escaped from. Now if you'll excuse me' – he gestured at his plate – 'I was *eating*.'

Professor Mallahide's smile widened. 'You think I'm mad?' he asked.

'As a hatter,' said Sir Reginald.

'You're not the first to think that, and I'm sure you won't be the last,' said Professor Mallahide airily. 'But it's as well to be sure of one's *own* sanity, I always think, before casting aspersions on someone else's. Here's a simple test for you.'

Sir Reginald heard a sudden sort of *fizzing* noise, then the professor brought his hands out from behind his back.

'How many fingers am I holding up?'

Sir Reginald's fork dropped from his own nerveless fingers, hitting the crockery with a crash. 'G-good Lord,' he stammered.

Professor Mallahide had decided to change his hands a little, just temporarily, for fun. Now the grossly misshapen palms with their fronds of digits spread in front of Sir Reginald like two giant fans or large pink sea anemones.

'Go on,' said Mallahide, waggling them at the old

gentleman. 'Take a guess! No? All right, I'll tell you: I'm holding up *twenty fingers*. Twenty-five,' he added gleefully, 'if you include all the thumbs!'

Sir Reginald blinked, gulped, stood up – and ran away. He'd got up so fast that his chair had fallen over.

'Thank you,' said Mallahide to Sir Reginald's retreating back. He waited until the lights on the lift panel told him that the building's remaining occupants were safely on their way back to ground level. 'Now,' he said. 'Time to get started.'

All over London – all over the country – TV screens abruptly filled with static, then went blank. Then, simultaneously on all terrestrial channels, a smiling but unfamiliar face hazed into view.

Professor Mallahide was ready to address his public.

'Good day to you,' he said. 'My name is Edward Mallahide. I'm sorry to interrupt your afternoon's viewing, but I've got some rather exciting news to share with you.'

In homes and pubs all over Britain, fingers stabbed fruitlessly down on the buttons of remote controls. But Professor Mallahide was broadcasting on all channels. Gradually, as the news began to permeate through to broadcasting corporations everywhere, the satellite stations started to show his broadcast too. As he continued to speak, the whole country stopped what it was doing and, curious, began to listen.

'Just two days ago now,' Professor Mallahide announced, 'I did something rather amazing. I stepped out of my body and became something . . . different.'

He paused, grinning delightedly.

'Two days ago,' he said, 'I was a human being. Now I am something else, something I've come to call *posthuman*. I believe that, as a species, this is the next stage in our development, and I have had the very great privilege of being the first to take that step. I can now do things you won't be able to believe. I'll never get tired, I'll never get old, I'll never die – and those are among the least of my gifts. But more important, I want to *share these gifts with everyone.*'

He paused again.

'Imagine a world,' he said, 'without physical limitations of any kind, where you can go anywhere, do anything, and *feel everything.* Imagine a world where man is finally able to escape the prison of his crude fleshy body and, at last, be *truly free.* There will be no age, no death, no disease, no hunger – only life and what you choose to make of it. My friends, that's what I'm offering you. Join me on humanity's greatest adventure. I promise, it will be the best decision you've ever made.'

'What on Earth's he talking about?' The question was being asked up and down the length of Britain – in this case, though, it was being voiced by David Sinclair, the prime minister.

'Ah,' said Dr Belforth unhappily. 'I was afraid of this.'

'What do you mean?' Mr Sinclair snapped back. 'I thought you told me Mallahide was dead! What's he doing on the telly, talking all this nonsense?'

'But that's just it, sir,' said Dr Belforth. 'I'm rather afraid that what he's saying may not actually be nonsense at all.' He took a step closer to where the prime minister was sitting. 'You see, now we know how the nanobots escaped,' he said. 'It wasn't an accident – they were being *controlled*! And now' – he gestured at the screen – 'we know who by.'

'Wait a second,' said the prime minister. 'Are you seriously telling me that Professor Mallahide has . . . become a part of this cloud of machine things?'

'That's correct, sir.'

'But if he can do *that* . . .' Mr Sinclair tailed off.

'If he can do that, Prime Minister,' said Belforth grimly, 'there's no telling *what* he can do.'

There was a short silence.

'First a giant monster,' said Mr Sinclair with feeling, 'and now a cloud of super-intelligent machines. Frankly, I'm starting to wish I'd never got into politics in the first place.'

'. . . Now, some of you, I'm sure,' Professor Mallahide was saying, 'will be thinking that I'm some sort of crackpot. "What's he on about?" you'll be wondering. Well, for those of you in London to answer your question, all you really have to do is *look out of your window*.'

'Go on,' said Mallahide, staring out of every TV screen in the country with a mischievous grin. 'Go on – take a look! You see that cloud over the centre of the capital? This weird orange-brown "haze" that everyone's been talking about? That's *me*. That's what I've become – or rather, that's how I currently choose to show myself. You see, *I can change my form at will*. I can take anything in the world and change that, too, into whatever I choose. I have absolute power over all matter, over everything I can touch – but I'm not a dictator. On the contrary,' he said, 'this power is something I want to share with every single one of you. Tomorrow morning, at eleven o'clock, I will appear again in Hyde Park. If anyone wishes to speak to me, I will answer all questions then.'

Back in the school sick bay, Anna looked at her father on

the screen. He had never looked happier. 'Oh, *Dad* . . .' she said.

'We've had our time as human beings,' Professor Mallahide announced – now speaking to the whole world. 'And you know what? We deserve *better*. With what I can offer, we can have it: we can all, every one of us, be *gods*.'

He paused once more, then started smiling again.

'Now, just so you know that what I'm saying is the truth,' he said, 'I've got a little demonstration for you.' He winked. 'I think you'll like this bit.'

His eyes took on a look of concentration for a moment, and the view on the screen suddenly changed. Instantly another small portion of his cloud of machines had converted themselves into a sort of makeshift camera: this one, unlike the one Mallahide's temporary body was speaking to, was *outside the building*. It swooped around the BT Tower in a vertigo-inducing tracking shot, better than anything that could have been filmed from a helicopter: even under the boiling orange-brown blanket of nanobots, the building's famous cylindrical shape was instantly recognizable to all who saw it. Then the view changed back to Mallahide's beaming face.

'I'm going to count down from five,' he said. 'When I reach zero, this whole building is going to *disappear* – each and every atom of it is going to be dismantled instantly. That should show any doubters, I think. So here we go! Five . . . ! Four . . . ! Three . . . ! Two . . .'

'Oh my God,' said Mr Sinclair. 'Get a squadron of helicopters over there right away!'

'I'm sorry, sir,' said Dr Belforth, 'but I think we're already too late.'

'One!' said Professor Mallahide. 'Everybody ready? And . . . *zero!*'

Abruptly all the windows of the thirty-fourth floor of the BT Tower seemed to burst inward. The restaurant behind where Professor Mallahide was standing suddenly filled with a boiling, rippling, seething cloud of orange-brown dust-like stuff – the nanobots that Professor Mallahide had just permitted to dismantle the outside of the building.

Professor Mallahide executed a low and mocking bow –

– then he too burst apart as the billions of nanobots that had temporarily coalesced into the shape of his old human body were allowed to rejoin the main mass of the swarm.

At the same instant, the part of the swarm that had turned itself into a camera panned backwards and out into the open air, the better to admire the view of what was happening to the rest of the tower.

By now, all over the UK, people were gaping. Tea slopped from the edges of overfilled teacups as their owners continued heedlessly to pour; sandwiches paused halfway towards mouths; people pointed, exclaimed, and swore.

It was true. Professor Mallahide was as good as his word. The BT Tower was disappearing.

All over the building's entire surface area, incalculable numbers of tiny machines set busily to work, taking apart every nanometre of concrete, steel, and whatever else they came across and reducing it to its constituent atoms. These they then *reassembled*, copying their own designs exactly, adding to the expanding swarm. It happened fast – the whole process took just less than three minutes. It also happened very quietly – a silence nearly perfect except for a faint sizzling sound. All 189 metres of the tower seemed to shrink inwards on itself, the column becoming narrower and narrower . . . until finally, shivering, it dissolved completely.

The Mallahide swarm scattered, hazing outwards again. This was so everyone watching could see what was left of the tower. And what was left? *Nothing*. Even the foundations were gone. All that was left of the BT Tower was a hole in the ground.

'Did you see that?' said Chris, unable to stop himself from grinning in what was probably a very uncool way. 'That guy dissolved the tower! The whole thing! *Zoosh!*'

Anna and the three men from the government looked at him. Chris couldn't help noticing that they weren't laughing or even smiling, come to that – so he recovered himself.

'I mean,' he said, 'sure, it was a little *fake*-looking, a bit too obviously computer-generated for my liking. But a nice little scene, I thought.'

No one answered.

'What's the name of the show?' Chris asked blithely. 'What channel's it on? Maybe I'll catch it next time it's on. I like it when they trash famous places.'

'It's on all the channels,' said one of the government men. 'Though not the terrestrial ones, obviously. Those got fried when the tower went,' he added pointedly.

Chris blinked. 'Wait a second. You don't mean . . . ?'

'He means it's not a show, Chris,' said Anna quietly. 'My father did that to the tower. And that . . .' She took a breath. 'That *cloud* is what he's become.'

Chris suddenly noticed Anna looked like she was about to cry. But—

'You'd better come with us, miss,' said one of the government men. 'For your own protection.'

Anna looked up at the men.

Chris watched her shining eyes take on a concentrated look.

'Come on, miss,' said another of the black-clad men. 'There's no time to lose. He could be on his way here right now.'

'Where will you take me?' asked Anna.

'Somewhere safe,' said another of the men, reaching for Anna's arm.

'No,' said Anna, taking a step back. 'Hang on: *no*. At any rate, you'll have to give me a better answer than that.'

The man pursed his lips. 'You'll be taken to a secure location,' he told her. 'Underground. One of the bunker complexes most likely: they're the safest places we've got. But you'll understand I can't tell you exactly where you'll be going, for security reasons.'

'We'll protect you, miss,' said another of the men. 'We'll keep you safe until we work out what to do about . . .' He trailed off.

'About the, er, current situation,' said the first.

'But you have to come with us,' said the third. 'Right now.'

Anna just stood there, considering for a moment. Her tears were gone. She was thinking clearly now.

'You know what?' she said. 'I don't think you're here to "protect" me at all. Not really.'

Chris looked at her.

'Your bosses want me,' Anna went on, 'because . . . yes, that's it: because I might be the only hold you've got over my father!'

'Miss, we don't have time for this,' said the leader of the black-clad men. 'You're in *danger*—'

'From my own dad?'

'And you have to come with us *right now*.' The man took hold of her arm, and the other two stepped forward to surround her.

'Get your hands off me!' said Anna.

'Hey!' said Chris weakly. 'Wait a second! If she doesn't want to come with you, then, you know, you can't force her – right? I mean, you've got no *right* to—'

But suddenly it seemed no one was taking any notice.

'Get – *off* me!' said Anna, struggling to escape, but the two government men on either side of her held her in an iron grip, and now they were heading towards the door.

Chris sat up on the bed, but—

'Stay where you are,' said the third government man. Unfolding his tree-trunk-like arms, he took a step closer towards where Chris was lying. 'Just keep out of this, all right? It doesn't concern you.'

'But,' Chris spluttered, 'you can't—'

'Yes, we can,' said the man. 'And don't try and stop us.'

Chris thought about this.

'Fine . . .' he said.

'Chris!' said Anna. 'Help me!'

'You asked for it.' An idea had occurred to him: Chris reached up to the wall behind the bed – and he hit the fire alarm.

The noise rang out, a hideous jangling din. But bad as it was, the sound of the alarm was immediately challenged by another noise, the sudden racket of a school full of kids who've just realized they're going to be let off at least a good half an hour's worth of lessons. The passageways were instantly packed with bodies. The air was filled with the vain shouts of teachers asking everyone to 'leave in an orderly fashion' and the total pandemonium as nobody took the blindest bit of notice.

'Now,' said Chris. He crossed his arms over his chest, enjoying the moment. 'You've got a bit of a problem, haven't you? I don't think you people are going to be able to take Miss Mallahide anywhere she doesn't want to go – not without the whole school out there watching you lot putting your paws on her. So why don't we all just discuss this a little bit further?'

The three men exchanged a look. Then the two who had been manhandling Anna abruptly released her.

Chris beamed. With just one slick move he'd rescued Anna from three burly government goons. Result! He felt enormously pleased with himself.

'Miss Mallahide,' said the first MI6 man over the continuing din from outside, 'I really do think you're in considerable danger here. Honestly, you'll be much safer with us.'

'Nope,' said Anna, coming over to stand next to her rescuer (which made Chris feel even better). 'Sorry. No way.'

'Seems we've got a standoff,' said Chris cheerfully. 'So . . . what's next? The head'll be wanting to know who set the alarm off, so I wouldn't take too long to decide if I was you.'

The first MI6 man gritted his teeth.

'All right,' he said. He looked at Anna. 'Here's a deal for you, Miss Mallahide. If this' – grimacing, he indicated Chris – 'young *gentleman* accompanies us, will you agree to come with us willingly, without struggling?'

'Now that your father's gone public, you're going to be something of a celebrity, miss,' another MI6 man put in. 'If you won't let us protect you from your father, at the very least you'll be needing some protection from the press.'

Anna considered this.

Hang on, Chris thought, his smile faltering as he watched. This wasn't part of the plan! He'd done his bit: now the goons were supposed to leave with their tails between their legs, not—

'Do we have your word we won't be mistreated?' Anna asked.

'You have our promise,' said the first.

Anna turned to Chris and smiled. 'Well, partner?' she asked. 'What do you say?'

There was a pause.

'Er . . .' Chris managed back. Then, 'I mean . . . yeah, *sure*, I guess.' He shrugged, trying to look as casual as he could. 'Why not?'

'Very well, then,' said the MI6 man. 'Get your coat, young man. You're coming on a little adventure.'

THE DEFENDER

'. . . So that's how it works,' the Kraken was saying. 'We're a little like the planet's *immune system*. When an organism's bloodstream senses disease, it reacts, producing antibodies to fight the infection, right? Well, every few million years, when the *planet* senses a threat, it reacts too, producing us.'

'Um . . . can I ask you something?' said Tim.

'Anything,' said the Kraken.

'How do you *know* all this stuff?'

'What stuff?'

'The stuff you've been telling me, about the world and its . . . "moon system"?'

'*Immune* system,' the Kraken corrected him.

'How do you know about all of it?' Tim repeated. 'Do you travel around a lot? Did somebody tell you about it? Or what?'

'Nobody told me,' said the Kraken patiently. 'And no: I don't move around much these days. The fact is, I just know.'

'But how?'

'Because,' said the Kraken, 'a long time ago, someone did to me what I'm about to do to you now.'

'Did what?' asked Tim.

'Did *this*,' said the Kraken –

– and grabbed him again. Before Tim even had time to register what was happening, six more of the Kraken's powerful tentacles shot out and wrapped around him, sealing him up tight in a complex knot of wriggling, pink, sucker-covered squid flesh.

Tim was bound almost completely, from the crown of his head to the tip of his tail. His eyes were covered; his mouth was covered; he couldn't even move enough to struggle. Only the stubby spines on Tim's forehead were exposed: everywhere else on his body was cocooned in the Kraken's coils.

'What—? *What are you doing?*' asked Tim.

'Don't fight me,' he heard the Kraken whisper in his mind. '*Trust* me.'

Tim's head seemed to fill with the gently pulsating patterns that he'd seen on the Kraken's body.

'*Calm,*' the Kraken's voice told him. 'That's it. Let yourself relax . . .'

Almost without realizing he was doing it, Tim found he'd gone limp and floppy in the Kraken's grasp.

'Yes,' said the Kraken. 'Be passive. Be still. It's time to receive your gift.'

Inside Tim's mind the pulsating patterns were lulling him into a feeling of warmth and serenity. The Kraken's tentacles blocked out all external sensation: for Tim, there was no touch, no sound and no sight – so he didn't see what the Kraken did next. Another tentacle, one the Kraken hadn't used yet, was snaking out of the surrounding darkness towards the exposed spot on Tim's forehead.

The Kraken's gigantic baleful eye narrowed for a moment as the ancient creature prepared itself for what it was about to do. Closer came the last tentacle. Closer still.

'Calm,' the Kraken told Tim. 'Calm. Calm.' Caressingly, the tentacle draped itself over Tim's skull.

Now. The suckers latched onto him, their secretions instantly permeating Tim's scaly skin –

– and Tim's entire body went rigid.

Soundlessly, helplessly, Tim screamed. Everything was on fire. Everything was burning, freezing, jolting, sizzling with a pain that arced through every nerve and every fibre of his whole being. It was like his mind was being . . . *stretched.* Something was pulling at it, pulling it away from its foundations. He felt a tearing, wrenching, splitting sensation—

Then suddenly his consciousness seemed to break away from his body! A kind of hideous, bottomless, lurching vertigo took hold of him as his mind broke free, plummeting away endlessly into the surrounding cold watery darkness. *WHERE AM I?* he wanted to scream. *WHAT'S HAPPENING? WHAT ARE YOU DOING TO ME?* But as loud as he wanted to scream, nothing came out. There was only the panic and the endless falling. For minutes-hours-days-weeks-months-years-centuries he fell, helplessly, rigid with fear. There was nothing but darkness all around him. Soundlessly Tim howled and shrieked out his terror, and just when he thought the darkness would go on for ever, just when he thought he was lost for good—

He saw something.

It was nothing more than a speck at first: he couldn't be sure if he wasn't just imagining it, but—

Yes! There, far away, was something like a tiny spark of light. Reaching out with his mind, Tim went towards the spark, willing it to grow bigger, anything to stop the plummeting empty feeling of the darkness around it, and yes—

Yes, it *was* getting bigger. It was taking shape now. It was . . . a ball. A *globe*, in fact, hanging there in the dark.

Tim could see now that its surface was rippling and shivering. Clouds of poisonous gases howled across the globe's surface, becoming shuddering rivers of sparkling red magma that coiled and darkened and clumped as they formed into masses and began to cool. Now the remaining gases were changing colour, becoming a blanket of white, then grey, then a heavy bruise-black before, finally swollen beyond endurance, the clouds abruptly dumped their condensing contents out onto the globe's new surface. The globe turned blue: a strange round blob of brilliant blue suspended in the endless night.

Tim saw the world, in every detail at once.

He saw the seas form their shapes and the continents slithering over them into their positions. He saw the vast tracts of land, barren at first, but then suddenly teeming with life. Billions of years were passing on the planet's surface and Tim watched it all, watched the different forms (plants, reptiles, insects, mammals) rising and evolving and struggling for dominance. And all the time the pretty blue blob just hung there, spinning, surrounded by darkness.

Gradually, as if from far away, Tim began to be aware of the Kraken. The ancient creature was a presence in his mind, sharing the vision with him.

'Is that . . . the Earth?' Tim asked.

'Yes, little one,' the Kraken told him patiently. 'That is the Earth.'

Tim knew that the Kraken was probably waiting for him to say something else, and yes, Tim *was* going to say something, he could feel he was, but he wasn't sure at first exactly what, so for a long while he just watched the Earth as it continued to spin and the cloud currents slid across its atmosphere. He waited, trying to get his thoughts into the order he wanted.

'But . . . it's so . . . small,' said Tim finally.

'Bigger than you,' said the Kraken's voice in his head. 'Bigger than me, bigger than lots of things. What do you mean, it's "small"?'

'I'm not talking about us,' said Tim, irritated not at the Kraken but at how difficult it was for him to say what he was feeling. 'I mean . . . the way it's *hanging* there like that, in the dark. There's so much dark all around it – dark and emptiness, for ever. But *there it is*, a little blue spot, with all the tiny things crawling around on it. It makes me feel . . .' Tim paused.

'What?' asked the Kraken.

'It makes me feel . . .' Tim repeated, trying to articulate it, 'sort of . . . *sorry* for it, in a way.'

'Why?' asked the Kraken.

'Because it's on its own like that,' said Tim. 'Because there's nothing else all around it but black.'

'There are other worlds,' said the Kraken. 'Other planets.'

'Like this one?'

'A little,' the Kraken replied. 'But none nearby carry life in the same way this one does.'

'Well, there you are!' said Tim. 'It *is* all on its own, this world, or as close to being on its own as makes no difference.'

'So?' said the Kraken.

'Well . . . don't you see?' asked Tim. 'Something could just come along and . . . I don't know, *step* on it or something.

That little blue dot – it could just vanish one day, and then there'd be nothing but darkness! But . . .' He paused again, thinking, while the Kraken waited for whatever he was going to say next.

'Well . . . there it is,' Tim repeated, 'the little thing, spinning and spinning. There it is, doing its best. That's actually, well, kind of . . . *brave*, really. You know,' Tim added, embarrassed now, 'if you think about it.'

The Kraken said nothing.

'What was that . . . "Defender" business you were telling me about before?' Tim asked.

'This is your vision,' said the Kraken, not answering Tim directly, not at first. 'From now on it will be with you, inside you, always.'

The little spinning blue planet began to slow: time was returning to its normal speed, and Tim watched – with a mixture of feelings he didn't really understand – as parts of the Earth began to stain and become dirty-looking as the tiny-people civilizations spread across its surface, leaving their mark.

'Anytime the world is under threat,' the Kraken went on, 'you will know: you will feel it. And that will be your signal. That will mean it is time for you to act.'

'Poor little thing,' said Tim, not really listening. 'It needs someone to look after it.'

'It does,' said the Kraken.

'Someone to stand up for it. Someone to fight for it.'

'Yes,' said the Kraken. 'I'm afraid that's true.'

'Hmm,' said Tim.

Something was waking up inside him. Whether it was to

do with the vision that the Kraken had given him or what, he could feel something changing in the way he thought about things. He felt a rush of something in his mind: determination.

'Yes,' he said. 'All right! I'll do it! I will be the Defender of the Earth!'

Tim thrashed his tail and felt very pleased with himself.

The Kraken did not reply.

'So, er, what do I do?' asked Tim. 'What's next? Who do I have to fight?'

The Kraken sighed. 'You are brave, little one,' it said. 'But you sure are stupid. I hope I'm not just sending you out to die.'

'What do you mean?' asked Tim, instantly defensive.

'Watch . . .' said the Kraken.

'Oh!' said Tim suddenly. He'd noticed something on the blue planet's surface. Something was happening.

Tim hadn't spotted it at first because, to begin with, it had just looked like something to do with the tiny-people civilization. They certainly were messy. But *this*, Tim realized, this was different. The clouds were beginning to change. A strange orange-brown tinge was creeping outwards across the globe, colouring everything it touched. It was slow at first, but it soon picked up speed: before long, everything was the same colour. Now the haze was spreading across the continents. Now it was spreading across the seas! And *now*, the blue planet wasn't blue or sparkling any more: it was a uniform dull orange-brown all over.

'What happened?' asked Tim, suddenly frantic. 'What just happened then?'

'I'm not sure,' the Kraken replied.

'But I didn't get a chance to do anything!' Tim yelped. 'Make it go back! MAKE IT GO BACK HOW IT WAS!'

'Easy!' said the Kraken. '*Easy*, little one. Remember how you felt: remember being calm. Calm! The answers are coming.'

Tim didn't feel calm at all. But he managed to quieten his mind down so that the Kraken could speak to him again. And in due course, the vision seemed to rewind. The awful dun-brown colour swilled back, like it was draining away. The lands and the seas returned to how they'd been a moment before, and the planet became blue once more. All that was visible of the orange-brown haze was a tiny speck, hovering over a spot on the globe that – Tim suddenly realized – was familiar to him.

'What *was* that?' Tim asked.

'That,' said the Kraken, 'was a warning.'

'A warning of what?'

'Of what is to come,' the Kraken replied. 'One of the tiny people has created something powerful – something he lacks the maturity to control. He has already changed himself: if he is not stopped, he will impose this same change on the *whole world*. Diversity will become conformity; grown will change to built; nature will change to machine. For ever.'

'But . . .' said Tim. 'How can we stop it?'

'There's no "we" in this,' said the Kraken. 'You, little one: if you're the Defender, *you* must face this thing. Alone.'

MALLAHIDE RISING

Hyde Park. 10:57 a.m. Standing in the turret of a Challenger tank, under cover of some trees within sight of Park Lane, Field Marshal Clement 'Clem' Thompson checked the perimeters of his field of operations one last time, then lowered his binoculars. He and his team were ready – or at least, as ready as they were ever going to be.

Whatever was about to happen, Professor Mallahide had picked a good spot for it. Covering 350 acres, Hyde Park was the single biggest open space in central London. It had been used regularly as a concert venue, most notably in the Live 8 event of 2005, in the course of which an estimated 200,000 people had crammed into its grassy environs.

But if Mallahide really had any hopes about attracting a serious crowd with his publicity stunt of the day before, he was going to be disappointed: today Hyde Park looked almost empty. It was closed to the public. All exits were sealed. Any groups of curious onlookers that formed around the edges of the park were being firmly encouraged to leave the area. Instead, a small but powerful tactical force – put together from the finest men and hardware that the British military had to offer – was currently lying in wait for the professor's arrival. Field Marshal Thompson had supervised their positioning personally. Professor Mallahide was walking into an ambush.

Thompson felt uneasy. A veteran of many military

engagements from all over the world, from Ireland to Afghanistan to Iraq, he had long learned to trust his instincts in combat, and his instincts were twitching powerfully. The problem was that there were so many unknown factors: Hyde Park was *too* open. It was impossible to tell where or how the professor was going to make his entrance, let alone what else to expect.

Thompson sighed. In all his long years serving his country, he had never had to deal with anything like what had occurred in the past week. First a rampaging dinosaur, now a man who'd turned himself into a cloud of machines. What on Earth could possibly happen next? He checked his watch: 11 a.m. exactly. The sky had been overcast for some time now, and a thin drizzle began to fall.

There! He saw something, a flicker, but it was enough to make him lift his binoculars again.

Six hundred metres away from where Field Marshal Thompson was waiting, the air over a patch of ordinary grass in the centre of Hyde Park seemed to shimmer for a moment. A column of something bright and sparkling shivered into view, and by the time Field Marshal Thompson's binoculars had focused on the spot, Professor Mallahide had appeared.

'This is Unit Six – target acquired,' murmured a voice in Thompson's ear.

'Unit Three – target acquired.'

'Unit Five – target acquired.' The other units called in with similar messages from their camouflaged positions all around the park.

'Hold your fire,' said Thompson into his throat microphone. 'All units, wait for my mark.'

In front of him, focused in the field marshal's binoculars, the professor appeared to be very relaxed. Blissfully unaware, apparently, of the array of large-calibre weapons currently locked onto his position, Mallahide spread his arms wide and stretched luxuriously. He bent down and ran a hand across grass that still had the fresh pale green of early summer growth. He smiled to himself. Then he looked up.

Field Marshal Thompson blinked, surprised, and looked through his binoculars again. The professor was staring right at him – as if he was standing in front of him, in fact. Worse yet, he had started to wave.

'Hello!' he shouted, his voice sounding faint and silly in the middle of the empty park. '*Coooo-eeeee!*'

Field Marshal Thompson gritted his teeth but said nothing.

'I wish you'd let everyone in!' the professor called out. 'There's absolutely nothing for people to be afraid of, you know. I've no wish to hurt anybody: quite the reverse, in fact!'

Nobody answered.

Professor Mallahide pursed his lips.

'I should have guessed you lot would look at this the wrong way,' he said finally. He shook his head to himself. 'All these years of people like you funding my research, and do you know? I don't think even *one* of you ever really understood its true significance.' He sighed and looked up again.

'OK,' he began, 'here's the situation. I know you've already decided what you're going to do.' Absently he wiped his grass-stained hands on his trousers. 'Believe me, you're making a dreadful mistake. But I'm going to give you one more chance.'

Still watching through his binoculars, Field Marshal Thompson touched the microphone at his throat. 'All units,' he whispered, 'prepare for my mark.'

'Move your men away from the park's entrances,' said Mallahide, 'and allow whoever wishes to meet me to come and do so. I'll give you ten seconds: I know exactly where all of you are, so the sooner you do what I'm asking, the sooner we can forget all this. Stop this *idiocy* of yours *this instant*,' he added with a flash of anger, 'or you're all going to be very sorry. Ten. Nine. Eight—'

Well, thought Thompson, *here goes nothing* . . . 'Thompson to all units,' he said. 'Fire at will. I repeat: *fire at will*.'

Instantly the spot where the professor was standing exploded in a flash of light and a gout of smoke. Crisp soil and grass fragments pattered down for hundreds of metres around under the continuing barrage of noise as the bombardment continued. All six Challenger tanks had loosed their main cannons almost simultaneously, vaporizing the target area in a deafening blast of thunder. While they reloaded, more of Thompson's group laid down a withering hail of suppressing fire from their machine guns, churning up the grass, shattering the peace of the park with an unending-seeming welter of noise. The second wave of shells from the tanks hit home a scant couple of seconds later, sending more clods of black earth high into the air. And as if that wasn't enough . . .

'Napalm,' said Field Marshal Thompson into his throat microphone –

– and a specially trained squadron of men in biohazard suits advanced through the smoke, dispensing searing chemical death across what little remained of the greenery.

'Hold your fire,' said Field Marshal Thompson. 'All units, I repeat: cease fire. Cease fire.'

For a long second the storm of noise echoed around and back across the empty park. The air was thick with smoke. Thompson's retinas were covered in the blossoming flashes of the explosions, and his ears rang. But he waited, his binoculars glued in place.

'All units, stand by,' he said.

The thick cloud parted, revealing the scene.

Thompson's team had been gratifyingly accurate in their grouping. The damage that the attack had caused was strictly confined within a radius of something close to ten metres. Outside this perimeter, with the exception of a few spots of sputtering flame where the napalm had set the grass alight, the park looked almost normal. Inside the ring of fire, how-ever, was a scene of utter devastation.

Where Professor Mallahide had been standing was nothing more than a large smoking hole in the ground. A great chunk of black London earth had been eaten away, scooped up by exploding ordnance and scattered to the winds. As an exercise in controlled destruction, it was definitely impressive.

'This is Unit Six: no sign of target.'

'This is Unit Three: no sign of target. Believe destroyed.'

'This is Unit Five: target appears to have been destroyed. Awaiting confirmation.'

A ragged cheer broke out over the radio. Clearly the men had enjoyed themselves, and in a sense Field Marshal Thompson couldn't blame them. Some of the tank crews had been on duty for the tyrannosaur fiasco the other evening: their confidence had been badly knocked, and they needed a victory – however minor – to build their morale back up.

Still: Thompson alone stood silent, searching through his binoculars. His instincts were still prickling. He had to be sure.

'All units,' he said, 'stand b—'

He fell silent.

A dreadful change seemed to have come over the scene in the park. The sky overhead, already overcast, suddenly seemed to turn black. There was a crackle in the air; it felt thick with pressure and something like electricity. Field Marshal Thompson's ears started popping.

He looked up – and dropped his binoculars.

An enormous storm had brewed up from nowhere, exclusively over Hyde Park. The clouds had sunk down, turning a menacing blue-black, bulging with rage. At the same time, the wind began to pick up in the park – but it was a strange kind of wind. Field Marshal Thompson's beret lifted and blew off to his left, but across the park (he couldn't help noticing) the branches of the trees were leaning to the *right* – the opposite direction.

The scattered clods of blackened earth began to twitch and tremble on the grass in front of Thompson's tank. The pressure in the air seemed to be dropping, and the massive black bank of cloud overhead flickered and licked with tiny tongues of lightning. Lower the cloud came, and lower still, the base of it extending into a cone and then a corkscrew of inky darkness that, slowly at first but with gathering speed, began to spin. Thompson blinked against the wind with streaming eyes, hardly daring to believe it.

In the last few seconds, for the first time in history, a tornado had formed in Hyde Park.

The wind had picked up savagely by now, rising to a howling banshee shriek as the whirlwind reached its top speed. The eye of the storm seemed centred on the hole Thompson and his team had just made, but the walls of the tornado were expanding outwards, blotting out everything: in another moment he could see nothing else. Before he really knew he was doing it, Field Marshal Thompson found that he'd ducked down into the turret of his tank and slammed the lid.

In the cramped interior of the Challenger the rest of its crew stared back at him: the air had heated up in there in the last few moments, but Field Marshal Thompson didn't feel it under the icy prickles that now crawled up his arms and the back of his neck.

'Sir . . .' said one of the men quietly, 'can you please tell us what's going on out there?'

'I . . . I don't know,' said Field Marshal Thompson honestly.

For a long second nobody spoke inside the tank as, white-faced, all four men stood listening to the rising shriek of the wind battering at the exterior.

Then there was a rocking sensation.

'What was that?' someone asked.

The rocking sensation came again.

'My God!' said Thompson. 'This tank weighs over sixty tons! How can the wind possibly be strong enough to—?'

The rest of his words were lost in the sudden rumble as the tank gave a sudden and definite *lurch*.

'Everybody out of the tank!' yelled Thompson. Touching his throat microphone, he added, 'All crews, abandon their vehicles! Everyone get to cover! Now!'

Nobody needed telling twice. In seconds, he and his men had leaped up the ladder and out into the screaming blackness beyond.

They weren't a moment too soon. Thompson jumped free, rolling to a stop on the sodden grass just as – with a piteous wail of protesting metal – the Challenger (all sixty tons of it) was dragged away towards the whirling black dervish dominating the centre of the park, and *swallowed*.

Struck dumb with amazement, Field Marshal Thompson watched as his own tank, the five others, and assorted other heavy equipment from all over his field of operations was plucked neatly into the air. For a second it all seemed to dance around above him like some sort of airborne carousel. He watched, still speechless, as all his finest military hardware was flung up like so much confetti, shrinking, shuddering, and finally vanishing as it was all stripped down to nothing. He felt a simultaneous tugging sensation himself – and grasped the ground. But the sensation seemed to be strangely localized, focusing only on his belt.

He looked down, eyes streaming, and saw . . . yes: the holster with his sidearm was twitching on his hip. Now it was opening, and his gun had flown out! Now, all across the park, men's weapons were being snatched out of their reach. Rifles, pistols, grenades, machine guns, napalm dispensers – all of it flew up into the air and vanished like the tanks had before them.

When the men were completely disarmed, when all of them just lay there in disarray, strewn around the grass wherever they'd landed, the tornado abruptly seemed to suck back up into the main mass of the cloud. The wind dropped. Then there was silence.

'Right,' said a voice. 'Are you ready to talk seriously now? Or are you still dead set on acting like idiots?'

Blinking, Field Marshal Thompson sat up.

There, standing only a few metres away, was Professor Mallahide. Behind him the patch of park that, up until a moment ago, was all that Field Marshal Thompson and his men had managed to destroy in their ferocious attack, seemed to have magically repaired itself. The black mass of cloud still loomed menacingly overhead, but apart from that – and the vanished weapons and equipment – there was absolutely no sign anywhere of what had just taken place.

Mallahide still wasn't smiling, though: he was getting impatient.

'Are you understanding this yet?' he asked. 'Is this getting through to you? *You can't hurt me.* You can't shoot me; you can't blow me up; in fact, you can't really do anything what-soever to stop me. So the only way you and I are going to make any progress is if you stop trying to cling to what little power you *think* you still have and just listen to what I have to say. *Listen to me,*' Mallahide repeated. 'That's all I ask!'

Field Marshal Thompson knew he had lost control of the situation. For a moment, as he lay on his back on the grass, blinking up at the figure of the professor, it felt to him like the whole episode – in fact, everything since last week – must be part of some sort of awful dream. Well, there was one more chance. He reached up and touched his throat microphone.

'Bravo Ten Zero,' said Field Marshal Thompson, 'this is Hot Spot, authorizing Operation Pandora's Box – code seven, seven, nine, seven, five. Repeat, Operation Pandora's Box, you are clear for your attack run. Acknowledge, please.'

'This is Bravo Ten Zero,' said a voice in his ear. 'Commencing attack run.'

'All right,' said the professor wearily, 'what have you done now?'

'Air strike,' croaked Field Marshal Thompson. 'I've just given the order to have the whole of Hyde Park carpet-bombed.' He smiled weakly. 'What do you think of that?'

'Oh, for heaven's *sake* . . .' Making a soft sucking noise of annoyance with his tongue, Mallahide looked in the direction the planes were coming from – even though, at that moment, they were still too far away to be visible or audible to any ordinary human being. 'You really are being very tiresome about this,' he added, looking down at the field marshal again. 'I think when I've dealt with this latest idiocy of yours, you and I are going to have to have *words*.'

Then – horribly – Professor Mallahide started to change.

A column of sparkling golden light seemed to extend downwards from the waiting mass of cloud above, covering the professor in an extraordinary orange-brown aurora. Instantly his arms, his legs – his whole body, in fact – began to thicken and turn dark.

Spots of shiny brown – so dark as to be almost black – were spreading and expanding all over him: running up his legs, pooling across his torso. At the same time, the professor seemed to be *growing* – expanding in size at an incredible rate.

His legs, completely covered now in thick plates of a kind of armour, stretched outward, swelling, lifting him into the air. Abruptly, with a soft crackling sound that Field Marshal Thompson found especially hideous, each of the legs then split apart right up the middle, dividing in two, then four, while the professor's lower body seemed to elongate out behind him.

Now Mallahide towered over the park. Multiple insect legs had suddenly arched up into shiny brown ridges overhead, like the vaulted ceiling of some unspeakable cathedral – and Field Marshal Thompson gaped. He'd been reminded of something: he was so appalled and absorbed in the terrifying transformation taking place right before his eyes that it took him a moment to work out what. But he knew where he'd seen the shiny brown armour before.

On a cockroach.

Professor Mallahide had reconfigured himself, condensing his swarm of machines into a single shape, the first one that had occurred to him that would still be long enough to protect the park from whatever these military idiots were about to come up with next: the shape of a cockroach. However, Mallahide had decided to leave his upper body more or less as it was. From the waist up, his proportions were the same as those of his human body – torso, two arms and a head – but all were now armoured in the same tough carapace as the rest of him, and magnified to incredible size.

Clicking his giant new jaws, Mallahide looked down at himself and smiled. The whole transformation had only taken something like thirteen seconds, but he had to admit, the effect was pretty spectacular. He was now more than 150 metres tall – and that wasn't even including the length of him from the waist down. His new compound eyes – each dinner-plate-size lens of which processed vastly more information than any insect eye had ever been capable of before – focused on the oncoming squadron of jet fighters.

No doubt about it: he was really going to enjoy himself now.

'Dear God – what the hell is *that*?' screamed a voice in Field Marshal Thompson's ear as one of the fighter pilots got his first eyeful of what Mallahide had now become.

'Cut the chatter, Eagle Four,' said another voice. 'All units keep it tight on my wing. Weapons systems armed and ready.'

Six Tornado fighter planes streaked through the air over London, making crockery rattle on shelves all over the city with the shattering *boom* of their jet engines.

In the cockpit of his plane, the squadron leader eyed the looming shape through his windscreen and suppressed a shudder.

'Eagle One, this is Eagle Five,' said a voice in his head-phones. 'Shouldn't we have missile tone by now?'

'Eagle Five, this is Eagle One,' said the squadron leader, 'hold your course and stand by.' But it was true. All the planes in the squadron had been loaded with the latest air-to-surface weaponry, supposedly capable of locking itself onto a target without any input necessary from the pilot. Sophisticated computer systems in each warhead were supposed to search for their marks by themselves before signalling to the pilot their readiness to be fired by a teeth-grating whine from speakers in the cockpit. The fighters were well within range, but so far no sound had been forthcoming.

'Eagle One, this is Eagle Two – I'm not getting a fix either! I can see the target visually, but it's not coming up on anything else – no radar contact! Nothing!'

'He must be jamming us somehow,' Eagle One replied. Running his tongue along his teeth, he made a decision.

'We're getting too close. We'll just have to do this the old-fashioned way. All units, prepare to release payload manually on my mark! Three! Two! One! *Now!*'

And just as it seemed the formation of fighters was about to overshoot the park, the warheads were released to find their targets as best they could.

*Wha*KHOOM!

WHUMP!

CRUMP! FUP! FOOM!

KaBOOM!

A roll of explosions echoed across the London skyline as the missiles – their sophisticated targeting equipment reduced to the simple 'on-impact' activation of the most basic bombs used in the Blitz – struck Mallahide's carapace and detonated.

Still frozen on the grass underneath the gigantic dark canopy of Mallahide's hind legs, Field Marshal Thompson and his men stared upwards, helpless with amazement and terror. The great pillar-like armoured black legs seemed to quiver for a moment as the bombs hit home. For an extraordinary fraction of an instant just before he heard the explosions, Field Marshal Thompson caught a flash of their light passing through the swarm – before it condensed even tighter to absorb the damage.

Instantly, without Mallahide even having to think about it, scores of millions more of his nanobots converged on the places where the bombs had struck, shoring up the parts of the swarm that had been destroyed by the bomb blasts.

But Mallahide hadn't felt a thing.

The fact was, he had told Field Marshal Thompson the truth. The vast cloud of machines that made up Professor Mallahide's body was now simply incapable of being seriously harmed by anything a conventional army could throw at him. Individual nanobots could be damaged or destroyed, sure, by the trillion if need be – but that wasn't going to stop Professor Mallahide. *He was too big*. He could just make more of himself! And as the squadron of fighters, their jet engines howling, wheeled round for another pass at the awesome creature bestriding Hyde Park like some dreadful half-insect colossus, their pilots did not have the faintest conception of what was about to happen to them . . .

Field Marshal Thompson was still lying frozen where he'd fallen. The grass of Hyde Park was completely overshadowed by the vast and looming shape of Mallahide's gigantic cockroach-like body. Thompson was staring upwards at the raging battle taking place high above – but he still noticed when a haze of something bright and sparkling shivered into being in front of him.

Professor Mallahide had reappeared.

There was a little blurriness about his face and the edges of his silhouette, and occasionally (a result of him being in two places at once: most of the swarm was concentrated else-where for obvious reasons) parts of him were a little *transparent*. But basically the professor's human form was exactly the same.

'Call off the attack,' Mallahide said.

'No,' said Field Marshal Thompson.

'Call off the attack,' Mallahide repeated, his features going out of focus for a moment in his annoyance. 'I won't ask you again.'

'Why?' said Field Marshal Thompson, with all the bluster he could manage. 'What's the matter? Are you *scared*?'

Mallahide pursed his lips – or did his best to. It was hard to get the facial nuances right when so much of his processing power was concentrated on the battle: Eagle Squadron was just making its second attack run. Suddenly the air was shuddering again with the crash and shock of another volley of missiles detonating – spectacularly if harmlessly – on Mallahide's back, high above.

'It's not me who should be scared,' he told the field marshal. 'It's *you*. This is getting dangerous: not for myself of course, but for this whole surrounding area. I mean,' he added, beginning to lose patience again, 'what do you think you're doing, launching an air strike like this *here* of all places? For heaven's sake, man, we're in the centre of London! What about the buildings? What about the *people*?'

'I could ask you the same thing,' said Field Marshal Thompson. Sitting up, he took a deep breath. 'I protect this city,' he told the shimmering form of the professor. 'I protect this whole country, and I'm proud to do it. You are a *threat*, an invading force, and as the head of Her Majesty's Armed Forces, it's my duty to respond to that threat with *any means at my disposal*.'

'Hot Spot, this is Eagle One!' Thompson's radio broke in suddenly. 'Hot Spot, this is Eagle One; please respond!'

'Hot Spot here,' said Thompson. 'Go ahead, Eagle One.'

'Sir — our missiles are having *no effect*. This thing, it's just taking everything we can throw at it!'

'Call them off,' said Professor Mallahide quietly. 'You see? It's useless.'

Thompson scowled. 'Eagle One, this is Hot Spot. There's only one thing left to try.' He paused, took another deep breath, and then — looking up at Mallahide — he said: '*You know what to do.*'

Professor Mallahide frowned. This made his eyes pixellate a little at the corners, but he didn't care about that any more. 'What have you done now?' he enquired.

'Hot Spot, this is Eagle One,' said the voice from the radio. 'Confirm, please: "Last Post"?'

' "Last Post," ' said Thompson. 'And may God have mercy on your souls.'

'All right, boys,' said Eagle One. 'You heard the man. Everybody form on my wing.'

'Thompson, *what have you done?*' Mallahide repeated.

'You'll find out,' said Field Marshal Thompson — and smiled.

'Oh no!' said Professor Mallahide. 'Oh no, no, no. Those poor pilots!'

But then, with a noise like thunder, all six planes from Eagle Squadron drove themselves screaming into the swarm.

It was the last option. Every member of the team was a volunteer. They had known what was at stake when they'd taken off from base: they'd known that if all else failed, the last chance was to hurl *themselves* into the fray. A suicide run, right into Mallahide's heart — assuming he had one.

In front of Field Marshal Thompson, the part of Professor

Mallahide that still looked human abruptly vanished. What was taking place up above now would require a concentration of almost all of his processing power. Vast millions of individual members of the swarm writhed and bunched into position, ready for the impact of the six full-size oncoming fighter planes.

At the last instant, all six pilots of Eagle Squadron closed their eyes, waiting for the shock, the flood of heat and flame that would wipe them out of existence.

Professor Mallahide reconfigured himself again –

The swarm rippled and quivered –

And one by one, when annihilation didn't come, the pilots opened their eyes.

Eagle One looked out of his cockpit and blinked.

His plane had stopped – brought to a halt gently but firmly before any damage could be done. Now, it seemed, pilot and plane were suspended in a kind of boiling cockroach-brown fog that seethed and shivered against the cockpit's windows.

For a long moment he stared out helplessly.

Then the windows – the nose – the wings – the whole plane was dissolved. A thick brown cloud poured in all over him. There was a moment of stinging and unbelievable agony—

Then nothing.

Eagle Squadron had vanished with all hands – or not *vanished*, exactly: they'd been *absorbed*. Mallahide had them now.

On the shadowed ground in Hyde Park, Field Marshal Thompson stared up at his enemy.

No change. The attack had failed.

The air shimmered in front of him, and Mallahide's human form appeared again.

'I am *very* angry with you,' Professor Mallahide announced – though from the way his eyes were flashing, Field Marshal Thompson hadn't really needed to be told this.

'How could you do that?' asked the professor, gesturing upward with one tweed-jacketed arm. 'How could you order your men to kill themselves like that? What gives you the right? And why did they *obey* you?'

'Professor Mallahide,' said Field Marshal Thompson wearily, 'for someone who has spent as many years working for the military as you have, you really don't seem to understand us very well. Look at yourself.' He too gestured upwards. 'Look at what you've become. You're a danger to the world, and my men and I are willing to die to stop you.' He drew himself up proudly. 'That's what being a soldier is all about.'

'I didn't want to have to absorb those people,' said Mallahide. 'And believe me, I don't want to have to absorb *you*. For what it's worth, I want you to know that you won't be harmed, and that I can bring you back whenever I see fit.'

'How very reassuring,' said Field Marshal Thompson.

'But *you* are the dangerous one here, to yourself and to others,' Mallahide announced, ignoring the sarcasm. 'You – and all those like you, who see the world only in terms of violence – are the last remnants of our caveman days. And now, I'm happy to say, humanity has outgrown you.'

'Oh, shut up and get it over with,' said Field Marshal Thompson.

'Fine,' said Mallahide.

DIPLOMACY

The Cabinet Room, 10 Downing Street, not far beyond the most famous black front door in the world. A long table dominated the room: the biggest decisions about the running of Great Britain were made, supposedly, around this table. This occasion was to be no exception.

At one end, the end nearest the room's soundproofed double doors, stood Mr Sinclair, flanked by a couple of very worried bodyguards. At the other – in his old human form, for the time being, at least – stood Mallahide.

Behind the professor, a pair of windows allowed the hazy grey light of the day outside to leak into the room. The windows were made of Plexiglas and a metre thick, a security precaution installed after they'd been shattered one time in a terrorist attack. To make his entrance, Mallahide had just reduced them to their component atoms, reconstructing them behind him.

'Well, Prime Minster,' he said, beaming widely, 'here I am. What can I do for you?'

Mr Sinclair cleared his throat: Mallahide's sudden appearance had scared him badly. But a lifetime's experience as a politician and public speaker helped the prime minister control his voice.

'Thank you for coming, Professor,' he began in his most ingratiating tone, 'but I think we both know it's more of a question of what *we* can do for *you*. Am I right?'

Mallahide raised an eyebrow. 'Sorry? I'm not sure I follow—'

'What do you *want*, Professor?' Mr Sinclair asked him, hoping this was plain enough.

'Oh,' said Mallahide. He shrugged. 'Well, it's like I said in my broadcast. I have taken humanity's next step up the evolutionary ladder. I now possess a gift, the most incredible gift you can imagine – and I want to share that gift with the rest of the human race.' He beamed again. 'That's about the size of it.'

'Yes,' said the prime minister with a wave of one hand. 'But what do you *really* want?'

'Pardon me?'

'Professor Mallahide,' said Mr Sinclair, 'let's be frank with each other, shall we?'

'Please.'

'Your ambitions for the human race are wonderful,' the prime minister began, 'or I'm sure they seem that way to you. I admire ambition in a man: I admire *you*, Professor Mallahide, truly I do. But . . .' He paused. 'Well, speaking as someone with some measure of experience in trying to convince large numbers of people to believe in him' – the prime minister tried for a smile – 'I have to say you're not doing a particularly great job so far.'

'Really?' said Professor Mallahide.

'I don't think people understand you,' Mr Sinclair said carefully. 'To be honest, Professor, I don't either. So, let me ask you again: what do you want? What can we give you,' said Mr Sinclair slowly, rephrasing his question, 'to make you *stop what you're doing*?'

'Oh!' said Professor Mallahide again, surprised. Then he smiled, in a way that Mr Sinclair found particularly infuriating. 'Prime Minister,' he asked in a tone of mock horror, 'are you trying to *buy me off*?'

'All right,' growled the prime minister, losing patience. 'Yes! Well, *can't we*?'

'I'm sorry, Prime Minister,' said Mallahide, 'but I'm afraid the short answer is *no*.'

'But . . . why not?'

'Well, for one thing,' the professor pointed out, 'I now have direct control of all physical matter, down to the atomic level. In layman's terms,' he went on, 'this means that anything I don't happen to have – anything I want – I can now simply *make for myself*. Here, let me give you an example.'

He held out a hand. The air over his open palm seemed to flicker for a moment, then an object appeared. It was crystalline and twinkly and about the size of a hand grenade. Mallahide tossed it to Mr Sinclair.

The bodyguards flinched, reflexively (if uselessly) going for their guns, but Mr Sinclair had caught the glittering object before he could stop himself.

'What is this?' the prime minister asked, dreading the answer.

'It's a diamond,' said the professor blithely. 'I made it, just now, from the carbon in this room's atmosphere. A simple process, really, just a question of arranging the atoms in the right configuration – and of course, the result is *much* purer than you'd get from digging it out of the ground, cutting it, et cetera.'

The prime minister gaped.

'You see,' Mallahide went on, 'now that I exist as I am, the human race as we know it is going to undergo some rather significant changes. One of the first things that will happen is that current conventional measures of *wealth* – jewels, gold, oil and so forth – simply won't count for much any more. Before long, everyone will simply be able to make anything they want for themselves: my machines will conjure it for them out of air or earth or whatever base materials are to hand. Imagine it!' he added excitedly. 'Total freedom for everybody!'

Seeing the prime minister's attention was still rooted to the giant diamond, Mallahide's expression fell a little. 'I'll take that, if you don't mind,' he tutted, gesturing – and the gem burst apart into a cloud of nothingness, its existence annulled as quickly as it had begun.

The prime minister blinked.

'My point is,' Mallahide told him, 'that if you were hoping that somehow you could tempt me with money, or power, or those sorts of things, then I'm afraid you're in for a disappointment. Quite simply, Prime Minister, there's nothing you can really offer me. So,' he added, putting his hands on the other end of the table, 'why should I want to . . . "stop", as you put it?'

The prime minister gulped. 'People are scared of you,' he said. *I'm scared of you*, he added, though not aloud. 'People don't want to be dissolved into atoms or whatever. People are happy as they are!'

The professor looked sad. 'Perhaps you're right,' he said. 'When I took the first step to becoming what I am, it wasn't easy, I can tell you. It certainly requires something of a leap of faith. But I believe,' he went on, brightening again, 'that when people see the benefits, they'll be begging to join me. And I'll be more than happy to oblige.'

'But what if they don't?' asked the prime minister. 'What if that doesn't happen? What's to stop you from . . . forcing them? Dissolving them against their will?'

The professor smiled. 'My dear Mr Sinclair,' he said, 'what do you take me for?'

The prime minister didn't answer.

'I'm not a barbarian, you know,' said Mallahide. 'If some people, for whatever reason, choose to turn down the chance to become what I can help them to become, then I'm certainly not going to *force* them. I abhor force in all its forms.'

'You do?' said the prime minister.

'Of course,' said the professor. 'There is, however,' he added regretfully, 'the, ah, issue of *safety*.'

'What do you mean?'

'Well,' said Mallahide, 'it's like this. The difference between being human, as I was, and posthuman, as I am now, is really so vast that – with respect – it's going to be difficult for you to imagine it. But I must ask you to imagine how much vaster that gulf will become once a significant proportion of the world's population has followed in my footsteps. Surely it's not too hard for you to grasp it: before long, those who are left behind will begin to find that the world they have known up until then will be . . . well, *incomprehensible* to them. Morality, technology, relationships – let alone the funda-mentals like birth and death – the old conventions on these things will simply no longer apply. And,' the professor added darkly, 'with ignorance and misunderstanding comes fear and, finally, danger.'

'*Danger?*' the prime minister echoed.

'There will need to be . . . certain *areas*, I think, set aside for those who choose not to join me. It's regrettable, really, to curtail their freedom any more than they'll have already curtailed it for themselves. But the fact remains that the world at large simply won't be safe for them any more.'

'Why not?' the prime minister pursued.

The professor sighed again. 'All right,' he said, 'you're not going to like this, but it's really the only way that I can explain it to you. Are you ready?'

The prime minister just looked at him.

'To those who choose not to take the path I have, we posthumans will be *gods*. We will be able to do whatever we want: we will seem so advanced to those who remain that anything we do will look like *magic*.

'For us, however,' he added regretfully, 'those who have not joined us will seem rather different. They will be weak, vulnerable, easily crushed, damaged, maimed, or – worst of all, obviously – killed. They'll present a tremendous burden, purely in terms of the care and attention with which they'll need to be treated. In truth, compared to us, ordinary humans will be something like . . . well, *ants*.'

The prime minister said nothing.

'Those who don't become posthuman,' Mallahide went on, 'will have to be kept separate from the rest of us for their own safety. We can set up – I don't know what you'd call them – reservations? They'd be offered every possible comfort and allowed to live out their limited lives in whatever way they see fit.'

'Zoos,' said the prime minister. 'You're talking about zoos. For people.'

'Well . . .' The professor shrugged. 'That's not the word I would have chosen. But something along those lines will have to be established, I imagine. Yes.'

The prime minister didn't answer. He was staring openly at Mallahide now.

'So?' the professor prompted. 'What do you think?'

'You're a monster, Professor Mallahide,' said Mr Sinclair. 'God help us all.'

THE SECOND VISIT

'Now,' said the guard, 'I'm just going to lock this door.'

'What?' said Chris. 'You're going to *lock us in*?'

'This is one of the most secret locations in the country,' the guard pointed out. 'I can 'ardly risk letting a pair of kids like you just go wandering around in the night, can I?'

'But what if we need the toilet or something?'

'There's a button to press by the door. Though come to think of it, I'm not sure if it's ever been used before,' the guard added nastily. He grinned. 'I 'ope it's connected to something for your sake.'

'Great,' said Chris. 'Terrific. Thanks a bunch.' But the door had shut. He heard the snick of bolts. Then silence.

The room Chris and Anna were standing in looked not much different from an ordinary hotel room. Two single beds lay along two of its walls, separated by a small chest of drawers with a lamp on it. The walls themselves were painted a fairly unappealing shade of beige. The room also contained a mirror, an armchair, a table, and a wardrobe that stood at the foot of one of the beds. The only thing that made the room different, in Anna's eyes, took a moment for her to figure out.

There was no window. Of course not: they were deep underground. And that made the room feel like a cell. Anna shuddered.

'Well,' she said, breaking the silence, 'I guess that's it for us for the night. We might as well try and get some sleep. Which bed do you want?'

'You choose.'

'Fine,' said Anna, pulling back the bedspread on the one facing the wardrobe. She grimaced. 'Do you know,' she said, 'I think that guard was right. I guess they keep the beds made up just in case a war breaks out or something, but you'd think someone would give the sheets an airing once in a while: these are *so* musty. Think I'll sleep in my clothes,' she added, taking her shoes off. She got into bed – and looked at Chris, who was still standing by the door like a spare part.

'Would you mind getting into bed yourself and turning off the light?' she asked him. 'It's been kind of a long day.' Without waiting for an answer, she turned over to face the wall.

'Oh . . . sure,' said Chris. Awkwardly he got in his own bed and reached for the lamp. 'Well . . . night, then,' he said.

Anna didn't reply.

For a long time Anna lay in the dark, listening to Chris's breathing. Anna didn't have any male friends or relatives apart from her father; this was the first time she'd shared a room with a boy before, and truthfully, she felt more than a little uncomfortable about it. Anna's own breathing sounded very loud in her ears, and she kept wondering if Chris (for his part) was listening to hers. But gradually his breaths became more even, if a little louder, and she realized that he was asleep.

The room was so dark that it made no difference whether Anna's eyes were open or shut. Encased in musty-smelling sheets, in the underground room, it was as if she'd been buried in her coffin. If it wasn't for the sounds of Chris's breathing, she thought, this could be what it was like to be dead. In fact . . .

'Anna?' a voice whispered.

She opened her eyes. She was still facing the wall, but the darkness had thinned somehow into a grey haze coming from behind her, just strong enough to cast her shadow.

'Anna?' the voice whispered again. 'It's me.'

Slowly, ignoring the cold sluice of fear in her belly, she turned.

Her father was sitting on the side of the bed.

For a weird, detached second, Anna was glad he hadn't appeared like this the first time he'd come to visit her: she would've had even more trouble believing he was real. He was *glowing*, flickering with the static grey light of an old TV tuned to an empty channel. He left no impression or weight where he sat, and his hand – where it gently stroked her side through the sheets – left no warmth or sensation. His hair and clothes and face and body looked the same as always, just in black and white. He looked like a ghost. He smiled at her.

'How did you get in here?' Anna asked.

'Shhh!' Professor Mallahide made 'keep it down' gestures with his translucent hands. His grin got wider. 'I used to work for the military, remember? This place might be top secret to some people, but not to me!'

'You look funny,' Anna whispered back.

'Yes, er . . . sorry about that,' said her dad, looking embarrassed. 'Getting through all the security and so forth was a bit of a challenge. I couldn't risk bringing any more of myself with me than this, I'm afraid.'

'So . . .' Anna said, 'what are you doing here?'

'Why, I've come to see you of course, silly.'

Anna didn't answer. For a moment there was silence, apart from the continued sound of Chris's breathing.

'Who's the boy?' asked Mallahide, smiling broadly. 'Friend of yours?'

'Just someone from school,' said Anna. 'Why?'

'No reason.'

'Then why,' Anna demanded, 'are you *grinning* like that? He's not my *boyfriend* or anything.'

'Shhhhhhh!' Mallahide said again delightedly. 'Quiet! You'll wake him!'

Anna scowled and changed the subject. 'You know,' she began – and having to whisper was infuriating to her – 'you're really causing a *lot of trouble*.'

'Change always causes trouble,' said the professor, unconcerned.

'But . . . the way you're acting!' Anna shook her head. 'You're not going to convince anybody like this. The things you're saying! It's much too *sudden*. You're too scary to them right now for anybody to believe you.'

Professor Mallahide smiled. 'But *you* don't find me scary,' he said. 'Do you, Anna?'

Anna looked at him: at the weightless way he sat on the bed, at the black-and-white flickeriness of him, and at the touch of his hand that was no touch at all. She swallowed.

'No,' she lied. 'Of course not.'

'Well, then,' said Professor Mallahide, 'perhaps we can help each other.'

'H-how do you mean?' Anna asked.

'Anna,' said her father, 'I want you to join me.'

155

Anna didn't know what to say.

'I think if you joined me,' Mallahide told her, 'then some of those other problems you mentioned would just go away. If someone like you took the step, then people would see the good in what I'm offering. They'd see that becoming post-human isn't something bad or frightening – in fact, it's the opposite! And here's the thing, Anna: *you would too.*'

Anna said nothing.

'You can't imagine it,' her father told her (*again*, Anna noticed). 'The implications of it just get bigger and bigger! Every time I think I've approached the limits of what there is to discover about the way I live now, I find something else, something new, something amazing.'

'Such as?' Anna asked.

The gleeful smile that had appeared on her father's face, just as it always did when he talked about his work, now dimmed a little.

'Well,' he said, 'there is one thing. As soon as I realized I could do it, I knew I had to tell you straight away.'

'What's that?'

'It's . . .' Mallahide paused. 'Well, it's about your mother.'

Anna looked at him.

Anna's mother had died when Anna was small. Almost eleven years before, just three weeks after Anna's third birthday, Mrs Mallahide – after complaining about a very bad headache – had suddenly collapsed in the kitchen. She never woke up.

It was a brain tumour, the doctors said, the most terrible thing: the disease had been progressing undiagnosed for quite a while before having its effect. It was nobody's fault, everyone said: just one of those things that happen. But the professor had never accepted this. After his wife's funeral, he'd thrown himself even further into his work. That was when he'd started taking military contracts in an effort to get enough funding – even though he'd always sworn blind before that he never would. That was when his and Anna's life together had become what it was. Everything dated from that time. From the time her mum had died.

'Anna,' he said now, 'what do you remember about her?'

'Why are you asking me that?' Anna hissed back at him, exasperated.

'Anna, please,' said Mallahide, 'just tell me. What do you remember?'

The fact that she remembered so little about her mother was a source of great pain to Anna. She had fragments – being taken to the park, ice cream, hugs, picnics – and she hung onto those as best she could, hoarding them and polishing them like precious jewels. But what hurt about them, what made these memories sting her whenever she took them out to examine them, was the fact that they were unreliable. Whenever she thought back, Anna couldn't help wondering: *Maybe that wasn't how it happened.* Perhaps, without realizing it, she was adding things, embroidering them. Maybe, when she thought of her mother's face, all she was really thinking about was a photo she'd seen or an impression of what she, Anna, would have preferred to remember – and she wasn't remembering the real person that her mother had been at all.

Anna hated that idea.

'Little things,' she said defensively. 'You know – bits and pieces. Why?'

'My mind has . . . changed,' said her father slowly. 'It works quite differently now, in lots of ways. Particularly,' he said, leaning towards her and fixing her with a look from his strange black-and-white eyes, 'my *memory*.'

'What do you mean?'

'When I allowed the nanobots to take apart my old body,' Mallahide explained, 'they recorded absolutely everything. That's the way it works: they store every single piece of information about a person, every single thing there is to know – including memories. The difference is,' he added, smiling again, 'that unlike the contents of my *human* mind, I can now access all of it whenever I want. Everything I've seen, heard, touched, tasted, smelled and done is mine again. Mine, to remember and savour instantly. Believe me, Anna, it's absolutely *amazing*.'

Anna couldn't really see where any of this was headed. 'So?' she asked.

'You'd be surprised how much humans forget, Anna,' said her father. 'Things slip away; they get stored in some dusty corner of the mind and your conscious brain forgets how to find them. But they're *still there*, Anna. Still there!' He paused. 'Do you see what I'm talking about yet?'

Anna looked at him.

'Do you want to know more about her?' asked her father. His eyes glittered strangely. 'Do you want to see what I saw of her, know what I know? Because that's one of the things I can offer you.'

Anna said nothing.

'It'll be like that for everyone who joins us, Anna. Everything will be shared – hopes, dreams, knowledge, wisdom, memory, all of it. If you choose, you'll know as much about your mum as I do. You'll know how much I loved her because you'll have seen her the way I saw her. You'll know *exactly* what you missed when she was taken away from us because through me you can see her for yourself, from the day we met to . . .' He paused. 'To the day she died.' He looked straight into Anna's eyes. 'Anna, I can give you that – and more besides. Well,' he added, 'what do you say?'

Anna looked at him. 'You can do that?' she asked. 'If I join you, we can share memories?'

'Memories, sensations, everything,' said Mallahide, grinning again. 'Think of it! And think, for a moment, of what it'll be like when *everyone* is like us too! True freedom of information at last!'

He was going off on one of his tangents again. 'Dad—' said Anna.

'A world of wisdom waiting to be shared!'

'*Dad*—' Anna repeated.

'Perfect understanding! Perfect communication! *Heaven on Earth*,' said Mallahide. 'For ever!'

'*Dad!*' said Anna.

'What?' Mallahide asked.

Anna took a deep breath. 'Dad, I'm sorry, but I've got to say it. What you're asking is just . . .' She shrugged. 'Well – *weird*. Don't you think?'

Mallahide blinked, astonished. 'How do you mean?'

'I *mean*,' said Anna heavily, beginning to lose patience, 'knowing a bit more about Mum than I do right now, all right, I can't pretend that side of it isn't a *bit* tempting. But you said it yourself: your memories of her will be through *your* eyes, not mine.'

'So?' asked Mallahide.

'*So*,' said Anna, 'to you, she was your wife! To me, she was my mum! It's different!'

Mallahide looked at her blankly.

'So,' Anna prompted again, 'sharing your memories of her isn't necessarily a good thing for me, is it? In fact, from my point of view, it'd just be . . .' She shook her head. 'Weird! Don't you see?'

Mallahide didn't answer.

Anna bit her lip. But she had to say it.

'What you're offering,' she went on, 'leaving our bodies behind, sharing everything, becoming what you are – all of it. I mean: we've talked about this stuff. I'm more used to your wild ideas than anybody. But to most people, what you're saying is just . . . *mad*.'

'People of vision,' said her father, with icy dignity, 'have always been called mad.'

'But can't you see how strange it is?' Anna pursued. 'To most people, thoughts and memories and feelings are *private*. They're not supposed to be shared around – you have them by yourself. That's what makes them what they are.'

'That's *old* thinking, Anna! Human history has been filled with the idea of "keeping things for yourself" – and look where it's got the world!'

'You're not listening to me,' said Anna, shaking her head. 'You're not understanding what I'm saying at all.'

'But I *do* understand,' said Mallahide. 'Believe me, I do! It's just that—'

Suddenly he stopped.

'What?' Anna asked.

'It's just . . .' Mallahide bit his lip and looked at her. 'All right, you've made me say it: I just *know more about this* than you do. All right?'

Anna looked at him.

'I've done it, Anna,' said her father, his face flickering as he spoke. 'I'm the one who took the step. I'm the one who knows what it's like to do this – and an ordinary human mind just *can't conceive it*.'

'What are you saying?'

'I'm *saying*, Anna,' said Mallahide, 'that we can argue about this all night, but at some point you're going to have to *trust me*. I am your father,' he said. 'I want what's best for you. And believe me, this is best. Better,' he added, smiling again, 'than even *you* can imagine.'

He held out his hand towards her – his translucent, black-and-white hand.

Anna sat up in bed – and as she did so, she noticed something.

The molecule-size machines reacted almost instantly, but it wasn't quite fast enough. For a tiny fraction of a second – a time so short that someone who hadn't been looking for it might have missed it – Anna had seen the truth.

The way her father was appearing to her then was a projection. It was a two-dimensional image, as if he was showing up on a screen. For a moment, when she'd sat up, she'd looked round the side of it. *There was nothing there.*

She took another deep breath. She'd been sure before. She was twice as sure now.

'I'm sorry, Dad,' she said. 'But no.' She shook her head. 'I won't do it.'

Mallahide's smile vanished. 'What?' he said.

'I just . . .' Anna sighed. 'It's the way you're acting. The way you speak. You don't seem like you were before. You're *different* now. Too different. And I . . .' She looked at him, pleading for his understanding. 'I'm just not *sure*. You know? I'm not ready to take the step. Not yet.'

Mallahide looked at her. 'That's your decision?'

'That's my decision.'

Mallahide shook his head. 'Then I'm sorry too, Anna. Sorry it has to be this way.'

Anna frowned. 'What—?'

'Relax.' Her father's face had already started to change, but enough of the swarm still looked like him to say, 'You'll soon see this the way I do.

'Believe me,' he added, 'it'll only hurt for a moment.'

'Dad?' said Anna. He'd vanished – but suddenly the room seemed to be heating up around her. There was a tingling, itching sensation on her skin, growing stronger every second. 'Dad, *what are you doing?*'

'I am your father, Anna,' said a voice that seemed to come from everywhere. 'I know what's best for you. It's a shame you've made me do this against your will, but in the long run, I promise, you'll thank me.'

The itching sensation grew to a sudden sharp sting. Her face, her arms, every part of her exposed flesh felt on fire with a spreading pain.

'It's for the best, Anna,' her father repeated.

'Dad, *no*! No! Please!'

'In a moment you'll see what I mean.'

'You can't!'

'*Yes*, Anna,' said Mallahide. 'I *can*. Now stop struggling, please, you're interfering with the process.'

'Stop it, Dad – you're *hurting*!' Anna could feel it now, all over her body, as her father's machines went to work. They were going to rip every cell of her into its constituent parts, to be examined and recorded and reproduced as something else.

They were taking her to pieces.

The room lit up in a blaze of light. Someone had switched on a lamp. Chris – heavy sleeper that he was – had woken up at last.

'Anna, what's wrong?' he asked blearily, rubbing his eyes. 'You woke me. What's the mat—'

Anna saw him freeze as he caught sight of her.

'Oh *no*,' he said.

'Chris! Chris, *do something*!'

'I'm thinking!'

'*Chris*—!'

'Yes!' He leaped out of bed –

– and pressed the buzzer on the door.

Nothing happened.

Perhaps the security guard was right. Perhaps the buzzer wasn't connected to anything and Chris and Anna were locked in a small, windowless room, deep underground, with only a cloud of all-consuming nanomachines to keep them company.

But Chris didn't spend a lot of time pondering the issue. With a last few despairing jabs on the buzzer, he turned,

taking in the room, thinking of what he could do or use:
then, yanking the blanket off his bed, he ran to where Anna
was still sitting.

If the swarm in the room with them now had carried anything like the numbers of nanobots Mallahide usually moved
around in, everything would already have been over. Even so,
the skin of Anna's arms and face was raw red where the tiny
machines had begun their dreadful work.

Chris smothered her like you would someone who was
on fire, swatting at her helplessly.

'Get off her, dammit! Leave her alone!' he yelled as the
very air around them both seemed to buzz with anger.

Under the blanket, Anna shrieked with pain and fright,
her bare feet drumming wildly on the floor by the bed.

It was happening, Chris thought. It was really happening.
She was being dissolved right in front of him. In a moment
the arms and head under his frantically rubbing hands were
going to shrink down and vanish and disappear—

'Stop it!' Chris yelled. 'Stop it!'

And there wasn't a single thing he could do! Worse than
the screaming had been, Anna had now gone silent. Her feet
had stopped drumming and were now pressed against the
floor, her whole body arching back in a sudden spasm.

At that moment, the door to the room crashed open.

'GAAAAAAAAAAAH!' said the burly security guard
who'd locked them in earlier, in his best approximation of a
war cry. He lifted the nozzle of the fire extinguisher he held
in his hands –

– and let rip.

When the security guard, whose name was Wilson, had

heard the buzzer and caught sight of what was going on over Chris and Anna's room's closed circuit TV feed, he hadn't had much time to consider how to react. In fact, apart from hitting the alarms to call for backup, he hadn't had any time at all: it was a pure fluke that the extinguisher had happened to be clipped to the wall of the passage outside, and simple instinct that had made him grab it as he ran past. But Wilson's instinct was a good one. The extinguisher was of the kind filled with aqueous-film-forming foam: Mallahide's reduced swarm was thinned out even further as the tiny machines malfunctioned or were simply swept aside by the continuing torrent of smothering gunk. Still Wilson kept the handle pressed, squirting away, until Chris and Anna were almost covered in the stuff. And as the extinguisher reached the end of its reservoir and the torrent of foam subsided to a dribble, it became apparent that Mallahide had given up his attempt: Anna was still there, still in one piece. Spluttering, Chris pulled the now foam-sodden blanket back from her face.

'Anna?' he yelled. 'Anna!'

She opened her eyes. Her face was red and starting to go puffy. Her eyelids were scored and scratched – flaky, like her skin was peeling from sunburn. But—

'I'm all right,' she said weakly.

Chris breathed out in relief, and for a moment there was silence.

'Where is he?' said Wilson, pointing the nozzle of the fire extinguisher around the room like a gun (even though it was empty). 'Where's he gone? Where is the bastard?'

'It's no good,' said Anna. 'We . . . can't see him. He's too small.'

But she was wrong.

Imperceptibly at first, the foam covering the room began to twitch and move. The particles of it all began to boil and wriggle as the tiny, and only temporarily stunned, molecule-size machines underneath it began to wake up again and re-form themselves.

All over the blanket of foam, large flecks and spits of the stuff began to shudder and lift themselves into the air. For a second it looked like the jet from the extinguisher was happening in reverse: the foam lifted from the blankets and furniture, coagulating into a strange bulging blob that hung in the air in front of the staring eyes of Anna, Chris, and Wilson the security guard. The blob extended itself downwards and outwards, flattening out . . . into another version of Professor Mallahide. He hovered in the air, a child's drawing of himself, daubed in foam.

'I'm very disappointed in you,' said the foam mouth – its lips two distended sausages of white goo, hunching out the shapes of the words. 'You're all of you being very stupid about this. I expected it, of course, but I'm disappointed just the same. Especially with *you*,' the foam effigy added, extending a pale bubbly streak of an arm and pointing it at Anna. 'It seems that you're every bit as childish as the rest of the human race.'

Anna stared at the apparition palely but said nothing.

'That's what *old* humanity is to me now,' Mallahide hissed: '*children*. Humans are *children* compared to me – compared to what you can become. The fact of the matter is,' he added bitterly, 'that as a race, you are simply not mature or capable enough to make decisions concerning your own future. As with any child, serious decisions must be made *for you*, by an adult. And as a responsible parent, it seems the duty and power to make those decisions falls to me.' Mallahide paused. 'You will all of you follow me and become what I have become. There is no other choice. And in the end, I still believe you will thank me. But tell your leaders, tell whoever you have to: if anyone tries to stop me in any way whatsoever, you will all be *very sorry*.'

'What are you going to do?' Anna asked.

'I've tried being reasonable. Thanks to *you*,' the foam face of her father added, 'I find I'm forced to try another approach. We will meet again, Anna. In time you will learn to appreciate what I'm offering you, and then, I hope, you'll understand me a little better than you do now. Goodbye.'

The foam effigy suddenly flew into pieces, making a headlong rush for the door.

'Oh no, you don't—' said Wilson, then, 'AAGH!' He flung his hands up over his face as the remains of this particular part of what had been Professor Mallahide swept past him like a gust of wind.

Chris and Anna looked at each other.

There was silence.

RAMPAGE

Instantly, or as close to instantly as made no difference, the microwave transmissions that Mallahide was currently using for thoughts had reached the edges of the main body of the swarm. In the night sky over London the cloud of machines immediately began to flatten and spread out. Tendrils of Mallahide reached for the surface: billions upon billions of his molecule-size machines drifted down towards the London streets like a rain of near-invisible ash.

Mallahide was angry and hurt by what Anna had said. To him, the situation was clear. The human race was failing to make the right choice. They were failing to join him. Without his intervention they would fail to reach their potential, fail to become like him. So (he told himself) only one course remained open to him.

It was time to make the choice for them.

In the West End below, the first bars and pubs were starting to close. For a frenetic hour or so the pavements and Tube stations would be bustling with humans, many of them rowdy, many of them happy, most of them in some state of intoxication.

They didn't know what hit them.

It wasn't at all how it had been with Anna. Perhaps (Mallahide reflected) that had been part of the problem: if there had been enough of him in the room with her to make the dissolution process as quick as he was now capable of making it, then Anna and that 'Chris' boy might not have resisted him in the way they had. When the main mass of the Mallahide swarm hit the crowds thronging the West End, it was quite different.

Now people just began to disappear.

It happened so fast that those whose turn had not yet come didn't even notice it at first. But young men and women all over the West End suddenly *weren't there any more*. Their partners and friends would turn and look: their last thoughts before being transfigured themselves would be, *Where's X gone? She was here a second ago* – then they too would vanish, rendered down into their constituent atoms and meticulously recorded by the expanding swarm of Mallahide's astonishing little machines. For a full three minutes, nobody realized what was happening. Then—

Pandemonium.

Everyone still standing made a rush to get off the streets – stampeding into Tube stations, desperate to escape. But they didn't escape. Escape was impossible. No matter how hard they struggled or screamed or cried, Mallahide caught them just the same.

To Mallahide, the sudden vast influx of information was almost overwhelming. Scores of entire lives – ambitions, dreams, griefs, loves – poured into him. His billions of pristine digital fingers sifted it all. And the skills and talents! Mallahide could take what he wanted: cookery, kickboxing, parkour, human resource management – *Human resource management?* he thought, interrupting himself. Well, why not? When the time came, everything might be useful. Anything was possible in the new world order that was coming – except one thing.

He couldn't let these people be free. He couldn't convert them properly – not in the sense that they would be allowed the ability to choose their own paths or make their own decisions – not for the time being. They might band together and try to stop him. They might overthrow him, taking control of the swarm. They might threaten his plan, and that was something he could not tolerate.

No. He was the first posthuman. As Anna had failed to understand, *he knew best*. The new converts would simply be stored, suspended, kept in a holding pattern until Mallahide was ready to return their freedom to them. And in the meantime the swarm would remain under his exclusive control.

It wasn't a betrayal of his principles, he told himself: not at all. He was doing this for the people's *own good*. There was plenty of time for freedom *later*, he told himself, once his task was complete. For now, all he needed was to get bigger, stronger, increasing his swarm until it was the size it needed to be.

There was, after all, a whole world to conquer.

'And – yes – following on from this morning's incredible events in Hyde Park, we're now receiving reports of some kind of incident taking place in the West End. It appears that the strange cloud that has formed over London – the freakish phenomenon newspapers have dubbed the "Mallahide Swarm" – is now *on the attack*. Exact numbers of casualties are hard to estimate at present because . . .'

Sitting in the news studio, Fiona Pilkington paused again. She ought, she supposed, to have become used to incredible things by now. But what she was hearing shocked her more than anything else she'd been required to announce so far.

'I'm sorry. All over the West End, men and women seem to be *vanishing into thin air*. Now, to explain these astonishing reports as best we can, we go live once more to Nelson Akubwe, who is there at the scene as we speak. Nelson . . . ?'

She spun in her chair to face the studio wall screen, unable to mask the small sag of relief in her back as she slumped a little once the camera was off her.

'Well, Fiona,' said Mr Akubwe breathlessly, 'I apologize right now for the jerkiness of the footage, but as you can see, the scene here is one of total panic and confusion, and I and my team, like everyone else, have been forced . . . to run . . . for our lives!'

The shrieks of the stampeding crowd were clearly audible in the background of Mr Akubwe's voice-over. The orange streetlights wove crazy trails across the screen whenever the cameraman turned in a new direction. But everywhere were people, running and jostling, screaming and crying. And whenever the soft grey tendrils of Mallahide reached down and found their marks in the crowd, people froze – opened their mouths – and vanished.

'We're under attack!' shouted the young journalist over the din. 'London is under attack! The cloud seems to be reaching down into the streets and . . . destroying us!'

On-screen, the view from the cameraman's shoulder rounded a corner, then juddered to a halt. Throughout the next part of the transmission the view slowly bobbed up and down as Mr Akubwe and his crew gasped for breath.

'I'm sorry . . .' he said. 'We're . . . we've just taken shelter in an alleyway off Leicester Square. From here, we'll . . .

continue to broadcast our report as best we can.' He straightened up and squared his shoulders as he faced the camera.

'Ladies and gentlemen,' he began, 'when Professor Mallahide first appeared, there were those who dismissed him as a hoax – some kind of publicity stunt that went out of control.' He shook his head. 'Tonight we've seen the truth. The attack began without warning: as we speak, innocent civilians are being targeted and . . . dissolved! And, ladies and gentlemen, I'm afraid this is only the beginning: I—'

He paused and went pale. 'Oh God,' he murmured. 'It's coming.'

The orange streetlamps that were lighting the scene seemed to go dim, as if an enormous shadow was falling across them.

'Get off the streets!' shouted Mr Akubwe as quickly as he could. 'Stay in your homes and shut all your windows and doors! What else can we do? *Who can save us now?*'

Then he froze. Silhouetted in a kind of orange-grey haze for a moment, the hapless journalist opened his mouth to scream. His face and body held their shape for another second – then burst apart into nothingness and TV static. The screen went blank.

'Nelson?' asked Fiona Pilkington. '*Nelson?*'

There was no answer.

SMACKDOWN

In the Crisis Room, Colin Wythenshawe took a deep breath. He hadn't been working as a military liaison for long: this was his first posting to the underground nerve centre. Also, he was nervous about speaking to the prime minister. But it was too late to be worried about that last point: Mr Sinclair had already noticed the way that he'd been hovering by the side of his chair.

'Yes?' Sinclair snapped up at him.

'Sir,' said Wythenshawe unhappily, 'we, ah, have a problem.'

The prime minister gave him a look that could have withered an Amazon rain forest. '*Really.*' He smiled mirthlessly. 'Young man, if you're referring to the fact that the West End is currently under attack by a cloud of super-intelligent nanomachines that appears to be gobbling up every civilian unlucky enough to be caught out on the street, I have to tell you that particular "problem" ' – he made air quotes with his hands – 'is one I'm already exquisitely aware of.'

'I – I'm sorry, sir,' Wythenshawe stammered, 'but – but I'm not talking about that problem. It's . . .' He gulped. 'It's something else.'

The prime minister looked at him grimly. 'Very well.' He sighed. 'Let's hear it.'

'Well, it's . . . it's like this,' said Wythenshawe, and took another deep breath. 'For the last half-hour I've been receiving reports from various points all along the Thames, from the coast right up to London's outskirts. I'm afraid there's no longer any room for doubt.'

'Doubt about what?'

'It's the monster,' said Wythenshawe. 'The *first* one,' he corrected. 'He's . . . well . . . He's back.'

'Oh *no* . . .'

'I'm afraid so, sir. If you look up on the main monitor, you'll see the satellite imagery now.'

Instantly everyone in the room stopped what they were doing and looked at the main screen. Anna and Chris, who'd been allowed to take refuge in the Crisis Room after their experience, looked up with them.

Thanks to the satellite's thermal-imaging camera, Tim was visible as a gigantic green-and-red *T. rex*-shaped blob; Mallahide, by contrast, appeared as a kind of a cool icy blue colour, drifting and slithering across the screen like some unspeakably magnified amoeba.

'But . . . what's it *doing*?' the prime minister spluttered. 'I thought the bloody thing had escaped into the sea and that was the last of it! What's it doing coming back to London?'

Chris knew. He'd known it when the extraordinary bracelet on his wrist had begun to heat up again. He'd known it in his heart too, as soon as he'd heard about Tim's return.

'They're going to fight,' he whispered. 'He's come to save us.'

Burning with righteous rage, Tim strode up the river. The water surged around his legs. His massive tail thrashed the air behind him.

He was ready to take on his first job as the Defender of the Earth. His claws were sharp, his jaws were ready to bite and he was spoiling for the first proper fight of his life. In fact, he could hardly wait. His muscles tingled as he flexed them. A surge of joy ran from his jet-engine-size heart to the tips of his claws.

The surrounding city seemed to have changed a bit since he'd last been there. Not thinking of much else except the upcoming combat, it took Tim's gently simmering brain quite a while to work out what the exact difference actually was, but he got it in the end: there were no tiny people. No tiny people! None anywhere! Or none that Tim could see. All there was, instead, was this enormous *cloud*, poised over the city, piled up like a thunderhead and growing, growing all the time just like it had in the vision. At the edge of where the Mallahide swarm now reached, just a little upriver from St Paul's Cathedral, Tim halted. Eyeing the cloud with ineffable contempt, he opened his mouth –

– and roared.

Windows blew out in the buildings to either side. The gigantic bells in the belfry of St Paul's shuddered where they hung. Londoners cowering underground to escape Mallahide's attentions suddenly found themselves on the floor on their knees, covering their ears, terrified even further by the incredible noise as it continued on and on.

It wasn't the same kind of roar that they'd heard before, that night Tim had made his escape. That night, Tim had been *scared*, scared of the size of the world he'd suddenly found himself in, the world outside his enclosure. But everyone who heard it now recognized the roar – and noticed the difference.

Tim wasn't scared now. This roar was a challenge.

Abruptly the roar came to an end. Tim stood there proudly. For a long echoing moment, silence hung in the air over London.

Intriguing, thought Mallahide. Tim's none-too-subtle message had reached him in a quicksilver flash of clarity almost the moment the tyrannosaur had opened his mouth. The only reason Mallahide was hesitating was because he was working out how best to respond.

Well, why not? he thought. And he began to reconfigure himself.

Bulging downwards, the swarm began to take Mallahide's favourite shape.

An object like an unspeakable multi-fingered hand reached down from the heavens, instantaneously splitting apart into two rows of gigantic arched legs that straddled the Thames. At the same moment, uncountable trillions of freshly created nanomachines poured themselves forth, forming a kind of chimney of tapering darkness. The chimney grew bigger, rearing and swelling into a shape not dissimilar to that of a human torso – albeit one of colossal size. With a soft crackling sound, the place where the ribs would be seemed to bud, swell, then finally shoot forth no less than *six* long and limber arms this time, three on each side, each one tipped with a serious-looking set of opposing lobster-style pincers. Now encased in an appropriately monstrous-looking form, Mallahide eyed his opponent.

Half human, half cockroach, Mallahide squatted on the London skyline. The entire transformation had taken about eighteen seconds – the professor had slowed it down for added dramatic effect. Big as he was, Tim was barely level with his chest.

So, Mallahide thought, regarding Tim with interest. *You're what came* before *human beings. I'm what comes* after. *So come on. Let's see what you've got.*

In the underground control centre, Chris felt the bracelet grow suddenly hot.

Bellowing his defiance, Tim lowered his head –

– and charged.

Water surged and boiled around his gigantic hind legs as he took a step and another step, building up speed. Watching Tim coming, Mallahide spread his arms as behind him and to either side his multiple insect legs tensed for the impact. And –

WHAM!

With a noise that seemed to shake the whole city to its foundations, the titanic struggle began.

Tim wasn't a scientific kind of fighter: being mostly dinosaur, he tended to favour a direct approach. His opening move therefore was simply to charge into Mallahide bodily, hoping to knock him off balance. Tim's forearms were unusually thick and strong, considering how much of him was *T. rex*: at the moment of impact he wrapped them around his opponent's middle – and squeezed.

Mallahide, for his part, had underestimated Tim. Not having fought anything remotely like Tim before, the professor suddenly found himself being pushed backwards. His multiple insect hind legs skittered for purchase on the pavement on either side of the Thames until, with a thin screech of rupturing concrete, the armoured points at their tips penetrated the paving into the topsoil below. Now Mallahide tensed his newly created muscles – and fought back. All six of his arms wrapped around the struggling body of the furious giant reptile.

Before the arms could close all the way, Tim responded by reaching up, craning his neck, then taking one of Mallahide's arms in his jaws, up near where it joined the rest of Mallahide's shiny black armoured body. Tim bit down hard, harder than he'd ever bitten anything in his life before . . . and for a long moment the two titans just stood there, locked together like that.

Tim bit down harder still. Drawing on every last bit of strength in his muscular jaws, he concentrated on forcing his long, razor-sharp fangs through his opponent's outer layer of armour and beyond, into whatever tender meat lay beneath. Biting was what Tim was good at. Biting was coded into every protein of his DNA, every cell of his being, running right back to his dinosaur ancestors. If this fight was going to be decided by biting, then Tim wasn't going to lose. He could bite harder than anything else on the planet. Tim bit down on his opponent's arm until gigantic fiery pinwheels seemed to dance before his eyes. And suddenly –

With an echoing SNAP –

– the arm that Tim had been biting *came off*!

Tim's jaws clashed shut as the other arms released him. Letting go of Mallahide, he staggered back . . .

And he stared.

The arm Tim had bitten off was simply hanging there in the air. Each one of Mallahide's arms was about twelve metres long: for another two seconds, the severed arm stayed like that, suspended a short distance from the stump that had attached it to Mallahide's body. Then, before Tim's startled eyes, the arm seemed suddenly to melt into a strange kind of haze before vanishing to rejoin the swarm that remained in the cloud above.

Tim blinked, astonished –

– and before Tim could react, Mallahide's other five arms with their pincers for hands were diving down towards him. They snipped shut: two grabbed Tim's own arms, two grabbed his hind legs and hoisted him bodily upright, while the fifth – the topmost one, the one that didn't currently have a partner – seized him by the throat.

With an effort – but not by any means an *impossible* effort, not for him – Mallahide lifted Tim up out of the water. Tim's tail whipped frantically from side to side behind him, but he couldn't do a thing to stop it.

Now, Mallahide wasn't sure how much Tim was capable of understanding him. Not much, presumably – he was a dinosaur, after all. But what he needed to show Tim wasn't especially hard to comprehend, so Mallahide decided to take a chance.

Holding Tim easily in his five remaining pincer-tipped arms, Mallahide concentrated.

Tim struggled furiously – then stopped. His attention was caught: at the place where he'd bitten his enemy, something was happening. The stump that was all that was left of Mallahide's sixth arm began to change.

The bare patch of black nothingness where Tim's fangs had shorn through seemed to liquefy – seething, bubbling, and then *expanding*. The stump bulged outwards, and then it started to grow. It happened quite quickly. One minute, it seemed to Tim, the stump was still just a stump – and then, as if it had been there all the time somewhere behind Mallahide's torso, the new arm, complete with its pincer tip, abruptly shoved itself out through the gap, extending to exactly the full length that it had been before.

Tim gulped. But Mallahide had not yet finished his demonstration.

With a titanic *heave*, Tim found himself jerked into the air. As the new arm reached back, the other five let go of him. For a moment Tim was airborne, weightless, but then, before he could fall back into the river below, and with a movement so fast that Tim almost didn't catch it, Mallahide's replacement arm swung forward and struck him in the chest.

All the air came out of Tim's lungs in a short, hard gasp. The shock made Tim see stars. But almost instantaneously came a second shattering impact, this time from *behind* him. Concrete buckled and split. Glass exploded, walls tumbled, staircases and rooms and concert halls and restaurants were smashed flat as he crashed through a building and, eventually, came to rest.

For a moment Tim just lay there, trying to work out what had happened to him.

With his newly regrown arm, Mallahide had punched Tim so hard that he'd been knocked clear across the Thames. A long, grey concrete structure on the river's southern bank, the South Bank Centre, had taken the brunt of the impact of Tim's landing. Tim was lying flat on his back in the building's remains.

Tim sat up and shook his head groggily. The fight was most definitely *not* going the way he had expected. Dazedly, shaking clouds of dust and bits of building from his hide, Tim got to his feet. His chest was very sore. His ribs ached when he breathed. What had just happened then? Tim didn't understand it. He was the Defender of the Earth! He was big and strong and important! Obviously, he reckoned, there had just been some kind of mistake.

While Mallahide waited to see what Tim would try next, Tim looked around. His eyes were caught by the orange-lit structure just next to where Mallahide was standing. At one end of it stood a tall thing that looked, to Tim, like it might be usefully pointy . . .

Tim had an idea.

Tim didn't get ideas very often, so he was particularly pleased with himself for this one, and he was very keen to put it into effect. He roared at Mallahide, hoping that was going to be enough to stop him from trying anything funny until Tim was good and ready. Then he walked over towards the Houses of Parliament.

The large clock tower at the eastern end of the Houses of Parliament is one of the most famous buildings in the world. It's best known by the name of the enormous bell that sounds its hours: Big Ben.

Keeping an eye on Mallahide at all times, Tim climbed easily out of the Thames and onto the bank. Shattering paving and flattening cars without even noticing, he strode quickly to the tower, which (at just shy of one hundred metres tall) was almost as tall as he was. Then Tim bent down, wrapped his arms around the clock tower's base . . . and heaved.

'Good God,' Chris heard the prime minister murmur. 'He's not going to . . .' Words failed him. 'Is he?'

The heat of the magical bracelet seemed to suffuse Chris in a warm glow.

'Yes,' he said delightedly. '*Oh* yes. Yes, I do believe he is.'

All through Tim – across his massive spiked back, down his legs and arms – muscles like trucks and sinews like freight trains bulged and rippled and quivered with effort. Then, with a thunderclap of imploding brickwork, the whole of the historic structure parted company with its foundations and lifted into the air, the illuminated faces of the clock winking out as it did so.

Big Ben had first rung its famous note on the 31st of May 1859. Now, as the thirteen-ton bell rocked and shivered helplessly in its belfry, its death knell sounded like panic. Bellowing with triumph and fury and effort, Tim straightened up, turned –

– and flung the tower, tossing it straight at his waiting opponent, caber-style.

Mallahide watched, astonished, as the most famous building in London inscribed a short arc in the air. He was still watching when its cast-iron spire caught him in the chest, followed by approximately 8,667 tons of falling building.

KER-*RASHHH!!!* The clock's four faces simply exploded apart as the upper part of the tower concertina'd against the resisting surface of Mallahide's armour. But the momentum of Tim's makeshift missile was unstoppable. Though the tower was already shattering in a cataract of bricks and iron and ruined stone cladding, its sheer weight hit Mallahide full on – and he fell back. The gigantic arch of his unspeakable insect hind legs collapsed inwards, punched clean through by the impact, disappearing from sight in a whirlwind of debris as pieces of the tower (the clock's arms, Big Ben itself) continued to splash into the Thames, kicking up fountains of spray for several seconds afterwards.

'YES!' yelled Chris. 'YEEEEEEEEEEEESSSSSSSS!' He jumped up and down and punched the air, and even when he noticed how quietly horrified everyone else in the underground bunker seemed to be, he still couldn't help the way he was grinning.

Outside, under the London sky, Tim froze. The dust was clearing, and he'd noticed something. Something that he didn't like.

He'd been expecting to be presented with a view of his fallen foe – Mallahide's body spread out liberally all over the landscape. But Mallahide wasn't there.

Confused, Tim waded through the waterlogged wreckage. The Thames – never all that deep at this point in the river anyway – was now shallower still due to the sheer volume of bricks and mortar that had just been dumped into it. Tim prodded listlessly here and there with his hind legs – but it was true: of the gigantic creature that had hit him so horribly hard earlier, there was now no sign whatsoever. He looked north, east, south, west – no sign of Mallahide there either. Eventually, because it took Tim a while to realize that it was the only direction he hadn't looked in yet, he looked up . . .

And got a nasty surprise.

'Oh no!' said Chris. There on the screen, the satellite feed, something terrible was happening. The unspeakable cool blue amoeba shape from before had returned. Far from being weakened, it now appeared to be even bigger.

Over Tim's head, the darkness boiled and shivered. The

entire London night sky seemed to be converging on a point just ahead of him: something between a tornado and a mountain was taking shape there. At last, Mallahide had suspended his efforts to convert any remaining Londoners left out in the open. Now the whole swarm was coming, concentrating here to face this latest and most surprising of the professor's enemies. At last Professor Mallahide was beginning to take Tim seriously.

Mallahide knew the whole world was watching: not just governments through their satellites in orbit far overhead – everybody who had access to the media. Someone, some-where would be recording the whole scene. At this very instant, jerky amateur footage from handheld cameras and phones was being uploaded to the Internet and sent out all over the globe. Those who could would be glued to their screens, breathless, watching the situation unfold – watching him, Mallahide, to see what he was capable of and whether what he was claiming he could do was true.

This creature, this 'Tim', had put up the only serious opposition that Mallahide had so far faced. So, he was going to have to make an *example* out of him.

First, the professor reconstructed himself. In moments, he was straddling the Thames again. His previous armoured half-insect shape had reappeared, exactly identical to how it had been before, right down to the atomic level. It only took him three seconds this time: the professor meant business.

Next, reaching out with two of his arms, he fixed his pincers on the rim of a convenient wheel shape that he'd seen beside him, standing on the southern bank of the river.

Until this moment, the London Eye had been an

observation wheel – one of the tallest and most beautiful in the world. Built to celebrate the coming of the year 2000, it had rapidly become one of London's most popular attractions. People had come from everywhere to step into its gleaming glass passenger capsules and ride the wheel to the top, there to see (on a clear day) one of the most spectacular views in the whole city. The Eye had been an almost miraculous work of engineering: 1,700 tons of steel had gone into its construction.

Mallahide's newly recreated armoured limbs flexed once, easily, and the London Eye snapped off its moorings. He shook it, dislodging the irritating bubble cars attached all around it: they plummeted to the ground and shattered, a sudden hail of thirty-two unfeasibly large – and fortunately empty – glass eggs. Then he advanced. Before Tim could do much more than raise his forelimbs in a token attempt to protect himself, Mallahide lifted the London Eye's 135-metre-diameter wheel, turned it to the horizontal –

– and drove it down smartly over Tim's head.

The impact was stunning: Tim's hind legs buckled, his vision filling with swathes of blurry green flashes. The pain was shocking. Tim wanted to reach up: he wanted to feel with his foreclaws whatever damage had been done to him – but strangely, his arms didn't seem to want to move. His vision cleared slowly, and he realized why.

When the wheel's hub jarred loose on Tim's thick skull, the Eye's bicycle-style spokes, which stretched from the hub to the wheel's rim, were forced upwards, bent out of true. But as the ruined structure was shoved brutally down past Tim's shoulders, something else had happened.

Tim's arms were now clamped to his sides. Tim was stuck. Tim was defenceless!

Mallahide swung out two of his great arms at once, striking Tim on both sides of the head simultaneously: the anvil-hard pincers collided around Tim's skull with the force and power of a train crash. Stunned, Tim fell back. Behind him, the rim of the Eye's wheel plunged into the Thames: it bit into the river's silty bed, bending too – but it didn't collapse. Instead, under the sudden weight, the thick cable steel spokes finally sheared clean away from the wheel's hub and jabbed their sharpened ends straight into Tim's back, hard.

Then Mallahide took hold of his tail.

Tim sat up, feeling the distinctive bite of all six pincers snipping shut on his flesh. Dimly grasping what was about to happen, he made a last effort to get to his feet: with an ease that bordered on contempt, Mallahide gave Tim's tail a painful jerk, and Tim fell back again helplessly.

While Tim thrashed in the river, Professor Mallahide concentrated and focused, preparing for what he was about to do. The front pairs of Mallahide's insect hind legs began to pivot on the spot: the rear ones began to walk sideways – and, slowly at first, Mallahide's vast armoured black hindquarters began to swing round. At the same time, Mallahide's torso leaned back, reeling Tim's tail in harder. Now Tim found he was being dragged *past* Mallahide – past him, and round (as Mallahide continued to turn) in the beginnings of a wide half-circle.

ZOOSH! A spate of river water was flung up in a wave as Tim was dragged through it, sloshing the Thames up and over its banks as far as Whitehall (on the north bank) and Waterloo (on the south). But Mallahide continued to spin. He pulled harder on Tim's tail, reeling him in, leaning back even further. And then Tim left the water. He found that he'd been jerked into the air!

Mallahide was whirling Tim around by his tail.

Tim felt the momentum taking hold in his skull as his poor dinosaur brain was forced outwards, swung around like water in a bucket. Tim flailed and kicked with his arms and legs, but there was nothing he could do. Tim's eyes watered with pain – the place where his tail joined his body was sending powerful signals to his brain that it just was not built to withstand this kind of punishment. But even worse than the pain was the *indignity*. He was the Defender of the Earth! He shouldn't have to put up with this sort of treatment! Tim mewled piteously, the sound taking on a strange Doppler effect as Tim and his opponent – locked together like a bizarre sort of spinning top – continued to revolve against the night sky over the Thames. Mallahide spun like an Olympic hammer thrower preparing to break the world record. Tim closed his eyes, waiting for what was coming, because then, at exactly the moment he wanted, Mallahide *let go*. The pincers scissored open. Tim's tail was released . . .

And Tim was flung, like a dinosaur-size stone from a slingshot, straight into – and through – the Houses of Parliament.

Tim punched through the House of Commons like it was tissue paper, passing straight through one wall of the Commons Chamber and out the other in the space of less than a second, barely slowing down. Its support fatally weakened, the chamber's ceiling collapsed utterly, effectively wiping the room from the face of the Earth: whatever other damage was going to take place that night, Britain's politicians were going to have to debate their differences somewhere else now, and for some years to come. But Tim didn't stop there. The oldest part of the complex by far, Westminster Hall had stood there since 1097: its ancient and hallowed walls, at last, seemed to have some effect on Tim's progress – though not, sadly, enough to stop him. Helplessly he continued to slide, cutting an awesome fifty-metre-wide swathe of destruction straight through the hall. As in his wake the ceiling collapsed in there too, Tim slid on, only finally coming to a halt in what remained of Parliament Square, a little in front of Westminster Abbey.

For several seconds afterwards the London night resounded with the reverberating thunder of the destruction. Then a breathless silence fell.

For a long moment Tim lay still. He opened his eyes, and he stared up at the stars.

There they still were, twinkling down at him mercilessly. For a second, Tim remembered the first night he'd seen them, the first night he'd emerged from under the ground and taken in the size of the world and his place in it for the first time. What had changed since then? *Nothing.*

He'd been fooling himself. Scared witless by the sky over his head, Tim realized he had grabbed at the illusions that the Kraken had offered him like a hatchling being hand-fed its first meat. A role in the world, something big and important – that had been what he'd wanted, and that had been what the Kraken and his visions had seemed to supply. But visions and illusions were all they were.

Tim wasn't important. He wasn't even big – not really, not compared to the world around him. *He was nothing.* That was what his first fight had shown him.

Groaning, hurting all over, covered in the dust of battle, Tim sat up. The crumpled remains of the London Eye had shattered, releasing his arms, but that was about as far as the good news went. He looked down the long valley of debris and mayhem that his latest fall had carved into the London skyline. There at the end of it, a hulking shadow of absolute darkness towering into the streetlit night, stood his enemy, watching him.

Professor Mallahide looked down at his fallen foe. It was time to stop playing. He began to change himself again.

As easily as a person might discard a set of clothes, Mallahide abruptly dropped his giant monster form. The arched ranks of colossal hind legs, the six jointed forearms, the armoured torso – they all vanished, dissipating into their component parts. For another second the remains of the monstrous shape hung in the air, a colossal and awesome pillar of black. Then, like the finger of some god reaching down from the heavens, it began to topple forward. Mallahide fell upon Tim and at once began to devour him.

What a prize he is! Mallahide thought gleefully: if he could successfully disassemble this monster and added its mass to the swarm, he would increase the numbers of his nanomachines by almost an entire *quarter*. True, the machines that were currently working on Tim were encountering some unusual difficulties in penetrating his tough hide, but surely those were nothing that wouldn't be overcome with time.

Tim, for his part, wriggled and kicked and thrashed and

roared as much as he could, but trying to fight Mallahide now was like trying to punch a cloud of gnats: it was impossible. No matter what he did, Tim simply couldn't hurt Mallahide enough to offer any real resistance. Besides, he was tired. His whole body was hurting — everywhere, all at once, all over. And of course, worse than all that: he'd *failed*.

This had been his first battle, his first task as the Defender of the Earth — and Tim had lost.

THE BRACELET

An eerie hush had fallen in the bunker room. Faces lit by the blue-grey glow of the screens, Chris, Anna, and the most powerful people in Britain watched Tim's struggle in silence.

Chris touched the bracelet at his wrist. The warm feeling that had radiated up his arm and through his whole body over the previous few minutes was receding. The metal was turning cool.

'Oh *no*,' he said quietly – then held his breath, caught by a moment of piercing clarity:

He was rooting for a giant lizard.

This was crazy! said Chris's brain. This was worse than crazy: this was *uncool*. His style was supposed to be all about keeping his distance, maintaining his detachment at all times. But that wasn't what he was feeling right now – not at all. He didn't have any idea at what point the insane events of the past few days had started to affect him, but affect him they had. *He didn't want Tim to lose.*

'Come on . . .' he said to the screens under his breath.

Instantly his face went red. He was sure everyone must have heard him: they would all be looking at him, probably grinning smugly or giving him pitying looks for being such a chump. For a second he didn't even want to look round to find out – but when he did, he was surprised to find that everyone in the room was, in fact, still looking at the screens.

'How much longer do you think Tim can last?' asked one

of the prime minister's aides, not taking his eyes off the satellite feed.

'Who can say?' said Colin Wythenshawe, the aide who'd first announced Tim's return. 'He's obviously quite a bit bigger and tougher than anything Mallahide's taken on before.'

'The fight's going out of him, though,' said the prime minister, pointing. 'Look.'

It was true. Out there under the night sky, Tim was weakening.

'You know,' said one of the generals, 'that creature *has* put up more of a fight against Mallahide than any of our forces have managed.'

'But look at the damage it's caused!' the prime minister pointed out. 'It . . . it destroyed the Houses of Parliament!'

Wythenshawe took his finger away from the receiver in his ear. 'Sir, I've got reports coming in that while the fight's been in progress, civilian disappearances seem to have ceased.' He paused awkwardly. 'If Tim is destroyed, it seems reasonable to assume that the swarm's attack may start up again.'

'What are you saying?' asked the prime minister.

'I'm saying, sir,' said Wythenshawe, 'that creature out there might be the only chance we've got.'

'Get up,' said Chris, out loud now. 'Come on, will you? Get *up*.'

But Tim didn't. He was all but invisible: the swarm covered him all over, wriggling and glistening. It looked like Tim had been dipped in some inky black tar-like substance: he'd stopped resisting and just lay there.

'Isn't there something we can do to help him?' asked Anna into the silence.

'What do you suggest?' asked the prime minister, rounding on her. 'We can't risk sending in any more people, let alone our tanks or planes. All our weapons are useless.'

'But . . . he's *dying*!' said Anna with a catch in her voice.

'He's dying for us,' said Chris.

He blinked. The words were out of his mouth before he could stop them. But as soon as he said them, he knew they were true.

His eyes met Anna's as she turned from the screens and looked at him.

'When Tim arrived,' she began, 'you said something. I heard you. You *said* that he'd come back to fight. How did you know?'

'I . . .' said Chris. 'I'm not sure.'

'Is that what Tim's doing?' Anna asked. 'Is that what this was all about? Is he fighting for us?'

'I . . . I think so,' said Chris. 'I think he's here to help us. But I . . .'

He touched the bracelet and fell silent.

Why is this happening to me? That was what he was thinking now. *Why me?*

There was a way to avoid it, of course. There was a way to avoid involving himself any further in this whole situation. It was simple: all he had to do was continue to resist what was happening to him – continue to pretend to ignore what was going on – and then the issue would be decided. Tim would die – or be dissolved, like the people caught out there on the streets when the Mallahide swarm had attacked. Then it would be over. Was that what he wanted to happen?

Chris took a deep breath.

'There's . . . something I haven't told you,' he said.

'What, Chris?' asked Anna. 'What is it?'

'Me and . . .' Chris gestured at the screens. 'Me and the monster – Tim. I think . . . there's kind of a *link* between us.'

Oh God, Chris thought, how lame it sounded! But that was nothing compared to what else he was going to have to say.

'How?' asked Anna.

'Through this,' Chris said, pointing to the bracelet.

He took another deep breath . . . and went for it.

'A lady gave it to me when we did that visit to the British Museum. It's got some kind of – of *magic* to it, I guess. It glows and gets hot whenever Tim is near. It's also supposed to connect me to all living things: I think that's maybe why I passed out in the biology class.'

Anna was staring at him now. So was everyone else. Chris's face now felt so red that he was sure it was going to explode.

'She said something to me, Anna,' he went on quickly. 'The lady at the museum: she told me something weird. She said . . .' He paused, trying to get the words right. 'Yeah, she said, "*The Earth needs her Defender once more, and you will be the channel of his power.*" ' He shrugged helplessly. 'I think that's, you know, got something to do with this. Maybe.'

'Young man – are you on some sort of medication?' asked the prime minister. He turned to look at his aides. 'Who let this boy in here, anyway?'

'Shut up,' Anna snapped, making the prime minister blink. 'Chris, what was that about a "Defender"?'

'That's *him*,' said Chris, gesturing at the screens. 'Tim. The dinosaur guy. I think he's the one the lady was referring to. But, well, that's not the most important thing.'

He paused. *Sheesh*. He'd got this far. He might as well say it all now.

'The important thing is,' he said, 'I think there might be a way we can help him.'

'How?' asked Anna.

'The night when Tim appeared,' said Chris, 'I was out with my folks in our car. He *looked* at us, and the bracelet started glowing and I . . . I felt something. I felt I understood him: I could feel what he was feeling. And I think, you know, maybe, well . . .' He paused again and said, 'If we all felt . . . something *back* – then maybe *he* might feel it too.'

'What in heaven's name are you blathering about?' asked Mr Sinclair.

You must unite Earth's population behind the Defender (Chris remembered) *so our power can be there for him when he needs it. You, Chris, must* join the world . . .

'I don't know,' said Chris miserably. 'But I think . . .'

He had to say it. There was no way to escape it.

'I – I think what it is,' he stammered, 'is that Tim needs us all to *believe* in him.'

There.

There was a short silence.

'I've never,' said the prime minister, amazed, 'heard such a load of utter drivel in all my life. Young man, I don't know if it's escaped your notice, but we do have something of a situation going on here. This young lady's father is threatening the whole of London, and here *you* are rattling on about . . . magic bracelets!'

Chris hung his head.

'Let's try it,' said Anna quietly.

'*What?*' said the prime minister.

'I said, let's try it!' said Anna. 'I'm going to do as Chris says.' She looked around the room. 'Who's with us?'

There was another short silence while the assembled bigwigs exchanged a long look.

'What, er,' said Wythenshawe – going pale because he knew that everyone was staring at him – 'what do you want us to do?'

'How's it work, Chris?' asked Anna. 'Do we need to hold hands or what?'

'Oh, for heaven's sake,' muttered the prime minister – and for once, Chris felt he agreed with him. Could this whole situation get any *more* uncool? Was that even possible?

'I, ah, I don't know,' he said.

'Well, do you think holding hands would *help*?' Anna pursued, taking charge.

'It can't hurt,' said Wythenshawe. 'Frankly, at this point, I think we should be prepared to try pretty much anything.' He stepped forward, took Anna's hand and reached for Chris's.

Reluctantly, Chris held his hand out.

'Now, come on, everybody,' said Anna. 'Let's give this a shot.'

'No *way*,' said the prime minister. 'There is *no way* that I'm going to get involved in this . . . *charade*.'

'I'll do it,' said the head of the Royal Air Force. He gestured at the screens. 'I've seen what Mallahide's capable of. I'm with Wythenshawe and the young lady. Since nobody else has any other suggestions, we might as well give this a go.'

'Very well,' said the commander of the navy, stepping forward grimly. 'But I just want to make it clear: this whole business is *very embarrassing* and had better never go outside this room. Understood?'

Sheepishly, three or four of the other people in the room walked over to join hands with the little group surrounding the prime minister.

'You've all gone barking mad,' Mr Sinclair opined.

'OK,' said Anna. 'Now what?'

'Er . . .' said Chris.

'I guess we just concentrate on sending Tim some, like, good vibes,' said Anna brightly. 'Right?'

'Good vibes,' said Chris miserably. 'Right.'

The prime minister made a snorting sound in his nose.

'OK,' said Anna, ignoring him utterly, 'here we go, then. Everybody concentrate.'

Silence fell in the Crisis Room.

Chris was doing his best, but it was difficult. There he was, standing in a row, holding hands with a bunch of people he'd never met before: this was somehow supposed to save the dinosaur currently out there under the London night, fighting for its life against a swarm of all-consuming super-intelligent nanomachines. The situation was beyond ridiculous: it was *insane*. If someone had told him a week ago that this was what was going to happen, he would have laughed them out of the room.

But . . . he had felt that connection that night in the car.

He didn't want Tim to lose.

The seconds ticked away.

'Chris . . .' said Anna sadly. 'I'm sorry. I was wrong. I don't think this is—'

'Shhhhhh,' said Chris. 'Wait.'

He thought he was imagining it at first. But the bracelet was becoming warmer, and now – yes! – just like before, that night in the car, now it was starting to *glow*.

'Anna,' he said, and his voice came out strangely quavery. 'Anna, I think it's—'

'I can see! Oh, *Chris*—!' She stopped herself. 'Come on, quiet now, we've got to concentrate.'

Chris noticed an odd fluttery feeling: tendrils of warmth and excitement were spreading out through his ribs, radiating out through his arms and legs and making his head go light and whizzy. At the same time, the bracelet was growing brighter every moment, taking on a weird undersea greenish-yellow light that quickly expanded until the whole of the room seemed to be filled with it.

Chris looked up at Tim's slumped body lying in front of Westminster Abbey, still swamped under the crawling black layer of annihilating machines.

'Come on, everybody. We can do it!' Anna commanded.

Something strange was happening to Chris behind his eyes. It was a little like the feeling he'd had when he'd woken up that morning after the bracelet had first been put on him: a weird, bulging, *swelling* sensation, like his brain was growing too big for his skull. There was an *opening* sensation at the back of his head. A connection was forming, coming straight up through the soles of his feet – and something . . . something was coming through.

The bracelet burned brighter.

The hands holding his held tighter.

And then . . .

Then it happened.

Something old and vast seemed to take hold of him and shake him, *rushing roaring racing shrieking bursting*. Every nerve and sinew in his body seemed to swell with power until it threatened to explode – but then, instead, it *relaxed*. At the same instant, the bracelet's glow flared to an intolerable brightness. And on the screens, out there under the London night . . .

Instead of giving up, Tim opened his mouth –

– and breathed.

A column of blinding whiteness split the night sky like a lightning bolt.

Tim – and the rest of the world – watched, eyes wide with amazement, as wherever Tim looked the column of whiteness followed. It struck the Mallahide swarm – and the swarm was driven back, shrivelling into nothingness under the sudden and incredible glare, the blast of unstoppable force, that was coming (Tim realized at about the same time as everyone else did) *from Tim's own mouth*.

He had breathed in air: he was breathing out light – light and a living energy of such concentrated power that Professor Mallahide suddenly found he had to pull himself clear before it wiped him from the face of existence.

Tim sat up, clean of the nanomachines now – and the blast of his breath travelled straight up into the main body of the swarm. The machines caught directly in the path of the blast vanished instantly into nothingness – and even when, at last, Tim's great exhalation ended, for several seconds afterwards tens of billions more of Mallahide's nanobots continued to flare briefly and expire where its edges had passed.

Gathering the tattered remains of his swarm – *half* of it

had been lost! – Mallahide fled, scattering into the four corners of the night.

Woozy, stunned, bleeding all over, Tim got to his feet. He bellowed, in a mixture of defiance, amazement and confusion. Then he staggered back to the Thames, splashed into the water and set off in the direction he had come.

There was silence.

'What—?' the prime minister spluttered finally. *'What the hell just happened there?'*

'We did it!' said Anna. Letting go of the military bigwigs whose hands she'd been holding, she turned to Chris and threw her arms around him, jumping up and down with excitement.

Chris grinned weakly, then collapsed.

DEVASTATION

Tim swam as far as he could: swam until his battered forearms stopped paddling and his poor, wrenched tail stopped going from side to side. Then he gave up and sank into the depths.

'Well, well, well,' said a voice presently. 'Let me guess: things didn't go quite like you expected?'

'He was so *strong*,' said Tim, feeling like he wanted to cry. 'And so mean! I grabbed him, bit him, lifted things up and hit him with them – but whatever I did, he just .. took no notice! He *hit* me and *ow*, it hurt! And *then* he picked me up by the tail and threw me. And *then* he turned himself into lots of horrible little biting and stinging things, and *then*—'

'Hush,' said the Kraken. 'Hush, little one. I was watching: I saw it all.'

Tim fell silent.

'Let me ask you a question,' the Kraken said. 'Did I ever tell you it was going to be easy, being the Defender of the Earth?'

'No,' Tim admitted. 'But—'

'Did I ever tell you that you couldn't be hurt? That bad things couldn't happen to you?'

'No, you didn't,' said Tim. 'But I had no idea he—'

'Yes,' the Kraken interrupted, 'you had *no idea*. And that, you see, was no fault of mine.' It paused. 'You were too confident.'

Tim said nothing.

'You must learn *caution*,' the Kraken told him. 'By charging in headlong like that, you only succeeded in putting yourself in more danger. Forethought, cunning, *discretion* – those must be your watchwords. Otherwise you won't live as a Defender of the Earth for even a quarter as long as I have.'

For another moment Tim thought about what the Kraken was saying: he gave the words the most thorough consideration he could. Then –

'No,' he said – now very angry. 'No, I'm sorry, that just won't do *at all*. I have just come back from a *colossal* battle, one that almost killed me – and you know what? I want a bit of sympathy and kindness. I want you to be *nice* to me,' Tim emphasized, warming to his theme, 'because I was scared, and it hurt, and I don't understand what's going on! And what do I get from you now that I've come back? A *lecture*!

'I'm not like you,' Tim added, shaking his head. 'I'm not the kind of Defender of the Earth who just sits at the bottom of the sea: I fight! I grab things and bite them! And you know what I think?'

'Do tell,' said the Kraken wearily.

'I think *my way is better than yours*.'

Tim paused, but he'd said it now and he knew it could not be taken back.

'When you showed me the world,' he went on, 'I noticed something. You didn't show me what *you*'d been doing all that time, did you? You know why I think that was? Because I don't think you did *anything*. You were a *lousy* Defender of the Earth,' he spat. 'You just sat here and – and *watched*! Well? Am I wrong?'

'Yes, you're wrong,' said the Kraken equably. 'Maybe

not about all of it, but you're at least wrong about that.'

'Oh yeah?' said Tim.

'I did my bit,' the Kraken told him, 'just . . . in my own way. I adjusted things to keep the whole operation running: a tectonic shift here, a change of the Gulf Stream there. Believe me' – Tim felt the Kraken's amusement in his mind – 'the Earth would be in a much worse state without me playing my part behind the scenes. But as to whether your approach is better than mine . . . well, who knows? Perhaps you're right. Perhaps what the world needs right now really is someone who'll charge in blindly like a fool. At any rate,' it concluded, 'it doesn't matter now.'

'What do you mean?' asked Tim, suddenly nervous.

'You did it,' said the Kraken. 'Or at least, you did enough. The channel was opened. Your power – the power of every living thing in this world – was granted. Now, truly, you are the Defender of the Earth. And now,' it added, 'at last, I can die in peace.'

'*What?*' said Tim.

'I told you,' said the Kraken. 'There can only be one of us. From this point on, you're on your own. You're the one with the power now. I'd tell you to use it wisely, but as you've pointed out, what would I know about it? After all, I've only been defending the earth for the last *nine million years* . . .'

In his mind Tim could hear the Kraken carry on, but it was muttering to itself. The words 'young whelp' (grumble, grumble) and 'show some *respect*' came out clearly enough, but the muttering and grumbling were fading in strength as if their origin was . . . going away.

'W-wait a second!' said Tim. 'You can't go *now*!'

The muttering stopped abruptly. 'Oh, really?' said the Kraken. 'And why not, may I ask?'

'You can't leave me here on my own like this!' said Tim. 'I – I don't know what I'm doing!'

'On the contrary,' said the Kraken. 'I think you already know *exactly* what you have to do. Hmm?'

Tim said nothing.

'Yes,' said the Kraken. '*Mallahide*. You surprised him, but you did not defeat him. You must face him again. And this time you must finish him.'

'But . . . I *can't*!' said Tim, panicking again. 'He took everything I threw at him! I bit his arm off and he just . . . grew himself another one! And if it hadn't been for what happened at the end there, I . . .'

'Yes?' said the Kraken.

'I was about to . . .'

'Go on.'

'I was – well, I was going to *give up*,' said Tim. He hung his head. 'When I was lying out there, under the stars, I didn't feel like the Defender of the Earth. Before that thing with my breath, I just . . . felt like . . .'

'Like you'd failed,' said the Kraken for him. 'It's all right. I know.'

'You do?' asked Tim, surprised.

'There's no shame in that,' the Kraken told him.

'There isn't?'

'Not at all. Tim . . .' The Kraken paused. 'You can't do everything by yourself. Sometimes you're going to need help. And that's why—'

'So you're staying?' Tim interrupted. 'You're not going to

die after all? That's great!' He was so happy, he started to thrash his tail.

'No,' said the Kraken heavily, 'that's not what I meant.' Tim heard it sigh. 'You've got a lot of good qualities, little one, but *brains* – it appears – aren't one of them. Very well,' it added, 'let's try and explain this another way.'

'Oh,' said Tim.

'Let me tell you about the Defender that came before me – my predecessor,' said the Kraken.

'All right.'

'Her name was Arachne. She was a powerful Defender, subtle and wise, and long ago, long before my time, she had a vision. Arachne foresaw that one day a new race of creatures would emerge. These creatures would have great power because they would have *consciousness*: they would be able to think for themselves, like we do.'

'The tiny people?' guessed Tim.

'That's right,' said the Kraken. 'Now, Arachne found this vision very troubling. You see: what drives us, what gives Defenders their strength, is the life force of the world. And for all the millennia up to that point, the living things of the Earth had supplied that life force *unthinkingly*. There had been no question of "permission" before because there had been no creature with sufficient intelligence, sufficient intellect, to think to give permission or withhold it. But with the coming of humans that certainty was gone. Humans would have the ability to choose. And Arachne felt she could not truly be the Defender unless they were offered the chance to exercise that choice *for themselves*. Do you understand me so far?'

'Not really,' Tim admitted.

'Never mind for now,' said the Kraken, 'just listen. Arachne came up with an answer. She created a device. This device would act as a focal point for the life-force energy, concentrating and magnifying its power. You saw one of the effects this focusing can have tonight.'

'Oh! The thing when I breathed!' said Tim.

'That power,' said the Kraken sternly, 'is the strongest thing on this Earth. It is nothing less than the wellspring of life: the source of the random mutations that cause life to evolve and develop. Focused and amplified, that power can be intensely destructive. Used with *care*, however, it *could* be employed against your enemy somewhat . . . differently.'

'How?'

'Mallahide is out of control. Unchecked, his swarm will eat the world – turning all it touches into more of itself, imposing his conformity on everything. You saw this in your vision.'

'Yes,' said Tim. 'But—'

'But nothing!' said the Kraken. 'Will you shut up and listen? This is crucial.'

'Sorry,' said Tim.

'Focused through the device – focused through *you* – the life energy becomes a force for *instantaneous change*. I believe that if you direct that force properly it will disrupt Mallahide's control, counteract the conformity he imposes, and return the swarm and its elements to a healthy randomness once more. Those he has consumed may even be released unharmed: *breathe your chaos upon him*,' the Kraken emphasized, 'and your enemy will fall.' It paused. 'But . . .'

'But what?' asked Tim.

'The *other* function of Arachne's device is as a way of giving the humans their choice. The device must be worn by a representative among them. And the decision over whether the power can be used will rest with that human. Actually,' the Kraken went on, a little ruefully, 'because of that, when I became Defender the first thing I did was throw the device away.'

'Why?'

'I did not think humans should control our power,' said the Kraken. 'I did not believe they had – or ever would have – the necessary judgement and wisdom to take on that kind of responsibility. So I cast the device deep into the rock of the Earth's upper mantle. For many years it lay there. The humans never even knew it existed, and I continued my work as Defender in my own way – *discreetly*. Until one day it was my turn to foresee something.'

'What?' Tim asked.

'I foresaw my time coming to an end,' the Kraken replied. 'I foresaw the new threats facing this world: I foresaw *you*. After that, I changed my mind. I decided to nudge the tectonic plates again. I caused an eruption: *Krakatoa*, the humans called it. It brought Arachne's device back to the surface. And in due course, as I had intended . . . it was found.'

Tim said nothing. He was beginning to see where all this was going.

'There is . . . a boy,' said the Kraken. 'He wears the device. I believe you saw him once.'

'Yes,' said Tim.

'Tonight he granted you your power when you needed it.

But you cannot be certain that he will do so again. He is . . .
hesitant. You will have to convince him. For without him, you
– and all the Earth – are lost.

'That is your path,' the Kraken concluded. 'Now you
know everything: I cannot help you any more. So now . . . it's
time for you to let me go.'

'*Why*, though?' Tim whined again, though he already
knew the answer. 'Why've you got to leave me all alone like
this?'

'Because I'm *old*, Tim,' the Kraken told him frankly. 'Old
and very tired. I've done my time, and now I'm ready to stop.
The fact is, I've earned it – *despite*,' it added, 'what *you* seem to
think.'

'I didn't really—' said Tim.

'I know you didn't,' said the Kraken. 'Don't worry about
it.'

There was a short silence.

'Well, so long, little one. I hate long goodbyes, so now I'm
going to head on my way.'

'But—' Tim pleaded.

'I've got a heavy date! Soon some human scientists are
going to find parts of me washed up on a beach somewhere,
and it's really going to mess with their heads!'

The voice was beginning to fade.

'You know,' it said, 'the last time they discovered something remotely like me, they had to invent a new species
name for it. They already *had* a "giant squid", but this guy they
found was about twice the size. So what did they call him? A
"colossal" squid! And the best part is, *he was only fifteen metres
long*! HEE HEE HEE *HEE*!'

Tim opened his eyes in the endless dark and listened to the laughter in his mind. He listened for as long as he could.

But then it was gone.

The sun rose over London's shattered skyline. Hazy light crept feebly over the ruins of the Houses of Parliament, filtered as it was by the awesome and unnatural formation of black cloud that still hung in the air over the whole of the city.

Those of the city's inhabitants who came under that shadow just waited, quaking in their homes. Those who lay outside its reach made plans to escape further, clogging the roads in a continuing and hopeless rush to get away from the city that had become a battleground for monsters.

Tickled by breezes, revolving his swarm slowly, Mallahide . . . pondered.

Mallahide's mind was now vastly powerful. With the combined processing power of his trillion-strong army of nanomachines, he could calculate at speeds that made the fastest computers in the world look like they were counting on their fingers. Yet for the past few hours since the battle had ended, Mallahide had found himself swamped by a question that he – even he, the God of Small Things – was entirely unable to answer.

What, he wondered, *am I going to do about Anna?*

The night before, everything had seemed simple. He'd had enough of letting people decide whether to join him or not. He was going to take the decision for her, take the decision for the whole human race in fact, and as soon as she and they saw how wonderful what he was offering really was, then they'd thank him.

But now . . .

He was confused. Somehow, despite all his knowledge and power, he had lost his way.

Anna had fought him as he'd tried to assimilate her: she'd pleaded with him, cried and begged. He had told her it was for the best, but Anna had not believed him. She saw him as a threat. *She hates me*, he realized. His own daughter, his only child, hated him. Here he was, at what should have been the summit of his achievements – the fruition of years of planning and research, years that had prevented him from being a better father than he was – and all he'd managed to do was hurt the person he loved most.

His work had been supposed to advance humanity, to take the human race to the next level of its continuing evolution. But to them and to his daughter (Mallahide realized) it was exactly as he'd been told: perhaps he *had* become a monster.

How had it happened? And what was he going to do now?

The situation in London had not gone unnoticed by the rest of the world. While Mr Sinclair and the rest of Britain's leaders dithered, the other nations of the globe – especially those nearest the UK – had begun to act.

One of the first things that happened was that the Channel Tunnel closed down. The Eurostar trains were held at their stations; those already en route were turned back. Then the tunnel itself, a direct link between St Pancras Station (in central London) and the Gare du Nord (in Paris) under the narrow sea between the British and French coasts – and as such one of the finest single feats of engineering in Europe

– was suddenly and permanently sealed off by a series of controlled explosions on the French side.

Flights too were abruptly cancelled. All aircraft entering and leaving British airspace were grounded without explanation until further notice. To the dismay of the flood of panic-stricken passengers already trying to flee the country, any planes or helicopters that ignored the warnings and *did* make it into the air were immediately forced back to earth again under threat of being shot down.

All ships leaving British ports – hovercraft, ferries, tankers, everything down to the smallest yacht – found themselves turned back to port by an international blockade of destroyers (and no less than *seven* aircraft carriers) that seemed to have mysteriously appeared, forming a ring of steel that surrounded the British coast.

Telecommunications were cut, crippling British Internet access even further since most of the Web's major hosts were on foreign soil. Satellite feeds were firewalled. Pipelines were sealed. All British exported goods that had recently arrived at their destinations were taken offshore again and destroyed. Even migratory birds fell prey to the guns of paranoid governments.

The UK was cut off. Nothing could get in or out.

Of course, this was just a temporary measure. As the rest of the world's leaders were acutely aware, if Mallahide took it into his seething hive mind to spread his influence beyond the British Isles, then even an entire globe's worth of conventional armed forces might not be enough to stop him. So naturally, the rest of the world had made other plans.

Not quite all Britain's international lines of communication had been cut. One remained: the hotline between the Crisis Room and a certain exclusive piece of real estate in downtown Washington, DC.

'Sir,' said Wythenshawe, 'I have the White House on line one. The president wishes to speak to you.'

'Er . . . right,' said Mr Sinclair. 'Put him on. Quickly!' he added. 'We wouldn't want to keep him waiting!'

Wythenshawe did as he was told.

'Mr President . . .' said Mr Sinclair, sitting back in his leather chair with the phone against his ear, 'what can I do for you?' Pasting a hideous, glib grin on his face that was all the more pointless for the fact that his counterpart was unable to see it, the prime minister then waited for whatever the president had to say.

It wasn't good.

'Well, *no*, Mr President,' the prime minister tried, frowning. 'That's true, but—'

He fell silent.

'Of *course* I remember signing the Nanotech Non-Proliferation Treaty,' he said after a moment. 'It was us who drafted it, if you recall. But—'

Again Mr Sinclair's efforts were met by a flood of crackling invective from the other end of the line.

'But . . . honestly, Mr President. It's not like you tell us everything *you're* up to with *your* military research.'

This was a bold sally from Mr Sinclair, and he instantly regretted it. The volume of the president's voice, already pretty loud, rose considerably, then suddenly turned icy quiet as he said what he said next.

'No,' the prime minister answered, 'I don't really know

why the tyrannosaur came back either. But I can assure you, Mr President, we're doing absolutely everything we—'

Once more the president's voice cut him off, and Mr Sinclair turned suddenly pale.

'What do you mean,' he said, '*only one thing to do?*'

Then he fell silent. Over the next few minutes, as the president continued to talk, Mr Sinclair's mouth fell gradually open as his jaw involuntarily dropped.

'But . . . you can't!' he squeaked finally.

The president could.

'Not the *whole country*, though,' said Mr Sinclair, 'surely! I mean, I could understand London – though I wouldn't *like* it, obviously. But really, Mr President! You can't seriously mean—'

He did. In fact, the decision had already been taken, at an emergency meeting of the United Nations. The only delegates who had opposed it were the ones who were worried that perhaps – catastrophic though it was – it just might still not be enough to counteract the threat that Mallahide now posed to the human race.

'How . . . ?' began Mr Sinclair, then stopped again, but this time it wasn't because the president interrupted; it was because, for a moment, Mr Sinclair didn't know how to say it. 'How much time do we have?' he asked brokenly.

The president told him. He told the prime minister how sorry he was. Then he ended the call.

Mr Sinclair sat back in his chair, stunned by what he had heard. He could barely take it in. In fact, he'd forgotten he was still holding the telephone, wrapped in his white-knuckled fingers. But he forced himself to go through it all, one bit at a time, to make sure he'd heard it correctly.

Mallahide was simply too dangerous to exist, the president had explained. The way he was, he could spread all across the globe, converting everything he touched into more of himself. And if that happened – and with Mallahide behaving the way he had been, there was no reason to suppose it wouldn't – then there was only a limited window of time in which the rest of the world could react to his presence.

It was brutally simple. The longer Mallahide was active, the more powerful he might become. It might not be possible to fight him later – and that was a risk nobody was prepared to take. Action had to be taken: Mallahide had to be stopped *now*, before the swarm grew any bigger.

To this end, a global operation had been set in motion. It would take time, of course, as these things do, but the clock was ticking and preparations were already well under way: they had begun soon after the news of Mallahide's appearance had first been broadcast.

Mallahide had to be destroyed: *utterly* destroyed. Ideally, not a single nanomachine could be permitted to escape, or – the fear was – the swarm would eventually simply reconstruct itself. Achieving this 'best-case scenario' would require an extraordinary amount of destructive power, so the deployment of the world's most powerful weapons was the only possible option. The use of nuclear missiles had been unanimously agreed to almost instantly. Where the nations of the world had debated was over the size of the attack.

If the attack failed, if Mallahide somehow survived, then the world's leaders and generals and thinkers would need time to work out their next move. Some way to hinder the swarm's ability to recover itself was required, so a 'scorched earth' policy – a tactic of destroying anything that could be useful to an enemy – had finally been settled upon.

The entire nuclear arsenal, of every nation of the globe that had one, was going to be launched at once in a combined surprise assault. The primary target was Mallahide's current location, London. But the secondary target was the rest of the British Isles.

As was inevitable in any large military operation (the president explained), there would be some collateral damage. Much of northern Europe would be radically altered. Even if the attack was a success, its side effects would be felt for hundreds – perhaps thousands – of years to come. *But*, as he'd told Mr Sinclair with genuine regret, *it is the only way to be sure*.

In just twenty-four hours, Britain would simply cease to exist. There would be nothing left but a smudge on the globe – a blot of cooling slag and radioactive ashes.

'Dear God,' said Mr Sinclair.

Nobody answered.

Hours had passed, but Chris's condition had not changed. His chest continued to rise and fall with his breathing as if he was soundly asleep, but his eyes rolled back and forth at high speed under his eyelids: he was dreaming, hard and constantly.

There was nothing Anna could do for him, she realized. She stood up from the chair at his bedside, stretched, and went out into the passageway.

She was in the medical wing of the bunker, where she'd been ever since Chris's collapse. His parents had not been informed – in the current crisis there was no way to contact them – so Anna, as the only person who even really knew who Chris was, had found herself taking their place, sitting at his side, watching over him. She'd done it willingly enough: though she wasn't quite ready to admit this to herself, she had become quite fond of Chris. But in the silence and waiting, her thoughts had been preying on her.

Anna was thinking about her father – about what he'd tried to do to her, about what he'd become. She was thinking about the way the whole world seemed to be running scared of him. An idea had started to form.

She started walking.

'Hi,' she said to the first person she came across in the passageway – a harassed-looking black-clad man running somewhere with a briefcase. 'Can you tell me where the exit is, please?'

'I'm sorry, I'm in a hurry—'

'I'll hurry along with you,' said Anna, matching his pace. 'Now, where's the way out?'

'Young lady,' said the man, the corners of his mouth tightening in a humourless smile, 'I'm afraid you don't understand. We have a crisis situation.'

'Yes,' said Anna.

'The skies of London are filled with airborne contaminants. Deadly ones.'

'Yes,' said Anna. She didn't exactly like her father being described in this way, but she let it pass this time in the hope the man would reach his point sometime soon.

'The bunker has been *hermetically sealed*,' said the man with great emphasis. 'I don't know how you got in here, but right now, to all intents and purposes, there *is* no way out.'

'Nonetheless,' said Anna, 'I need to get outside. There are answers out there, and I'm the only one who can find them. Now, who knows how I can do it? You? Or someone in charge?'

THE EMPTY CITY

Mr Wythenshawe's background was in counter-terrorism. Before his promotion, he'd spent six years as a field agent: he'd seen plenty of dangerous situations in his time, but *this* . . .

'Miss Mallahide,' he said, 'I think you're making a dreadful mistake.'

The lift they were standing in was military issue: no fancy chrome or mirrors here, just steel plate walls with a studded metal floor. Anna and Wythenshawe were its only occupants. There was no readout by the sliding doors to show what floor they were on – with only two choices, the bunker or the surface, there was no need for one. But Anna could tell from the way her feet seemed to be pressing into the floor that they were heading up at great speed.

'It's an awful risk to take – don't you think?' Wythenshawe prompted when Anna didn't answer him. 'If the prime minister himself hadn't given his agreement, then I'm sure we wouldn't be letting you do this. I mean, Mallahide attacked you before. What makes you think he won't attack you now?'

'He won't,' said Anna quietly.

'You can't be sure of that,' said Wythenshawe.

'No,' said Anna. She looked at him coolly. 'You're right. I can't.'

Seeing the expression on her face, Wythenshawe didn't press her any further. For another moment the two of them stood there without talking. Then the hydraulic whine of the lift's motor died away into silence. The doors slid open.

'Well,' said Wythenshawe, 'this is as far as I go. Head straight on through the decontamination chambers and you'll find exit seven, like I told you.' He shrugged helplessly. 'Good luck.'

'Thank you,' said Anna. She looked out into the empty corridor. But before stepping out, she looked back at Wythenshawe.

'Listen,' she said, 'if Dad was here before . . .' The word 'Dad' felt strange coming out of her mouth. Forcing herself to ignore the feeling, she pressed on: '. . . then that means he knows how to get through your defences. He could come back anytime, so you'd better start thinking about how to get everyone to another shelter. This place just isn't safe, not any more.'

'Where is?' asked Wythenshawe bleakly.

'And . . .' Anna paused. 'Look after Chris, OK? I rather think he just might be very important.'

'Will do,' said Wythenshawe. He frowned. 'Do take care of yourself, Miss Mallahide.'

Anna nodded and stepped out of the lift.

Wythenshawe pressed a button. The doors slid shut.

She was alone. Quickly, before she could think about this too much, Anna turned and set off down the corridor.

The decontamination chambers were fully automated. However, since she was heading out of the bunker rather than in, the machines remained silent, making no effort to stop her. She reached the bank-vault-style door that Wythenshawe had instructed her would be there; she entered the seven-digit code she'd been given into the keypad. The locking bolts slid back. The foot-thick steel slab swung ponderously forward to reveal a surprisingly small room with an ordinary wooden door at the end. This door was painted grey, with an old brass door handle. Anna grasped this, turned it, stepped out – and had a surprise.

She was standing in the open air, just over the road from the mysterious Egyptian obelisk known as Cleopatra's Needle. She was on the north bank of the Thames, just five minutes' walk from where her father's titanic battle with Tim had taken place.

Watching the fight unfold on the screens earlier, Anna had imagined the way the ground must have shook as Mallahide and Tim traded blows – but she'd felt nothing. Then she realized: the bunker was buried so far underground that nothing, theoretically at least, could reach it. That was its purpose. No wonder she hadn't known.

The second thing that surprised Anna was that the door to the British Establishment's most secret stronghold just stood there in plain sight. It was a plain grey door in a facade of plain brick: on an ordinary day millions of Londoners would have walked past without sparing it a second glance.

But this was not an ordinary day.

Anna stood there looking all around herself for a full minute before she could begin to take it all in. All she could grasp were random details at first.

To her left, the upside-down beached hulk of a pleasure boat loomed upwards, blocking the whole of the road. She saw the broken paving and severed pipes jutting into the air like the exposed bones of ghastly fractures. She looked at the river and the stumps that remained of London's bridges. She looked at the skyline, or what was left of it – the gap-toothed grin of the row of buildings that faced the water.

Then she looked at the sky itself. She looked up at what her father had become.

A vast disc of darkness hung over London – almost blotting out the sun and casting the entire city into shadow. Six strange raised ridges radiated out from its centre: you could see that the whole thing was revolving, slowly, and in absolute silence. It was about as far from what a living person looked like as you could possibly get.

It – or *he*, Anna reminded herself with an effort – was her dad.

Anna felt raw fear open a sluice in her insides again. She waited, watching the vast mass overhead, gripped with a vertiginous certainty that at any second it would reach down a delicate grey tendril and boil her away to nothingness where she stood.

The radio at her hip gave out a burst of static, almost making Anna have a heart attack.

'Miss Mallahide?' said Wythenshawe's voice, crass and crackly in the silence. 'Anna? Do you read me? Over.'

'Yes,' said Anna through gritted teeth, with her thumb on the transmit button, just like she'd been shown. The handset she'd been given seemed woefully old-fashioned, but with the cellular network down like most other communications, it was the only way she could keep in touch with people at the bunker. 'Please don't shout. I can hear you just fine. Over.'

'Oh,' said Wythenshawe. 'Er, sorry. I just wanted to say, all the closed-circuit TV cameras in the whole city are hardwired to us here at the bunker. Wherever you go, we'll be watching:

if you get into trouble, we'll know and we'll do our best to help you. Over.'

'Great,' said Anna crisply. 'If you don't mind, though, I think I'd rather keep radio contact to a minimum. It's very quiet out here, and I don't want to make any more noise than necessary. Over.'

'What was that, Anna?' Wythenshawe's voice crackled back. 'I didn't quite catch that. Over.'

'I said,' said Anna, 'I'd rather you didn't call me too often on this thing. Over.'

'Sorry, Anna, we can't quite hear you. Please repeat. Over.'

'I DON'T WANT TO MAKE ANY NOISE!' Anna shouted. 'Don't call me again,' she added, turning red. 'Over.'

'Oh,' said Wythenshawe. 'I see. Sorry. Er . . . be seeing you, then. Over and out.'

The radio fell silent.

Shaking her head to herself, Anna started walking.

It was as if she was in some kind of dream city, not the London that she was used to. The light – obscured as it was by the looming shape overhead – lent everything she saw a muted, grey kind of look. Not a breath of wind stirred the air around her. There were no birds in the air or the trees – not one solitary pigeon. No animals of any kind. And there were no people.

The London streets were empty. The only cars she passed were abandoned, parked, or crushed. There were no sounds apart from those she made herself: her own breathing and the tiny scuffles and crackles of the rubble underfoot as she picked her way along. Anna moved as quickly as she could, keeping to the sides of the pavement to be as out of sight from above as possible. And after twenty minutes, she reached the British Museum.

Its gates were open, which was a bonus. She made her way along the tarmac drive and up the museum's wide stone steps, wondering how much longer her luck would last.

'Hello?' she asked the echoing silence of the lobby. 'Anyone here?'

No answer.

Anna took another deep breath and – glad to be indoors at least – set off, trying to retrace the steps that Chris had taken on the afternoon of the school visit.

Anna's footfalls echoed off the surrounding marble walls as she made her way into the Great Court. Of course, she realized, she had no real idea where she was going. She was looking for some clues to what she should do, some way some opposition could be put up against what her dad was doing . . .

Well, she asked herself. *What is that about?*

Say she did find a way for Chris and Tim to team up and defeat him. Was that really what she wanted? What if it worked? What if they killed him? What then?

All around Anna, treasures from all sorts of times and all sorts of places sat in their glass cases, waiting to teach her amazing things: Anna ignored them. Wrapped in the confusion of her thoughts – dancing lightly but definitely on the edge of just giving up on the whole situation and freaking out completely – Anna was oblivious to everything around her. When an arm snaked out around her throat from behind and another hand pushed one of her arms up her back in an agonizing half nelson, for a moment Anna was so surprised that she didn't even scream.

'Who the hell are you?' said a gruff female voice. 'What do you think you're doing here?'

'I—' Anna gasped. 'I'm – please . . . do you mind? I'm *choking*—'

'Oh. Sorry.' The arm around her throat released its grip. But the one holding Anna in a half nelson – she couldn't help noticing – did not.

'Well?'

'My name is Anna,' said Anna. *OK*, she thought, *no point trying to hide it* . . . 'Anna Mallahide.'

'You're his daughter,' said the voice from behind her, 'aren't you? They showed your picture on the telly.'

'Yes,' said Anna.

'That must be why you haven't been taken to bits like the others.'

'I imagine so,' said Anna as patiently as she could, 'yes. Now – could you let go of my arm, please?'

'Keep your hair on,' the voice muttered, 'I'm just doing my job.'

'Thank you.' Released, Anna turned.

The lady security guard's grey flannel uniform looked a size too small for her: its tautness on her stocky frame and the glint of its buttons made it look like a suit of armour. Her henna-red crew-cut was pretty intimidating too, Anna thought, as were her eyes: grey-blue and hard as flint, they focused on Anna in an appraising look, and Anna found that any complaints she was about to make about being manhandled (again) had suddenly died on her lips.

'So,' the woman prompted, 'what can I do for you?'

'There's . . . a boy,' Anna began hopelessly. 'His name's Chris. Someone here gave him a bracelet.'

'Oh yes?'

'He's . . . sick,' said Anna. 'Unconscious. But dreaming. The doctors can't figure it out.'

'No,' said the woman, to Anna's surprise. 'No, I guess they wouldn't.' She looked thoughtful.

There was a pause. Anna held her breath.

'This thing,' the woman said, pointing upwards – but that was enough for Anna to know exactly what she meant – 'that's really your father?'

'Yes,' said Anna. 'Yes, I'm afraid so.'

'Well, if you don't mind my asking,' the woman went on, 'what concern is the bracelet of *yours*? Call me suspicious, but I'd've thought that you and the Defender would be on opposite sides.'

The woman's tone was casual, but Anna hadn't missed the way the set of her feet had shifted and her hands had bunched into fists. Anna's relief and amazement at having found the person she was looking for suddenly turned to horror. *Oh God*, she thought. *She thinks I'm going to attack her.*

'I thought,' said Anna, her eyes beginning to fill with tears, 'that you might have some idea of how we can help him. To be honest, this whole thing with him and the, um . . . *dinosaur* is – well, it's a little hard to understand. Do you know what's going on? Do you know how it works? I mean,' she added, the words beginning to pour out of her in a rush, 'I didn't want the monster to die, but we didn't know what to do to help it. Chris said something about the life force of the world, we all held hands, and suddenly there was this bright light.

My dad kind of fell back, and the dinosaur creature escaped, but then Chris collapsed. I sat with him for a while until I realized that I didn't know what else to do, so I came out of the bunker. I made my way here through all the empty streets, and I—'

'Whoa!' said the woman. 'Whoa, there!'

It was Anna's turn to fall silent. The tears were dripping down her face now, and she was immensely annoyed at herself for coming to pieces like that.

'Sorry,' she said. 'It's been kind of a weird few days.'

'Think nothing of it,' said the woman. 'My name's Eunice. Eunice Plimpton. You . . . er, want a cup of tea or something?'

'No,' said Anna, wiping her nose and straightening herself up. 'No, I'm afraid I honestly don't think there's time. What I really want are *answers*. Can you help me?'

'I think so,' said Ms Plimpton. She sucked her teeth. 'But you're going to have to take me to him.'

ACOLYTES

The UK is a small country, but it has over two and a half
million closed-circuit TV cameras – an estimated ten per cent
of all such cameras in the world. Of these two and a half
million, by far the biggest proportion are set up and focused
on London: they're used mainly for crime prevention, anti-
terrorism and enforcing the charge all motorists must pay for
entering the city. Many of these cameras can focus in close
enough to pick out individual licence plates, even the faces of
people driving: sophisticated computer programs can cross-
reference these details against databases such as police records,
and armed response teams can be dispatched when appro-
priate within as little as four seconds. The population of
Britain is under constant surveillance. These facts are matters
of public record. What's less known is that all the images, from
every one of these cameras, are fed into a single room.

The room is in the bunker, deep under Westminster. From
there, almost every street in London can be monitored and
watched, around the clock if necessary.

Wythenshawe, watching the screens and what they were
depicting, sighed.

'What do we do, sir?' asked his second in command.

'Not much we can do,' said Wythenshawe curtly. 'It's too
risky to send anyone out to intercept them. All we can do
really is watch and wait, and hope against hope that these
fools don't get their wish.'

They had heard the call and had come from all over the country. Most had been forced to abandon their cars or trains at the edge of the city, dodging what limited quarantine arrangements the government had set up and continuing their journey on foot. Most had been walking for a long time – days, in some cases. All were tired and sore and grubby. But as they neared their destination – as they sighted their goal at last and it loomed ever larger in their vision – all of them were also almost delirious with excitement.

There was nothing coordinated or organized about they way they came: they were arriving from all points of the compass. Their numbers weren't vast, but they were growing all the time as more came out to join them. At that moment, perhaps six or seven thousand people were out on the streets, converging underneath the shadow that lay over London.

Not everyone was cowering in their homes, terrified of what Mallahide could offer them. Some had listened to his message. Some had welcomed it. Some were eager to leave their fleshly bodies behind and become something better. Some *wanted* the chance to become posthuman.

And they were coming.

Joe Bennett was nineteen years old. A year before, he had started to experience a lot of bad stomach aches: he had gone to his doctor, been referred to a hospital, and now, after a succession of painful and undignified treatments, all of which had failed, he'd been told he had something less than six months to live. Pancreatic cancer: a genetic predisposition. Those were the words that the doctors had used, but they weren't Joe's words. To Joe, it was much simpler.

His body was crap. It was as straightforward as that. His

body – which had been supposed to last the length of a decent lifetime at least – had instead packed up and failed him. Now, Joe was a person with big plans for his life. He wasn't prepared just to give those up simply because the useless lump of a body that fate had doled out to him wasn't up to the job. He wanted more. He wanted something better. And when he'd heard Mallahide's message, he'd set out from home straight away.

It had been a long journey. His treatments made him constantly tired anyway, but getting all the way to the centre of London on foot had completely exhausted him. He walked the last of the distance to the banks of the Thames almost on pure adrenaline alone. He was one of the first to arrive there, under the giant disc-shaped shadow that continued slowly to revolve over the London skyline. He stood there, breathing hard, clinging to a railing for support.

The crowd was full of people like Joe. Not just people who were sick or in pain – and not just people who saw what Mallahide offered as an easy way out of the problems in their lives, either. There were people there who believed. People who had longed for the day to come when human beings could reach out beyond the limits of their bodies and become something else, something beautiful and eternal.

But Joe was the first one that Mallahide spoke to.

'Sir!' said someone in the camera room warningly. 'I'm reading some kind of increased activity in the swarm.'

'I know,' said Wythenshawe grimly – and shrugged. 'Well . . . here we go again.'

On the north and south banks of the river, the crowd finally stopped. Their numbers carved in two by the swathe of the Thames – the gap between them rendered uncrossable by the shattered remains of the bridges – they faced each other, and waited.

The gigantic shadow reached down a hazy grey finger. A soft wind blew, and out in the centre of the river something a little like a column of ash whirled into being, shivering in the air like a small tornado. Then Professor Mallahide appeared.

He was standing there on the water, as if this was the most natural thing in the world. His rumpled tweed suit was exactly the same. His tie was skewed, and his cheeks were wet. He was crying.

'H–hello,' he said with a smile.

The crowd to either side didn't answer. They just stood there watching, and a pregnant hush settled over the river.

'You came,' said Mallahide, looking around. His eye was caught briefly by a homemade banner that someone had brought with them: the banner showed an arrow pointing down at the person holding it with, above, the words GET ME OUT OF HERE in big red letters.

'You heard me,' he said almost to himself, as if he could hardly believe it. 'You understood me, and now you're here. I . . .' He paused. 'I can't tell you how happy that makes me.'

With shining eyes, he glanced around the crowd again until they locked on something else.

With a shudder of joy in his heart, Joe realized that Mallahide was looking at *him*. And now he was coming towards him! Casually striding across the surface of the choppy grey water, Mallahide made his way to the north bank of the Thames. The professor floated up over the embankment, alighted on the tarmac, and walked slowly through the crowd towards Joe. The crowd reached out to touch Mallahide's tweed suit as he passed as if he was some kind of god.

'You,' he said, standing in front of Joe and grinning hugely. 'Hi! What's your name?'

'Joe,' said Joe.

'And you've also come to leave your body behind? You've come to join me on humanity's greatest ever adventure?'

'Well . . . yeah,' said Joe.

'You're so young,' said Mallahide, frowning. 'What made you decide, if you don't mind my asking?'

'Cancer,' said Joe. He shrugged. 'It's inoperable.'

'Oh, Joe.' Mallahide looked sad. 'My wife, Katherine – I lost her to cancer. As a matter of fact, that's what set me on this path in the first place. Now that I've succeeded, I . . .' He hesitated. 'I hope she'd be proud.'

Joe had nothing to say to this, so there was a pause.

'When you . . . change,' Joe began, 'what's it like? Is it really as good as you say?'

'Joe,' said Mallahide, 'believe me, it's *even better*. You know what? Even with everything that's happened, I wouldn't go back to the way I was, never in a million years. In fact, Joe' – he winked – 'in a million years, you can ask me about it yourself! How about that? Now, are you ready?'

Joe smiled. His heart was pounding. 'I've always been ready,' he said.

'Then you'll be the first,' said Mallahide, smiling back. 'You!' he added, addressing the crowd. 'All of you! You're a shining example to the rest of the human race. Where others cower in fear in the face of change, you people reach out and embrace it. You are pioneers,' he added. 'You're an inspiration. And it's people like you who will help me lead humanity out of the darkness, into the light of the future.'

The small crowd clapped and cheered, grinning at each other eagerly.

'Now,' said Mallahide. Overhead, the swarm began once more to reach down its gentle grey fingers to the waiting crowd below. 'Close your eyes. This will only hurt for a moment . . .'

THE TRAP

'How do you know all this stuff?' Anna asked. She and Ms Plimpton had left the British Museum and had set off back towards the bunker without incident – so far.

'I'm sorry?' said Ms Plimpton.

'This business about the Defender and the bracelet and everything,' said Anna. 'How do you know about it? And how come,' she added, 'you and the bracelet were just waiting here until *Chris* came along, of all people?'

'Yes,' said Ms Plimpton, 'he's not the most prepossessing person you could ever meet, is he? If the bracelet hadn't started glowing like that, I never would have guessed.'

'He's got . . . hidden depths,' said Anna judiciously.

'He's certainly hidden them well,' Ms Plimpton agreed.

They smiled at each other.

'But seriously,' said Anna. 'Have you always known about the bracelet and the Defender and the rest of it? I mean . . . how long were you waiting before Chris showed up?'

'Seriously?' said Ms Plimpton. Her face took on a faraway look as she worked it out. 'Twenty-two years.'

Anna stopped walking. For a moment she was speechless.

'Quite a while, eh?' said Ms Plimpton, enjoying Anna's reaction. 'Yes, I guess a normal person would've given up. But there again,' she added darkly, 'being "normal" is something I've never had much talent for.'

'How did you get involved in all this?' asked Anna.

Ms Plimpton took a deep breath and said: 'Ah. Well, to cut a long story short, that would be when I decided to die.'

Anna blinked.

'I'd picked a pretty good spot for it,' said Ms Plimpton, smiling grimly. 'Thailand, one of the south islands. One beautiful evening I walked down to the shore. I stood there a while: the sky above was this extraordinary shade of pale purple. Then I turned, walked out into the sea, and started swimming.

'I'm a good swimmer,' Ms Plimpton went on as Anna stared at her. 'I swam a long way. And at that exact point where they say you're supposed to turn back – that point just *before* you start to feel tired so you've got plenty of juice left for the return trip – I kept going. I just kept on swimming into the night and the darkness, until finally I couldn't swim any more. The warm water closed over me and I let myself slip down into it.'

Ms Plimpton broke off her story and looked at Anna.

'Now, what you've got to understand,' she said, 'is that I wanted to die. I wanted not to feel anything ever again: no me, no nobody – nothing. But instead . . . I had this *dream*.

'Somewhere ahead of me in all that darkness, I started to think I could see a little speck of something. It was like a spark, tiny to begin with, but it soon got bigger and then it started changing colour. There was white stuff all over it, with blue and green underneath, and then I knew what I was looking at: the globe. Our planet. Planet Earth.

'It looked so small, surrounded by all the dark. I thought of all the people going about their lives on its surface, as if everything they did was so important, and all the while this vast hungry darkness was waiting all around – waiting to swallow them. I was watching the little planet, holding us and keeping us all safe, with nobody doing much to look after it in return. And I suddenly decided: I didn't want to die any more. Instead, I wanted to know what I could do to help. And *then* – and here's the really weird bit,' she said, turning to Anna again, 'as soon as I thought that, I found out that *I could.*'

'How do you mean?' Anna asked.

'It was right there in my mind, all of it, instantly. I saw the bracelet, where it was being kept. I saw what it was for. And I saw my place in it all: not to be the channel myself but to watch and prepare and wait and be ready when the time came. That was what I had to do. That was the task I was given. And as soon as I accepted it . . . that was it.'

'What was?'

Ms Plimpton grinned. 'Next thing I knew, I was on the beach. It was morning. I was very stiff, full of all sorts of cramps; I was pretty sick too and very sunburnt. But I sat up, brushed some sand off me and looked around. I thought for a moment that I was on the same beach where I'd started. But in fact I'd washed up all the way over on *Nassau*, in the Bahamas.'

Anna frowned. 'But that's . . .'

'Practically on the other side of the world?' Ms Plimpton's grin widened. 'Yup. I had a hell of a time explaining it to the immigration people! Now, is it my imagination,' she asked suddenly, 'or has it been getting kind of dark around here?'

Anna had been so wrapped up in what Ms Plimpton had been telling her that for the past five minutes she hadn't been thinking about her father at all.

Big mistake. All around them on the eerily empty London streets, a shadow had fallen. It was as if a storm cloud was forming overhead. But it wasn't a storm cloud.

Anna's hand went to her mouth. 'Oh no . . .'

The sky seemed filled with a looming bruise-black. A long drifting fringe of hazy grey tentacles now reached down through the air, combing the streets. Mallahide was on the move again.

For a moment Anna just stood there, frozen by indecision. They had almost reached the bottom of Charing Cross Road. The remains of Trafalgar Square opened out around them – the shattered paving and raw black earth underneath. There was no cover to speak of. For however long it took them to cross that space, Anna and Ms Plimpton would be totally exposed.

'All right,' Anna said. 'We're going to have to run for it.'

Ms Plimpton gave her a grim look. 'Ready when you are.'

'OK . . .' Anna took a deep breath. 'Go!'

They set off.

Anna hated running. She always had. But she ran until the air was like knives in her chest. And all the time she knew it was useless.

Up ahead, two of the tentacle things suddenly froze and changed direction. They converged at the top of Whitehall. They merged, twisting and glittering for a moment, and then Professor Mallahide was waiting for them.

There he was, in his tweed jacket and corduroy trousers, his hair still sticking out in a ruff around his head.

'Anna!' he said, grinning delightedly as his daughter

gasped painfully for breath. 'What are you up to out here? What's the rush?'

'We were trying to avoid you, actually,' said Ms Plimpton.

Anna gave her a look that she hoped would shut her up, then looked back at her dad. 'Hello,' she said eventually.

It was a strange combination of emotions that she was feeling at that moment. Her father looked so ordinary, so exactly like his everyday self, that it was almost impossible to connect him with the vast shadow above and the drifting horror of the searching tentacle things. She had missed him, she realized: missed him dreadfully. But at the same time she remembered what had happened the last time they met and what he had tried to do to her.

She still loved him. Of course she did: he was her dad, and what she felt for him was so strong that it couldn't be changed in one day, even by something as powerful as his attacking her. But now she was scared of him too – more scared than she'd ever been of anything in her life. Feeling both those things at once was almost unbearable.

'Hello, Anna,' said Mallahide. Without thinking, he reached out his arms to give her a hug.

Anna took a step back. The look her father gave her then almost broke her heart. For a second there was silence.

'And, ah, who's your . . . friend?' said Mallahide, with an immense effort to be casual that fooled absolutely nobody. His arms dropped to his sides and he nodded at Ms Plimpton. 'How do you do? I'm—'

'I know who you are,' she replied.

Mallahide's eyes narrowed. 'Then you have me at a disadvantage, Ms . . .'

'Not as much of a disadvantage as I'd like.' Ms Plimpton gave Mallahide a long look up and down, then shook her head and made a sucking noise in her teeth.

'You scientists,' she said with utter contempt. 'All you do is find new ways to screw up the world! Why can't you people do anything that helps humanity to live in *harmony* with the planet for once?'

Mallahide frowned. 'But . . . that's exactly what I've done,' he said. 'Don't you see? That's what this is all about! No longer will our bodies separate us from our world or from each other. Instead, for the first time, the whole of mankind will be truly united in its common purpose.'

Anna sighed. *Here we go again*, she thought. 'Dad . . .' she said quietly.

'What "common purpose"?' asked Ms Plimpton. '*Your* common purpose, I suppose – namely making more of yourself!'

'Well, yes,' Mallahide admitted. 'To start with, our primary motivation will be to increase the swarm, to protect it from those too shortsighted to see its full significance. Those, if I may say so, like *you* seem to be—'

'Dad . . .' Anna repeated.

'But my ambitions stretch far beyond that, I can assure you,' Mallahide went on, ignoring her. He smiled. 'Further than you can imagine!'

'Oh yeah? And what if people don't *share* your ambitions?' Ms Plimpton shot back. 'What if people don't want your perfect future? What if people don't trust you because what you're saying is a crock of—?'

'Will both of you PLEASE JUST SHUT UP!'

Anna's voice echoed around the empty square. Mallahide stared at his daughter, so surprised that, for a moment, all over the city, the drifting tentacles of the swarm stopped their searching and froze in place like stalactites. Ms Plimpton, shocked, stared too. Her mouth was open.

'Thank you,' said Anna. Using the pause to gather her thoughts, she added, 'Ms Plimpton, I don't mean to be rude, but these kinds of arguments are ones that me and my father have had a number of times before. And I don't think this is the time or the place to be going over all that again.'

Ms Plimpton closed her mouth and frowned.

'But . . . Anna,' said her father, smiling uncertainly, 'this is *exactly* the time and place. My swarm is growing. The first people have volunteered to join me, showing the way for the others. I hit a sticky patch, true, but now my plans are moving ahead at last, and soon you'll see what—'

'Dad,' said Anna, looking at him hard, 'I told you, I'm not going to talk about this now. If you're *not* a monster, if there's anything left of you after what you did to yourself, anything *real* about you any more from how you were before – then you'll understand and respect that and keep quiet.' She waited, looking at him. 'Well?'

Mallahide looked back at his daughter. He blinked. Then, simultaneously horribly ashamed of what he'd tried to do to her before and suddenly and intensely *proud* of her and what she'd become, he looked down at his feet.

'All right,' he said. 'What do you have in mind?'

'Tomorrow,' said Anna. Her heart began to pound as her plan fell into place in her head. She held her hands tight behind her back to hide their shaking, hoping that nobody noticed how scared she was. 'I'll meet you tomorrow, just you and me. Bring the whole swarm,' she added as she thought of more details. 'I want to see everything: exactly what you've become and exactly what you're hoping me and the rest of the world are going to turn into − *if* we decide to join you. Be at' − she thought for a second − 'St Paul's Cathedral at eleven a.m. Then we'll talk.'

She fell silent. Anna and her father looked at each other.

For the last few moments a sound had become audible, growing louder and louder through the surrounding empty streets as what was causing it came closer and closer. Three armoured police vans were making their way up Whitehall. They were approaching Trafalgar Square at top speed, their engines roaring and complaining as their drivers forced them on, crashing across the potholes in the tarmac. The vans were painted black, with wire-mesh riot shielding over the wind-screens. They swung to a gravel-spitting halt behind Mallahide and their side doors slid back, disgorging some twenty men with police shields and armour.

'Go! Go! Go!' roared Wythenshawe. The men fanned out, jabbing threateningly but uselessly at Mallahide with their guns and waving their truncheons. They were all, Anna noticed, plainly scared out of their wits.

'Step away from the girl!' called Wythenshawe through a megaphone. He was still hanging back at the passenger-side door of the van, ready to take off at a moment's notice. 'Get back, Professor, or we shoot!'

'And what do you think that's going to do?' Mallahide asked.

'Come over to the van, Anna,' said Wythenshawe

doggedly. 'Come on, quickly now! And bring your friend with you. Stay back, Professor! I'm warning you!'

'Well?' said Anna quickly. 'What do you say?'

'All right,' Mallahide told her. 'Eleven at St Paul's it is, then.'

'And,' Anna added, '*no more dissolving people*. At least not until then.'

'Not even if they want me to?'

'Not even if they want you to.'

Mallahide frowned and kicked a small stone with his shoe. 'All right,' he said.

'Then see you there,' Anna answered. 'Come on, Ms Plimpton, we're leaving.'

Ms Plimpton opened her mouth, then closed it again. With a last scowl at Mallahide, she followed Anna, climbing into the middle police van. The men jumped back in. The doors slid shut and they were off, on their way back to the bunker.

Bouncing up and down on her seat, surrounded by the insanely brave men with the useless weapons who'd come to rescue her when she hadn't needed rescuing, Anna sat in silence. She was thinking about her father.

He had taken the bait, as she'd known he would.

Now . . . she thought, *what was the trap?*

CHRIS THE CHOSEN ONE

When Chris was small, his mum and dad had taken him skiing.

The first trip had been the best. After that Chris had started to become jaded. But there was still one memory from that first holiday that Chris had always kept with him. He was thinking about it now.

Chris must have been about eight years old at the time: young enough still to get excited by things. The thing that made him most excited was . . . a chairlift.

It was a three-person chairlift. Chris sat in between his parents: his dad was on the left, his mum on the right. The lift was a steep one: it took them straight up the side of a mountain ridge that marked the boundary of one of the resort's valleys, and would shortly take them over the top and down into the next. The open air all around was crisp and sweet in Chris's nostrils, and Chris was happier than he'd ever been in his life before. Or, indeed, since.

I've never seen anything like it, a voice was saying. *His brain activity's reading way above normal, but everything else? Zilch. He's unresponsive to stimuli, his pulse is way down, but his brain's going faster than it would be if he was awake! What do you think he's—?*

It was late afternoon, and Chris and his mum and dad had been skiing all day. Chris's legs ached and tingled with the exquisite sensation of a day's hard and pleasurable use. The sun was already setting. In fact, where Chris and his parents were sitting, it was already dark. The sun had dropped below the line of the mountain ridge the lift was climbing, plunging everything Chris could see into shadow. Beyond his ski goggles the blinding blue and white of the sky and landscape had now shrunk to a near-uniform grey. Out of the sun it was colder too. The three of them huddled together a little against the gathering crosswind. The metal chair started rocking, just strongly enough to make Chris not mind his dad putting his arm across his shoulders. They sat there like that in a long and happy silence.

Nurse, what have I told you about patients wearing jewellery?

I know that, Doctor, but you don't understand – his bracelet just won't come off –

'Look, Chris,' said his father quietly (but still much louder than the other voices had been). 'I think you're going to like this.'

The lift was nearing the top of the ridge now.

'What, Dad?' said Chris. 'What is it?'

'Wait for it,' said his dad. 'Are you ready?'

The darkness was thick all around, thicker even than Chris remembered it. But at that moment, as the lift reached the top of the mountain . . .

'Now!'

The darkness blazed with light.

The setting sun struck Chris full in the face. The force of it hit him like a blow, annihilating everything else in his head in a heart-stopping blast of beauty. His retinas pulsed with glimpses of glittering blue-white snow crystals; the mountaintop was so close he could touch it with the tips of his skis.

'Wow!' he and his mum said both at the same time, and he felt his father's arm tighten, holding them both.

They hung there, at the top of the world, swamped with light. And in that moment, that perfect instant, Chris was utterly happy.

He's . . . Is he? Is he . . . smiling?

In his memory, Chris closed his eyes. The next second, in the past, he and his parents would start their descent down into the valley, and the rest of the fragment would recede into a blur. He didn't want to open his eyes because that would mean that the moment was gone, and nothing that came after it would ever be as intense, as pure and good, for Chris, again.

Still, he opened them. He had to. And he had a surprise.

The first thing Chris noticed was that his parents were gone. The chairlift, his skis, they were gone too. So were his clothes, his legs, his body, everything except the landscape – the valleys and peaks, stretching out all around him, as far as he could see in every direction.

The next thing he noticed was that he was still rising.

He was going upwards at an even pace that felt not much faster than the chairlift had been. But it wasn't: the details of the world shrank beneath him quickly. The horizons rolled back, their curve becoming more pronounced, and still Chris continued to go higher. For a brief moment his view was obscured by a clammy layer of wet whiteness, then the view around him turned a beautiful pure blue, which darkened and then finally turned black.

He had left the Earth's atmosphere. He was looking at the world from space.

He stopped.

And after a while he started to get restless.

The thing was, Chris had seen it before – hundreds, maybe thousands of times. He'd seen NASA footage of the way the Earth looks from the moon. He'd seen movies: shots of the Earth surrounded by flying saucers or whatever, special effects designed to suggest global peril. Although a part of him knew that what he was looking at at this moment was something else, something stronger, something different, the rest of him couldn't help but feel a bit . . . well, *disappointed*, really. He'd preferred the flying stuff. Why had that stopped? What was he doing, hanging here in space?

At this point – almost obediently – the vision began to change.

In a tiny area of what Chris was able to identify as northern Europe, the creamy cloud cover suddenly gave a great shudder. There was a succession of tiny blinding white flashes: the clouds were shoved aside roughly like a fist had punched through them, and the place where the flashes had been was replaced by an eruption from below – another cloud, but dirty-yellow coloured and rapidly expanding.

When the cloud thinned enough for Chris to see through it, he had another surprise.

Britain wasn't there. All there was, in fact, was a sort of wet brown smear. But then the smear, or rather something that *came* from the smear, started moving.

It was growing, spreading thin, dusty brown tendrils of itself across the seas. It spread over Europe, swallowing all in its path, as if the explosions had only encouraged it. It spread south, over Africa, and east, into Asia. It stretched a thin brown pseudopod right across the Atlantic, lassoing and finally swallowing the Americas. Soon the seas and the clouds were changed too, the whole world becoming a uniform seething brown as Mallahide assimilated it completely.

Chris knew what he was watching. This was the future as it would be if Chris failed to take up the responsibility that had been given him. If Chris didn't do what he was supposed to do, then humanity would respond to the threat of the Mallahide swarm with nuclear weapons. This response would fail, and Mallahide would eat the world.

Gradually, Chris began to be aware of another presence in his mind sharing the vision with him. Through the medium of the magical bracelet that connected them, Chris realized he could feel Tim's thoughts again: slow and ponderous, a little nervous and scared, but eager and ready to be brave if Chris would only say what he was supposed to say.

Chris had been chosen. Chris was the link between Tim and the natural life force that was the source of his power. Chris could help Tim become the world's saviour. It was all down to Chris.

Chris thought about it. Then he said,

No.

No! Why should he, Chris, have to be the one? Why should it be him? See, he didn't need all this stuff about giant monsters and clouds of all-consuming super-intelligent nano-whatsits. Sure, he cared about the world. Sure, he didn't like either of the alternative endings the future seemed to be serving up for him – being wiped out in a nuclear holocaust *or* becoming another flock of specks in Mallahide's swarm. But why should it have to be *him* who did anything about it?

Why couldn't it be people who were into this sort of stuff – people who were heroic or whatever?

Chris was sick. The way the bracelet worked was too intense for him: it had made him ill before, and now – now he was hallucinating! If he wasn't dead already, he was probably sitting in a hospital bed somewhere. The sacrifice was too much. They'd got the wrong guy, that was all.

No, Chris repeated.

There was a pause.

Chris felt, in his mind, the way that Tim turned away from him then. He felt the rising panic in Tim's slow dinosaur brain; he felt the sick twinge of despair, the loneliness of his vigil at the bottom of the sea, and the slow cold way he sank into it even further. Chris felt these things, and, sure, he was a little guilty about it. But he gritted his teeth and refused to change his mind. And then he woke up.

Chris opened his eyes. He only opened them a crack, but the light was like someone was jamming screwdrivers into his eye-sockets: for a moment all he could make out were silhouettes.

'Chris? Chris, are you awake?' said a voice he knew.

'He's coming round,' said a second voice he recognized.

'Step back everybody, give him a bit of space,' said a third briskly.

Anna was there: Chris had known it was her straight away, and he was pleased to see her. The government aide guy, Wythenshawe, he was there too by the sounds of it, plus a couple of others, nurses or doctors most likely: it was a full room he was waking up to. But that middle voice . . . he knew that one too; he just couldn't place it straight away.

'Chris,' it said. 'Chris, can you hear me?'

It wasn't . . . was it? Oh, *great*, Chris thought, it was! The crazy lady from the British Museum. The one who'd first got him into all of this.

'*You*,' he said. Then he paused.

His own voice had shocked him. It had come out as kind of a husky croak. He sounded like an old man. Come to think of it, he *felt* like one too. He ached all over: a bone-deep weariness that filled every particle of his body. His eyes hurt. His brain hurt. His ribs hurt. Breathing hurt.

'Hello, Chris,' said Ms Plimpton. 'Remember me?'

'Anna,' Chris asked, ignoring Ms Plimpton completely, 'what's going on?'

'You're a very lucky young man,' said Wythenshawe earnestly. 'You've been in a coma for nearly a whole day. The doctors here honestly weren't sure whether you'd be able to snap out of it. I—'

'I was asking Anna,' croaked Chris.

Anna and Wythenshawe exchanged a look.

'He's . . . telling the truth, Chris,' said Anna. 'I sat with you for as long as I could. But there didn't seem to be anything I could do. So . . . I decided to fetch Ms Plimpton.'

'And it's a very good thing that she did,' said Ms Plimpton primly. 'If you're to fulfil your purpose and help the Defender to save us all, then we've got a lot of work to do. Now . . . have you had your vision? Has the Defender linked minds with you directly yet?'

The look she gave Chris was very eager. Chris, looking back at her, was surprised to find that – though it hadn't seemed possible a moment ago – he now felt even more tired than when he'd woken up: her looking at him like that was making him feel that way. But since no other answer suggested itself, he said:

'I . . . had a dream.'

'And you linked minds with Him – right?' Ms Plimpton pursued.

The *H* in 'Him' was a capital letter. Chris just knew from the way she'd said it.

'Maybe,' he replied. 'Yeah. Yeah, I think so.'

'Wonderful!' said Ms Plimpton. She was so happy, she almost clapped. 'Oh, that's wonderful! I can't imagine what that must have been like for you. What I wouldn't give to trade places with you now!'

'Really?' said Chris with sudden interest.

'You actually joined minds with Him,' Ms Plimpton burbled on. 'You actually swapped thoughts with the Defender Himself.'

'Kind of,' said Chris. 'I guess. Yeah.' He would say anything now, he decided. Anything in the hope that it might make Ms Plimpton get herself and her obnoxious enthusiasm out of his face.

'Then you must know what you have to do,' said Ms Plimpton.

'Er . . .' said Chris.

'Mr Wythenshawe,' said Ms Plimpton suddenly, turning to the government aide, 'have you done as we asked? Is everything ready for the emergency broadcast?'

'We're . . . having some trouble getting hold of all the remaining channels,' said Wythenshawe.

Ms Plimpton looked stern.

'But,' he added quickly, 'I'm sure they'll all fall into line eventually.'

'Good,' said Ms Plimpton. 'It's time to spread the word. It's time to make everyone in London – everyone in the *world* – sit up and take notice of Tim, and what He is, and how we can help Him to do what He must do.' She turned to Chris.

He shrank under her gaze, wanting to sink through the bed, the floor, the Earth's crust, anywhere to get away from this woman and the way she was looking at him.

'Chris,' said Ms Plimpton, 'it's time to make you a *star.*'

For a long time Tim did nothing. He just stayed there, at the bottom of the sea, alone in the cold and the emptiness and the dark.

What had just happened exactly? He wasn't sure.

Tim had felt the tiny person in his mind. He had felt the hot, fast, sticky strangeness of tiny-people-speed thoughts: he had felt it like some sort of insect was wriggling in his brain. He and the tiny person had shared the vision: the tiny person, like Tim, had been shown what would happen if Tim failed. But instead of acceptance, instead of agreement, something else had taken place. A strange burst of feelings had squirted into Tim's mind – and then the answer had come. The tiny person had turned away. The tiny person had refused to help. And Tim was now stranded. Alone.

How had this happened? How could this be? Had Tim done something wrong? He ran what had happened through in his mind, searching for answers in his slow dinosaur brain, but of course, none were forthcoming. And, Tim realized suddenly, *it didn't matter.*

In a sense, nothing had changed. He still knew what he had to do. He was the Defender of the Earth. His task was to face up to the threat as best he could, no matter what the cost. He was still aching, still hurting all over, still smarting from his defeat and how close he'd come to being utterly destroyed. But there was no choice. He had to try. He had to face Mallahide again – and *now*, he realized, before his enemy had the chance to recover either.

All right, Tim thought. What else? Had he learned any lessons from the first time he and Mallahide had fought? Perhaps he had exposed some hidden weakness of Mallahide's, something he could exploit. Dutifully, already knowing what he would find, Tim played the fight through in his mind again, every last humiliating instant of it. Nothing. In fact, all he could find were the *opposite* of weaknesses: everything that Tim had tried, from the biting to the wrestling to the throwing things to . . . well, all right, actually that was all Tim had tried, all he knew how to try. The point was, it had all *failed*.

Mallahide was stronger and faster than Tim; he never got tired, he never got hurt – there was nothing for Tim to get hold of. How could he, Tim, possibly defeat an opponent that couldn't be bitten or hit? It simply didn't seem possible. But he had to do it. It had to be done. He had to find a way. Without him, the world would be destroyed. He was the Defender of the Earth, and he—

Alone in the dark, Tim froze. The surrounding deep-sea chill met a cold seeping feeling inside himself that penetrated his leathery skin and ran all over his dinosaur body in a way that Mallahide's nanobots had only just failed to do. Tim stopped kidding himself and looked at the clear facts of the case. They were these:

Tim couldn't defeat Mallahide. Tim was going to lose. He was going to fail, and die, and soon after the world would die with him.

Slowly at first, but with gathering speed, he started to swim.

ENDGAME

'No,' said Chris again. 'Absolutely not. No way.'

'Chris!' Ms Plimpton shouted at him – then sighed. 'Let me explain this to you again.' She spoke quietly now, but her words were filled with no less urgency. 'You are the channel for the Defender's power. You are His link to the life force of the world. *Everything depends on you.* Understand?'

'Yes,' said Chris, 'so you keep saying, but why—?'

'For the duration of this ritual,' hissed Ms Plimpton, cutting him off, 'you are humankind's link to every other living thing on this planet. Two-thirds of the world is covered by water, hence the pool – but tell me, Chris,' she said, poking him in the chest for emphasis, 'do any other creatures you know of on this earth wear *jeans*, or *T-shirts*, or *trainers*? Does any animal, apart from human beings, wear clothes of any kind?'

'Well, *no*,' said Chris, 'but I don't see why—'

'Our clothes may make us feel and look different from other animals,' said Ms Plimpton, 'but they don't make us different on the inside. We're *all* animals,' she added. 'Every single one of us!'

'I guess,' said Chris, 'but—'

'No buts, Chris!' said Ms Plimpton. 'Don't you understand what's going on here? Mallahide is a threat to every living, breathing creature on this Earth! Anything that makes you feel closer to other animals has got to be a good thing. So,' she finished, drawing herself up, 'you're doing this *naked*, and that's final.'

'Look, at least let me wear some boxer shorts!' said Chris, desperate now. 'In fact, if I can't wear my boxers, I'm leaving right now. The whole world can come to an end if it likes, but there's no way I'm doing this in . . . in the buff!' He crossed his arms. 'No way in *hell*.'

Ms Plimpton gave him a long look.

'All right,' she said. 'But you'll have to wear extra body paint. Now, where *is* the make-up guy? CAREFUL WITH THAT WATER TANK!' she yelled suddenly, catching sight of one of the studio technicians over Chris's shoulder.

So that was how it happened. Before Chris really knew what was going on, he was sitting hip deep in a small pool of water, clad only in his boxer shorts.

'Action!' said someone.

And now Chris was on TV.

He couldn't see his audience, of course. All Chris could see were cameras, and even they were indistinct and shadowy behind the dazzling brightness of the hastily erected studio spotlights. But from the trembling in his stomach, the raw sick taste of his embarrassment that backed up in his throat until he felt like gagging, he knew that made no difference. He could kid himself they weren't there, sure, but he knew the truth: right now the whole country, perhaps even the world – was staring at him, in a tank of water, on TV, clad in nothing but his boxer shorts and the bracelet on his wrist.

How had it come to this? He blinked, looking down at the way the lights glinted off his goose-pimpled skin. How had this happened? What was it about his life before that had invited this, now? Footage of this would be circulating the Internet for ever. For as long as he lived, he'd never be allowed to forget it. From this moment on, he was always going to be 'that guy, the one on TV'. In his underwear.

'People of Earth, listen up,' Ms Plimpton began. All over the country, all over the world, her face had appeared on the screens. The words EMERGENCY BROADCAST flashed in red letters just under her chin. 'My name is Eunice Plimpton. And your world is about to come to an end.'

Chris hung his head: it couldn't come to an end soon enough, as far as he was concerned.

'Do not adjust your set,' said Ms Plimpton. 'Do not try to change channels. This is a government broadcast going out to everyone who can hear it. And I'm here to tell you, one thing – and one thing alone – is all that stands in the way of the total and final destruction of this planet.' She paused and gave a thin smile. 'But don't just take my word for it. Take the word of the British prime minister here, David Sinclair. Mr Sinclair?' she questioned, beckoning. 'Over to you.'

Mr Sinclair blinked. He'd been standing at the back of the studio, hoping that nobody was looking at him.

'Come on now, Prime Minister,' Ms Plimpton coaxed. 'No need to be shy.'

Numbly Mr Sinclair watched as the cameras and spotlights swung round and targeted him mercilessly.

They were going out live. Everyone could see him hesitating. There was no choice.

'That's right,' said Ms Plimpton. 'Up you come. Wonderful. Now, Prime Minister: why don't you tell your electorate what you told me?'

For a second Mr Sinclair just gaped at her. His mouth closed a little, then opened again, giving him the look of a landed haddock. Bad enough that this woman had asked him up here without warning or preparation, but *this*. This was . . .

'Let me jog your memory,' said Ms Plimpton with contempt. 'This afternoon you attempted to *escape the country* in your private jet. But before you could leave British air-space, you were halted and forced to land by one of the international fighter squadrons currently patrolling our British coasts.

'Chances are you must have noticed them, ladies and gentlemen,' Ms Plimpton added, turning to the cameras. 'Perhaps you heard about it from other people who've tried to escape. The media has been forced to keep the details quiet, but the fact is that for the last forty-eight hours, this country has been in a state of total lockdown. In an attempt to stop the spread of the Mallahide swarm, the international community has clubbed together to ensure that nothing – *nothing* – has been allowed to get in or out of the British Isles. Including' – she smiled – 'Mr Sinclair here. Now, Prime Minister,' she asked silkily, 'could you tell us what exactly you were trying so hard to get away from?'

'I . . .' said the prime minister. 'Er . . .'

'What's going to happen to us?' Ms Plimpton pursued, losing patience. '*What did the president tell you?*'

Behind her, still sitting in his tank of water – and beginning to get a bit cold, not to say *wrinkly* – Chris watched.

The prime minister gulped. 'The president told me,' he began, 'that the Mallahide swarm was a threat – not just to us here in the British Isles – but to the whole human race. The possibility that the swarm might spread to other countries – might grow until it was impossible to defeat – could simply not be tolerated. A . . . decision was made' – he paused – 'unanimously, by the United Nations. In one hour . . .'

He coughed.

'Go on, Prime Minister. Tell the people. They need to know.'

'Britain,' said Mr Sinclair shamefacedly. 'They're going to destroy Britain.'

Ms Plimpton let the words hang in the air for a moment.

'There you are, ladies and gentlemen. You've heard it from the prime minister himself. Don't bother to run; you won't get far enough. Don't bother to hide; it won't make any difference. In less than an hour, a nuclear attack is going to be launched at Britain, and the whole country is going to be wiped off the face of the map. *Unless*,' she added, 'Mallahide can be stopped. And there's only one way that can happen.'

She took a deep breath. This was the moment. This was where it counted.

'He's green,' she said. 'He's a hundred metres tall, and he's all that stands between us and annihilation. Ladies and gentlemen, I give you . . . Tim, Defender of the Earth!'

St Paul's Cathedral. The last set of double doors slammed shut, releasing a tidal wave of echoes that crashed back and forth against the walls and the enormous dome above. They faded, and Anna was alone.

She looked at her watch. 10:53. Wythenshawe and his team had cut things pretty fine if they were going to get clear in time. But then again, she supposed, with the situation being what it was, where was 'clear' anyway?

She walked down the cathedral's central aisle. She chose a seat right under its three-hundred-year-old dome, as close to the centre as she could. Then she forced herself to sit down and wait.

The dome's gigantic hollow-egg shape loomed over Anna's head. It seemed to suck all the air and the light where she was sitting straight upwards, leaving her breathless. The silence gripped her like a bear hug.

11:00. It started.

Darkness fell across the stained-glass windows, as if the sun had been snuffed out. Anna felt tiny prickles of sweat at her temples as the temperature rose in the whole cathedral at once. A pencil beam of light lasered down in front of the altar; there was a faint fizzing sound . . .

And there he was. Her father.

'Anna!' he said, smiling.

'Dad,' said Anna, not getting up.

'Well, I'm here like you asked,' said Mallahide, as brightly as he could.

'No, you aren't,' Anna pointed out.

'I'm sorry—?'

'All of you,' said Anna. 'That was what we agreed. It was going to be all of you. The whole swarm, all of it, right here and now. Why d'you think I picked this place to meet in?'

'It is rather dramatic-looking,' Mallahide agreed. He pursed his lips for a moment and took a step towards her down the aisle. 'Anna . . .' he said.

She didn't move. 'Yes?'

Mallahide shifted awkwardly from one foot to the other. 'Well, there's no easy way to say this, so I'll just say it out straight, and you mustn't take it the wrong way. Promise?'

Anna said nothing.

Mallahide sighed. 'Anna: this isn't supposed to be . . . some sort of *trap*, is it?' He looked at her carefully. 'This isn't something you've cooked up with those government fellows you've been hanging around with? Some silly nonsense about getting all of me in one place, making me a little easier to attack, something like that? I mean, if it *was*,' Mallahide plunged on, 'I wouldn't get angry with you or anything. But I wouldn't be able to stop myself feeling a bit . . . disappointed.' He looked at his feet and forced a laugh. '*Huh.*' It echoed around the cathedral hollowly. 'Of course not,' he said. 'Darling girl, you wouldn't do anything to hurt your old dad!'

Anna let that hang in the air for a moment. Then she stood up and pulled the switch from her pocket.

'Microwave emitters,' she said. 'They're positioned all over the place: enough to charge the air particles and create a pulse a little like an EMP. Wythenshawe thought they might disorient you for a moment. That's all they had.' She laid the switch down on a chair beside her and looked at her father again. 'Right. I've been straight with you. Time for you to be straight with me. Where's the rest of you?'

'Not far,' said Mallahide, pursing his lips again. Anna had never spoken to him like this before. For all his vastly increased intelligence and powers, for a moment he wasn't sure how to react.

'So, what are you waiting for?'

'Anna . . . I'm not sure you—'

'What?'

'Well, I'm not sure you're ready to *see* me like this,' Mallahide admitted. 'I'm quite strange to look at en masse, I should imagine – especially up close. I don't . . .' He trailed off, twisting his fingers distractedly. 'Well, I don't want to *scare* you.'

Anna blinked and took a deep breath. For a moment she was so annoyed with her father that she had trouble getting her words in the right order.

'Making me think you were dead,' she began. 'Becoming what you've become. Trying to do the same thing to *me* against my will. After all that, don't you think it's a little late to be worried about scaring me?'

Mallahide bit his lip. 'Yes, of course,' he said, chastened. 'You're quite right, my dear: how silly of me.'

'*So . . . ?*' prompted Anna.

'Yes. Just a moment.' Mallahide closed his eyes.

It happened very fast. The shadows over the cathedral's stained-glass windows seemed to thicken as the darkness outside pressed against them. There was a second of nervy horror, then the swarm dissolved the ancient walls and remade them behind itself, passing through as easily as boiling water passes through a tea bag. Now the dome, the nave, all of it was teeming with machines, an orange-brown tornado that filled St Paul's to bursting.

They didn't touch Anna: they kept their distance. It was as if she was encased in a kind of invisible glass bell jar. She looked down at her feet in their round-toed black school shoes: a circle of floor around them, perhaps sixty centimetres in diameter, was clear. Beyond that, glittering and fizzing in uncountable trillions, was her father.

Abruptly the swarm rose up into the dome. Revealed once more, the professor's human projection stood a little way up the aisle, an umbilicus of tiny buzzing machines linking him to the boiling mass above. He looked nervous. Strangely, Anna thought that he looked almost as nervous as she was.

'So,' said Mallahide, the distant hum of the swarm just audible under his voice. He shrugged and tried for a smile. 'What do you think?'

Anna gestured upwards. 'This is what you're like now, isn't it? *This* is what you are,' she emphasized, jabbing a finger at the whirling mass, 'not what I remember of you. Isn't that right?'

'How do you mean?' Mallahide asked.

'That body,' said Anna, pointing at the figure standing in front of her. 'That face you're wearing now. It's not really *you* any more. Is it?'

'Anna,' said Mallahide, 'I . . .'

'*Is it?*' Anna repeated.

Mallahide pursed his lips.

'A body isn't a person, Anna,' he said. 'A body is just a machine for carrying a person around: one day, for whatever reason, the machine stops working and the person inside it dies. We've talked about this before.'

'Yes,' said Anna irritably. 'But—'

'We could improve the machine, of course. But here's the thing,' said Mallahide, grinning again, 'I've done something even better!'

'Dad . . .'

'Soon everyone in the world will have the ability to step *beyond* the boundaries dealt us by biology. At last we can *break out* of the prison of meat we're all locked into from conception and—'

'DAD!'

Mallahide blinked. 'Sorry, my dear: what did you say?'

'You promised!'

'Promised what?'

'Promised you wouldn't start spouting any more of your same old claptrap,' said Anna, exasperated. 'That stuff may sound good coming out of your mouth, but it won't work on me – and I'll tell you something else: I don't think it works on other people either.'

'I'll have you know,' said Mallahide, 'that a number of people offered themselves up to me to be . . . *translated* just yesterday afternoon. Why, that's what I was doing before—'

'Not *enough* people,' said Anna, shaking her head. 'Not for what you're talking about. Not a majority. Not the *whole world*.'

They looked at each other in silence except for the faint crackling buzz of the swarm.

'Bodies are . . . what separates us from each other,' said Anna, doing her best. 'Bodies are the line between us and other people. That's the way it's always been; that's the way people are. If you take that away from people against their will, then that's just . . . wrong!'

'Anna,' said her father, 'I am so, *so* sorry for what I did. I can't tell you how sorry I am. I lost my temper. It was a terrible mistake, and I would *never*—'

'Really,' Anna cut in. 'So what about all those people

you've already done your thing to? What are you going to do? Set them free?'

Mallahide froze. Suddenly he looked awkward. 'Anna, I . . .'

'It's a straight question,' said Anna. 'Are you going to let them go or aren't you?'

'Anna, it's not quite as simple as that,' Mallahide blustered. 'All those people I . . . translated, I can release them anytime, bu—'

'So why don't you?'

'Well, there are particular circumstances right now,' Mallahide went on with gritted teeth, 'that make that rather difficult.'

'Such as . . . ?'

'Right now, my dear, I need to be as strong as I can be. Until people realize it's pointless to resist me, I just can't release anyone. One day, yes,' he finished primly, 'but right now – no.'

'And what if those "particular circumstances" last longer than you think?' Anna asked. 'What if every time you get to the point of allowing the people whose lives you've stolen to be free again, something else just comes up? No, Dad.' She shook her head. 'Maybe you mean well, but I think you've gone too far to turn back. At any rate,' she added, 'most people won't trust you now, not after what you've done.'

'So what are you saying?' Mallahide snapped. 'Are you saying that's it? They're always going to fight me, down to the last human *cell*?'

'I . . .' Anna thought about it. 'I don't know, Dad.' She shrugged. 'I think so. Yes.'

For a moment Mallahide stared at her. Then, crestfallen, he looked at his feet.

'But . . . I've so much to offer!' he said quietly, almost to himself. 'A whole new way to live! A new era full of new sensations, a new way to share the universe – to share our knowledge and feelings and work together, in harmony, as a collective. And *the only reason*, the only reason why people won't take it, is that they're scared. Scared of the unknown.'

Anna looked at him. 'That's what people are like, Dad,' she told him. He really could be very slow on the uptake sometimes. 'Maybe if you hadn't spent so much of your time in research laboratories, you wouldn't be so surprised.'

There was a pause. Mallahide looked up.

'What about you, Anna?' he asked.

'What about me?'

'Do *you* trust me? Are *you* scared of the unknown like the others? Or are you prepared to take a chance?'

Anna's heart lurched in her chest: here it was, the moment she'd known would come. When she spoke, she was amazed at how calm her voice sounded.

'I'm sorry, Dad,' she said sadly. 'But I'm with the human race on this one, I'm afraid.'

'Oh, Anna . . .' said what her father had become. 'Not you too.'

BOOM! A sudden eruption of noise, followed by a rumble like thunder.

BOOM! The noise came again, closer this time, then—

WHAM! A jagged crack appeared straight up the side of the dome.

'It couldn't be,' said Mallahide, blinking.

In answer, there was a piercing noise like a squadron of jet engines taking off, like two aircraft carriers being grated against each other – a mashing blast of sound, a groaning tearing screeching bellow, inconceivably, immeasurably loud . . .

Tim's next blow smashed the dome of St Paul's like an egg.

The air went thick with plummeting tons of masonry. Mallahide's human projection vanished as the swarm formed a shield to protect Anna – and not a nanosecond too soon. Without an improvised umbrella of machines to deflect them, the tumbling ruins of Christopher Wren's masterpiece would certainly have crushed her to death.

Anna had dropped to her knees and held both her arms over her head. Useless as the gesture would have been, it was instinctive. After what seemed a very long time, the wreckage stopped falling – and she opened her eyes.

Sunlight poured into the cathedral, turning the dust in the air into a glittering shaft of gold. Anna was momentarily dazzled. But then the light was blotted out again.

To an answering groan from the cathedral's ancient walls, Tim leaned against the side of St Paul's. He stood on the tips of his hind claws, peering over the lip of the shattered dome to inspect the contents beneath.

Anna just stood there gaping.

She'd had read an Internet essay once about how the laws of physics made it theoretically impossible for a bipedal creature to live beyond a certain size. No bones (the theory went) would be strong enough to support it: the creature would literally collapse under its own weight. Yet there he was: here Tim stood in defiance of physics, of reason. But the strangest thing for Anna at that moment was the way Tim was looking at her.

Tim's eyes were like nothing Anna had ever seen. They glittered with ancient power. They looked into her and all through her, as if the mind behind them was examining every thought or memory she'd ever possessed. For a second all Anna could do was stand there, hypnotized.

Then – blasting past so fast Anna's hair blew about her head – Professor Mallahide took up Tim's challenge. The swarm poured out of St Paul's like a huge cloud of angry wasps.

And then the final battle began.

MORTIFICATION

'Tim is now all that stands between us and the end of the world.' Ms Plimpton's eyes were bright and moist. She sniffed, blinked, pulled herself together. 'And he needs our help. Cameraman? Can we get a close-up on *Chris* here?'

Chris watched with helpless horror as, cannon-like, the camera swung its muzzle onto him.

'People of the Earth, this is Chris Pitman,' said Ms Plimpton. 'I guess some of the sharper-eyed among you will be wondering what he's doing sitting here in a tank of water, clad only in his underpants. Well, all is about to become clear.'

Chris was blushing. He was blushing so hard it felt like his whole body had gone hot and red with shame.

'Chris here may not look like much, I grant you,' said Ms Plimpton with a dainty grimace. 'But he's an extremely fortunate young man. You see that bracelet on his wrist? Chris: hold it up, would you? And can we get a close-up on that too, please?'

Obediently – if reluctantly on Chris's part – both Chris and the cameraman did as she said.

'That's what brings us all here. For twenty-two years I've been watching over that bracelet, waiting for this moment.' Ms Plimpton held up a hand. 'Allow me to explain.

'The Defender exists to protect all living things on this planet. He is our world's Guardian Spirit, a living, breathing, fighting force of nature. The Defender doesn't work alone: the

Defender is an aspect of the life force inside every one of us. *That*, ladies and gentlemen, is why he needs our help. And that's where Chris comes in.'

She took a breath.

'Each time the Defender rises to protect us, a *representative* is called. One among us is chosen to be a channel, a point of focus for the energy that crackles and breathes in every cell of every living thing on Earth. That person – that ordinary, everyday, *fallible* person – will be the only one who can wear the bracelet. And the bracelet's wearer – Chris here – will form the connection between the Defender and the source of his power. Now, ladies and gentlemen,' Ms Plimpton added, drawing herself up to her full height, 'here's what we're going to do – and I don't want you to question me or think too much; I just want you to do it. First of all, I want as many of you as possible to come together and *hold hands . . .*'

She stepped up to Chris's side and took hold of the hand that had the bracelet on it.

'Don't be shy now,' she said. 'Don't be embarrassed. Believe me, if this doesn't work, then feeling like a bit of a fool is going to be the *last* of your problems. Come on, everyone!' With her free hand she gestured at the various people standing out of the line of sight of the camera. 'We need to lead by example on this one. And that includes *you*, Prime Minister,' she added sternly.

Gradually, with varying degrees of sheepishness, Mr Sinclair, Mr Wythenshawe, other military aides and any spare studio staff all stepped forward. Wythenshawe went round the other side of the paddling pool to take Chris's right hand. Before long, everyone except the cameraman and the sound guy had formed up in a line with Chris at its centre. The scene was pure theatre: if it wasn't for Chris sitting almost naked in the paddling pool, everyone would've looked like they were about to take a curtain call.

'All right,' said Ms Plimpton. 'You at home: are you holding hands? You'd better be, ladies and gentlemen, because here comes the important bit. I want you all to *concentrate*.'

Chris sat in the water, at the centre of it all, waiting. The studio lights beat down on his eyes and body like miniature suns. His arms stuck out to either side (Wythenshawe's grip was dry and firm; Ms Plimpton's was faintly clammy) and he was getting a headache. 'Feel it,' Ms Plimpton commanded. 'Feel the energy of the world all around us. Feel it inside you, quivering in every cell in your body. Feel it . . . and *summon it*.'

The silence stretched out.

'Close your eyes if you think it'll help. But concentrate, concentrate as hard as you can. Make that connection between us all as strong as you can make it. And reach out, reach out to the Defender, because this is when he needs us most . . .'

Chris bit his lip. *When was she going to realize?* he wondered. When was Ms Plimpton going to figure out how ridiculous she was being? Did she seriously expect – with two monsters out on London streets and the whole country just minutes away from nuclear apocalypse – that in the middle of all that, people were going to sit down in front of their TVs and all hold hands? It was pointless: completely pointless, and embarrassing, and stupid . . .

Wasn't it?

Chris closed his eyes and reached down into himself, remembering how he had felt last time, searching for the slightest sign that he was feeling that way again. With his eyes shut, the image on the screens of Tim and Mallahide facing off for Britain's future disappeared from view, if not from Chris's thoughts. He concentrated, and the flow of exhortations from Ms Plimpton to concentrate gradually faded in his ears, taking on a distant, lulling quality.

You, Chris, must join the world . . .

The fact was, he thought he *could* feel something. Much as he wanted to deny it, it was there. It had been there ever since the morning after he'd first been given the bracelet, sometimes strong and sometimes weak but constant, like the distant seething hiss of a TV tuned to an empty channel. He concentrated on that sound, that feeling in his mind.

It grew stronger. The constant sizzling and rattling seemed to expand in his brain as he focused on it. Perhaps this sound really *did* come from every living thing on the planet. Was it working? Was all this hand-holding and concentrating actually *doing* something?

'Yes,' said Ms Plimpton inanely. 'Can it be . . . ? Yes! Yes, ladies and gentlemen, I think I can feel something! Come on! You can do it! I think I can—'

No, Chris told himself savagely. No! It was stupid. This whole thing was ridiculous and stupid. What he was feeling wasn't this guff about the energy of the world: what he was feeling was an effect of the lights beating down and the attention and cameras on him – those things and being tired and embarrassed and *really pissed off*. He shouldn't be sitting there in a pool of water, in his pants, holding hands and concentrating on nothing. It was so uncool it was a joke – beyond a joke. What he should be *doing*, he realized . . .

. . . was helping Anna.

The idea came to Chris so suddenly he actually flinched. The water sloshed around him; Wythenshawe's and Ms Plimpton's grip slackened on his hands – and Chris snatched them away.

'Chris . . . what—?' asked Ms Plimpton, eyes wide.

Chris stood up. 'I'm sorry,' he told her – and, he realized, the world. 'Look, I'm sorry. But I just don't think this is going to work.'

Everyone stared at him.

'My friend's out there,' he said, pointing at the screen. 'She's in danger.'

He looked around the room, at the grown-ups all holding hands and still staring at him numbly.

'Fine,' he said. 'I'll go by myself.' And with (the footage showed) surprising dignity for a young man dressed only in his underwear, he strode from the room.

PUNISHMENT

The torrent of seething machines shot out of the dome.

Caught by surprise by Mallahide's sudden rush, Tim staggered back, swatting at his own face with his forepaws in an instinctive effort to wave the swarm away – but he needn't have bothered. Mallahide wasn't going to attack him. Not just yet. Not until he was *ready*.

Professor Mallahide was furious. He'd thought he'd taught the stupid creature enough of a lesson before, but clearly it hadn't taken the hint. Time to speak more plainly.

Released from its temporary captivity in St Paul's, the swarm expanded, casting Tim into shadow. Its edges began to droop downwards, stretching and forming points that – with sudden and eerie speed – thrust down, like stalactites, around where Tim was standing.

Javelins of darkness jabbed straight through buildings: they buckled concrete, shattered paving and impaled parked vehicles, which were then lifted helplessly into the air. While the lower half of the swarm returned to its insect shape, the upper body reared out of the boiling mass of machines, towering over Tim, great claws spreading.

Shaking the debris from his giant cockroach feet, Mallahide attacked.

Professor Mallahide was no martial artist: experimental science was his forte, not hand-to-hand fighting – but he'd been human once, and he'd been to school. Playground encounters had taught him a few essential moves, and those were what he used on Tim first. Encased in armour, faster than a freight train and denser than a tank, his first fist lashed out, punching Tim in the stomach. Tim bent double, all the air in his monstrous body huffing straight out in a helpless rush. The sudden gust of his exhalation tore trees out by the roots; billboards tumbled like playing cards – but Mallahide didn't notice or care. Knocking the wind out of Tim had just been a means to an end, an echo of the opening gambit of playground bullies the world over.

What came next was the headlock.

While Tim was still bent over round where the first punch had struck him, Mallahide wrapped two of his right arms around Tim's neck. Instantly the arms constricted, coiling up tight under Tim's jaws, tighter than would have been possible if they were filled with bones and muscle. Cutting off his breath with absolute thoroughness, they *bunched*, becoming almost impossibly dense and heavy as the professor concentrated more of himself into that part of his body.

Tim was trapped. His forearms flailed weakly, trying to reach his attacker, but with his shoulders now right up against Mallahide's armoured midriff it was impossible.

Once again, he was at Mallahide's mercy.

Almost casually, with his two free left arms Mallahide swung back and punched forward again – catching Tim two hammer blows that each landed with unerring pinpoint accuracy exactly where the professor had struck before. Enjoying the way Tim's entire body spasmed with pain under each blow, Mallahide struck him twice more just for good measure. Then, his playground-bully-fighting repertoire temporarily exhausted, the professor decided to get creative.

He shifted his weight, the vast mass of nanomachines moving smoothly and easily to do his bidding.

His left arms changed shape – spreading, hooking, grabbing across Tim's back.

The professor gave a great *heave*, jerking Tim bodily into the air –

– and let go, upending his hapless victim in a credible (if gargantuan-size) wrestling-style *throw*, right over his shoulder.

For Tim, the world swung, turning upside down. One second he was staring at the ground; the next, his world exploded into stars that, when they cleared, revealed sky above. Mallahide had flipped him, whiplashing Tim's entire body over onto his back.

The Old Bailey, the nearby building that had taken the brunt of Tim's fall, was squashed all but flat. Of the historic courthouse that had seen some of Britain's most famous criminal trials, nothing was now left but the outside walls. The centre of the building – when at last Tim struggled groggily to his feet again – had been instantly and permanently pulverized into a kind of dinosaur-shaped silhouette.

Gasping and shuddering, Tim shook his poor head to clear it, and groaned.

He got to his feet, staggering a little, and flexed his tail: he didn't even feel it shattering the remaining walls behind him, it was so numb.

Woozily, he looked up at his enemy.

Mallahide just waited.

The professor's first fury was gone now, its flames banked down into burning coals. He knew he could destroy his prey whenever he liked, so now – cat-like – he was going to toy with Tim a while. What was the nonsensical beast going to come up with next? Tim was pretty predictable. The professor reckoned he could hazard a guess.

Tim, for his part, prepared himself as best he could. His throat and lungs felt crushed and raw: he couldn't roar aloud any more, it would hurt too much, so he roared in his mind instead.

He was the Defender. It was down to him. He would succeed or die trying.

He lowered his head, scratched a great trough in the paving with his right hind claw –

– and charged.

MEANWHILE . . .

Chris's ears were burning. The doors to the makeshift studio swung shut behind him: he was alone. The linoleum floor was cold on the soles of his bare feet, but Chris was blushing so hard it felt like he was on fire.

First problem: his clothes weren't where he'd left them.

The room was now empty. His clothes were nowhere to be seen. And of course, everyone who'd been out here before had gone through into the studio to join in the hand-holding.

Chris glared at the cold silver bracelet on his wrist with real loathing. How had he got into this? *Why him?* Suddenly pinpricks of tears were pushing at the back of his eyes: he was just thinking of doing something really stupid like breaking his bare toes giving the walls a good kicking, or maybe just screaming his head off, when the doors opened again.

'Mr Pitman?'

Chris turned, ready to unleash his fury, and froze.

Wythenshawe had a towel in his hand. He threw it: Chris caught it.

'Thanks,' Chris muttered.

Wythenshawe nodded, then he gestured at the doors.

'That was . . . quite a scene in there,' he said.

Chris and Wythenshawe looked at each other. Wythenshawe was staring at Chris, and there was a strange kind of tension around his mouth, but Chris couldn't decode what emotion this was meant to express. Chris shook his head, stopped trying, and set about towelling himself down instead.

'You, er, don't happen to know where my—?' he asked.

'Your clothes? They're hung up on a rail outside in the passageway.'

'Thanks,' Chris muttered again. He took himself off through the second set of double doors. To his discomfort, Wythenshawe followed him.

'What are your intentions?' the government aide asked, watching him dress.

'Like I said: Anna's still out there. She needs help. I'm just going to try and see what I can do.' It was hard to sound brave, Chris was finding, while attempting to put one's jeans on over one's still-damp legs: *irritable*, that was how he sounded. Yes: irritable he could do just fine.

'How are you going to get over to St Paul's?' Wythenshawe asked. 'You'll never make it in time on foot.'

'I don't know,' Chris replied through gritted teeth as he put his socks on. 'Maybe I'll call a cab.'

'That would be quite difficult in the circumstances, I should imagine,' said Wythenshawe, apparently missing the sarcasm.

'You don't say,' said Chris. He sighed and stood up. 'Look, Mr Wythenshawe . . .' He stopped, put a hand to his brow, and took a moment to get his words in the right order. 'Thank you for the towel, and for telling me where my clothes are. Sincerely: I appreciate it. But can you help me in any other ways, at all? Or are you just going to stand there stating the bloody obvious?'

For a moment they looked at each other. Then suddenly Chris realized what that expression on the government aide's face, that weird tension around the sides of his mouth, actually was.

Wythenshawe had been *trying not to smile*. And now, at last, he was failing: Wythenshawe was beaming at him, with a secret glee that was all the more powerful for it having been pent up for so long.

'What?' said Chris.

'Follow me,' said Wythenshawe.

rrrRRRNNNNN!

Chris's head pressed helplessly into his seat back as, beside him, Wythenshawe floored the accelerator. Before the steel plate hatch had risen all the way up they'd shot out of another of the bunker's secret entrances: with a scream of rubber they skidded round a corner and set off.

Gripping the leather of the seat beneath him, Chris turned to look at the government aide. Wythenshawe was still grinning wildly.

'I'm not cut out to be a desk man, Chris,' Wythenshawe said out of the corner of his mouth. 'Action, not words, that's always been my motto, and *field ops*,' he added, emphasizing this with a yanking hand-brake turn that threatened to separate Chris from his breakfast, *'that's* where my heart's always been.'

'Er, right,' said Chris. 'Look, do you know where we're going?'

'Oh yes,' said Wythenshawe. 'We'll be there before you know it.'

If you don't kill us first, Chris added mentally. Which was worse? he wondered. Wythenshawe's driving or what waited for them at St Paul's? At that moment, Chris was having trouble deciding.

Chris and Wythenshawe were in one of the bunker's special black armoured police vans. Apart from the van there was, mercifully, nothing else on the roads – which was why Wythenshawe felt able to go so fast.

'So, Chris,' the government man said, still grinning, 'have you had any ideas about what we're actually going to do when we get there?'

'It's funny you should ask that,' Chris said miserably. 'No.'

'Good man!' said Wythenshawe, his grin only widening, 'act first, ask questions later. Chris, you're a boy after my own heart!'

The events of the previous few days had played a certain amount of havoc with Whitehall's road surfaces: there was a sudden BUMP, a lurch, then a ringing CRASH as Wythenshawe tested the van's suspension to the limit.

It was amazing how fast you could get through London without any traffic to stop you. In minutes the speeding police van was approaching their destination. The sounds of battle grew clearly audible over the noise the van was making. The juddering and quaking of the ground vibrated up through the seats. And then . . .

'Oh no . . .' Chris breathed.

Then he could see them.

Until that moment, the titanic hulking shapes of Mallahide and Tim had been obscured from Chris's view either by buildings or simply by the van's roof: the two monsters were just too big; there was just no way for Chris to crane his head down far enough to look out from underneath, even if it had occurred to him to do so. But Chris and Wythenshawe had passed the remains of the Old Bailey now: they'd entered the epicentre, the heart of the destruction, and looking down the vast swathe of carnage that the battle had caused so far, Chris was now able to see everything.

He saw Mallahide first. This was the first time that Chris had seen for real the whole of what the professor had become, and the experience was quite different from seeing it on a monitor: suddenly Chris found he couldn't look at anything else.

Mallahide was still in his half-insect form. His huge black humanoid torso reared up over the skyline like a mountain. The pincers on the ends of his various arms, each one big enough to guillotine a truck, snipped slowly and colossally on the empty air. At that moment Mallahide's craggy black armoured hind legs were still: he was waiting for something.

'Stop the car!' said Chris.

Obligingly Wythenshawe stepped on the brakes. The van lurched to a halt.

Where was Tim?

With a sudden wheezing shriek that was still loud enough for Chris to have to put his hands over his ears, Tim emerged from the wreckage of another hapless building. Covered in dust, shaking off clumps of brickwork, Tim struggled to his feet –

– *Right next to the van.*

'Oh, *sh*—!' Wythenshawe barked, the word drowned out by a protesting scream from the police van's engine as he abruptly slammed it into reverse. The interior of the van went dark. Chris experienced a drawn-out moment of utter and absolute terror, then—

WHAM!

The gigantic hind paw that had been about to squash them flat came down just a scant two metres in front of the van's nose. The impact tremor bucked the van upwards – Wythenshawe and Chris both hit their heads on the ceiling – but the spinning tyres greeted the shattered remains of the tarmac below them, and held. The van shot back, but the darkness in the windscreen remained as – for two whole seconds – the full length of Tim's massive scaly tail slid by overhead with a great SWOOSH.

'Well,' said Wythenshawe once he'd brought the van to a halt again, '*that* was a bit close for comfort!' His terrible grin was still fixed firmly in place: in fact, Chris reckoned, it was now even wider.

'We need to get to St Paul's,' he reminded him.

'By all means, dear chap,' Wythenshawe answered. 'But let's just sit here a spell and wait and see what our two large friends are going to do first, shall we?'

They watched.

Punch-drunk, Tim shook himself – an awesome sight. As the gigantic tail threshed the air, Chris couldn't help flinching in his seat: it seemed close enough to whip down and smash the van out of existence at any second.

Tim took a step forward: the van's interior filled with light again as the foot that had nearly squashed them came clear of the ground. Then, screeching defiance, Tim set off on the attack once more.

Tim was now bleeding from multiple wounds to his face, chest, and legs: he had clearly taken one hell of a beating already, but Chris could tell from the easy, unhurried way Mallahide moved into position to receive him that there was plenty more punishment left where the first lot had come from. With a pang of guilt Chris watched the armoured black legs brace for impact. Mallahide's pincer-ended arms spread wide as if welcoming their victim, and with a shattering concussion that left the van trembling the two titans clashed together again.

Four of Mallahide's arms locked around Tim's back. Tim's arms locked around Mallahide's waist. The two of them stood there in a bear hug, struggling for dominance.

'Right,' said Wythenshawe, gunning the engine. 'Off we go, then.'

'Now?' asked Chris.

'Of course,' said Wythenshawe. 'Best get this done while those two are occupied, don't you agree? I don't think we'd like it if they noticed us.'

Realizing the wisdom of this, Chris tore his eyes away from the struggling giants and started searching outside the window for St Paul's.

Chris's geography of London wasn't brilliant, as he would have been the first to admit. His knowledge of what should have been where was hampered even further by the fact that most landmarks in the area had been flattened. But even *he* knew that St Paul's shouldn't be this difficult to find: it was so big, you couldn't miss it. Unless . . .

Chris gasped when he saw it. Even Wythenshawe let his mouth fall open.

There was almost nothing left. The dome, of course, was gone and the rest of the roof had collapsed: without it St Paul's looked so different it was almost unrecognizable. The area around the cathedral was littered with chunks of masonry. Two entire sections of the walls were missing, and the remainder were sagging dangerously.

'Anna!' Chris yelled as the van pulled up. He'd got the door open, and was on the point of running straight up the steps into the cathedral, before Wythenshawe laid a warning hand on his sleeve.

'Steady on, old chap,' he said. 'Poor old St Paul's looks a bit shaky. You'd best let me take the lead on this, I think.'

Chris just wrenched his arm away. 'Anna? *Anna!*' he called.

Stepping out from behind one of the pillars of the main entrance, she put her hands on her hips.

'Chris,' she said, sounding exasperated, 'what do you think you're doing here?'

It wasn't quite the response Chris had been expecting. He gaped.

'I . . .' he said, then tried again. 'We . . .' He shrugged. 'Well, we're here to . . . rescue you, I guess.'

For a moment, Anna just stared at him.

'Honestly, Chris,' she said. 'You're sweet in a way, but you can really be incredibly dense sometimes. What about the plan? Why do you think I lured my father here? Why aren't you back at the bunker with Ms Plimpton, where you belong?'

'It didn't work out, Anna,' Chris told her. 'We did the hand-holding, the TV, the whole bit. But it just didn't work. I don't know, maybe what happened before was . . . a fluke or something. Anyway, I gave up, and here I am. So why don't you come with us?'

'Come *where*, Chris?' said Anna. She gestured outwards at the shattered landscape around them. 'Where do you think we're going to go? Haven't you been listening to what's been going on? You were the last hope. If Tim doesn't defeat my father, it's the *end*. The fate of the whole world is resting on how this fight goes, and Tim can't possibly win without your help!'

'But it's not *my* help, is it?' said Chris, losing patience at last. 'I'm not fighting this bloody battle! I'm not doing anything! My job, apparently, is to sit there in my pants in a bath of water on TV while everyone holds hands around me. My job is to look like an idiot! How do you think that makes me feel?'

'There's rather more at stake here than your feelings, Chris,' said Anna through gritted teeth. 'Wow. I thought you'd changed – you know? I thought there was a bit more to you than this constant obsession of yours with trying to be cool – but I guess I was right that first time. Being cool is really all you're about, isn't it, Chris? Every thought in your mind is all, *How will it look if I do this?* Well, I've got news for you.' She glared at him. 'I don't claim to know much about cool, but I do know this: *Trying to be . . . isn't.*'

She shook her head.

'You're not even shallow, Chris. You're *nothing*. And now . . .' She paused. 'Now, you've killed us all.'

THE CRUNCH

Tim felt Mallahide's arms lock around him and begin to tighten. That was when he knew: the final facts of it at last penetrated even *his* dinosaur brain. One way or the other, this was going to be the end of the fight.

Plumbing the bottomless blue depths of himself, Tim brought out everything he had. A burst of animal rage lit up in him like a bomb behind his eyelids. He locked his own arms behind Mallahide's back; his hind claws dug into the ground – and he hung there, squeezing with every cell, every particle of his being.

Time seemed to stretch. The arms around Tim's great sides tightened slowly, inexorably. In response, all the muscles in Tim's colossal ribs and back began to bulge and ripple as he tensed them, straining against the intolerable inward pressure that – if he once allowed himself to succumb – would crush the life out of his body. At the same time, though the effort make him snort and wheeze through his nostrils, Tim tightened his own arms – harder, harder still, until every muscle, every fibre was quivering.

The two titans stayed like that, locked together, and the world waited, holding its breath.

'This is Fiona Pilkington of the BBC, bringing you the latest from the battle. As you can see, we're flying in the BBC helicopter and we've got about as close as we dare. Military choppers have stopped bothering to police the area: now the whole world can watch as this astonishing battle enters its last moments . . .'

On-screen, though the footage wobbled and shook, the two monsters sprang into focus.

All over the globe people sat frozen in front of their screens, locked on the events unfolding on the London streets. Since Ms Plimpton had gone off the air, the helicopter coverage had become all there was to see. The emergency broadcast might have ended in farce and confusion, but everyone – everyone – was watching this titanic struggle as, now, it reached its climax.

Mallahide poured on the pressure. He could have changed his shape again: he could have turned himself into anything he liked and escaped Tim's grip without effort, but instead he concentrated every last bit of himself on his final move against his opponent.

There was something strangely fascinating about how Tim always got up, always came back for more. Tim's tenacity would be admirable if it wasn't so stupid: it was a shame, really, that Mallahide wouldn't get the chance to study this determination and where it came from in more detail. But it was clear to the professor that simple punishment was no longer going to be sufficient. There could be only one outcome now. Tim was going to have to die.

Imperceptibly at first, the sky over London began to darken.

It wasn't Mallahide's doing. From across the whole world storm clouds were rolling in to bunch overhead. A strange pressure seemed to be building in the air. Weird little gusts of wind caught up scattered bits of paper and rubbish and whirled them into the sky. Bin lids bowled along crippled streets, hot dust hissed on the breeze, shattered brickwork trembled where it fell, and Chris – suddenly and unaccountably cold – found himself folding his arms and pulling his sleeves tight about him to trap what warmth remained in his body.

'Something's happening,' he said.

'Oh no . . .' whispered Anna. 'I think this is it.'

Mallahide's arms crushed at Tim's sides. Tim could feel the great bones of his ribs grinding as the pressure began to take its toll. The pain was intense. Tim's whole body was a mass of it. So for the last time, knowing what the answer would be, Tim reached inside himself and concentrated. Gathering his slow woolly thoughts as best he could, Tim reached out, crossing the distance to the mental presence he'd felt before – the tiny person that stood between him and the source of his strength.

Chris felt it. He shivered and bit his lip, but his mind remained set: he had tried, he had failed. He wanted to help Tim, a part of him knew what was going to happen, but there was nothing to be done. Inwardly, he turned his back again.

Tim tried to roar, but all that came out was a kind of low whine. He squeezed, just once more, a last-ditch effort.

No answer. It was no good. Exhausted, he gave up.

Instantly the pressure surged inward. Feeling Tim's defences finally weaken and fail, Mallahide rushed to make safe his triumph. There was a sudden dreadful sound: *crack*, like a cannon shot. It was heard around the world.

Tim's eyes rolled up in his head: a fine green drizzle sprayed up his throat and out over his teeth. His great arms released their hold on Mallahide's armoured black back, and fell to his sides.

Tim went limp.

For a long second, Mallahide just held him like that. Then slowly, knowing the whole world was watching, Mallahide's arms lifted Tim up into the air. As the swarm bulged and fizzed with effort and concentration, Mallahide hoisted the tonnage of Tim's slack body overhead in a final gesture of victory.

Then he threw his defeated foe down onto the ground.

WHAM! The shock wave spread outwards, knocking Chris and Anna helplessly to their knees. Another of St Paul's great walls collapsed. The wind, which had been steadily rising, blew up into a terrible shriek. Then died down.

Chris opened his eyes. Mallahide was coming towards them.

His ranks of bristling legs rippled eagerly. He grew even bigger in Chris's eyes as he got closer, a heaving black mass of clashing limbs and snipping scissor fingers, a mobile factory of death.

'Anna!' Chris yelled weakly.

The look she gave him then made Chris feel like his heart was turning to ashes.

'It's me he wants,' she told him hollowly. 'You'd better go.' She turned and stood between him and her father.

'Wait a second,' said Chris. 'This' – he shook his head – 'this isn't right. This can't be happening! It can't be!'

That was how he felt. Tim's defeat, the impending nuclear catastrophe, the hulking nightmare figure of Mallahide coming towards them – it was all like a bad dream. But it was real. Slowly, almost gently, two black trunk-like arms swung down on either side of where Anna was standing. Closer they came, closer still, their edges blurring, becoming translucent. The scissor hands passed straight through her. They caused no wounds. There was no blood. One set of the great blades swept through Anna's torso, the other through her legs. Then the arms went back to Mallahide's sides again.

Anna began to take on a grainy, effervescent quality. Chris blinked; his eyes were watering, but it wasn't that: Anna had frozen in place, like the image on a photograph, and now she too was blurring – her outlines, her skin going translucent for a moment, then bursting apart. For a last long second her afterimage hung in the air . . .

Then Anna was gone. She had joined her father at last.

'No!' said Chris. 'No! No! No!'

'Ladies and gentlemen,' said Fiona Pilkington from the helicopter overhead while her cameraman's eye remained glued to his eyepiece, 'what you're seeing is coming live from the scene. Mallahide has won, and – in this corner of the world at least – it seems humanity has lost. Is there nothing that can stop the professor and his nanomachines? Is there nothing that can stand between the British Isles and Armageddon?'

At the emergency session of the United Nations, the room had fallen silent. Each representative was equipped with a hotline to their respective military commanders; each had the day's codes for missile launch memorized and ready to be given. At bunkers and silos all over the globe, nervous but resigned military personnel stood ready to receive them, ready to press the buttons and start the processes that would wipe Great Britain from the face of the Earth. They had made their peace with what they were going to do. They believed they were ready to face the consequences. But as Mallahide's claws reached down again – for Chris this time – they waited. Poised to unleash Britain's utter destruction . . . they paused.

Chris didn't care about that. Chris didn't care about any of it: Chris was thinking about Anna.

He stood there staring at the spot where she'd been standing.

He thought about the first time he and Anna had spoken, back at the British Museum. He remembered how he'd felt then, and since. Chris had never met anyone like Anna before: someone who could throw herself into things and not care what people thought. She was sharp, she was brave, she was *cool* – and, until a moment ago, Chris had been hoping one day they might be friends.

Anna had been right, Chris realized. Through most of the events of these extraordinary few days he'd managed to keep his distance and not let himself get fully involved. Now, at last, that changed. He cared about Anna. He cared about what had been done to her.

Chris was angry.

The bracelet grew warm.

'What's that I just saw, back from where Mallahide is standing?' asked Fiona Pilkington. 'Can it . . . can it be? Is . . . is the tyrannosaur *stirring*?'

The cameraman blinked. His attention had been caught too. He focused on Tim: there! There it was again! It was true! His tail was twitching!

And now . . .

Chris felt that weird, bulging, *swelling* sensation, like his brain was growing too big for his skull. It wasn't just rage, he realized: it was the bracelet. The bracelet was doing something! *How?*

Suddenly he understood.

Ms Plimpton had got it halfway right. He, Chris, had been picked to represent the human race. But it wasn't a question of making everyone hold hands. It was him. He'd changed. He'd begun to care about something outside himself.

He, Chris, had *joined the world*.

Mallahide's scissor fingers reached down towards him. Chris ignored them. There was an opening sensation at the back of his head. A connection was forming, coming straight up through the soles of his feet – and something . . . something was coming through.

On Chris's wrist, the bracelet flared. The world brightened around him.

'Come on,' he said. 'Come on: get up. Let's do it.'

Woozily, wheezing, Tim sat up. Shaking the masonry dust from one of his enormous arms, he wiped the blood from his jaws – and looked around.

Tim was as surprised to be alive as anyone. Stranger still, considering the battering he'd taken, he felt *amazing*. There was a weird feeling building inside himself, a sudden kind of strength – something (Tim realized) he'd felt before.

Something old and vast seemed to take hold of him and shake him, *rushing roaring racing shrieking bursting*. Every sinew in Tim's body seemed to swell with power – and then it *relaxed*. Joyfully, hardly believing it, Tim opened his mouth . . .

. . . and breathed.

The blast struck Mallahide like a spear of light, punching straight out the front of his chest. He froze, arms spread and pincers outstretched, his half-insect form looking like he'd been pinned that way for some entomologist's cosmic-scale collection.

They stood there like that. The boy, the bracelet, the breathing giant monster, and their enemy. And then Professor Mallahide began to change.

The edges of the swarm went first. All over the surface of Mallahide's cockroach-brown armour, tiny spots began to form. Flaws and imperfections swelled into clusters and clumps as – struck by the torrent of light – the nanobots spontaneously began to change their interactions. Drawing on the information they'd stored at their creation, they began the process of reconstruction.

The insects came first, a dispersing hail that pattered on the pavement. Pigeons poured, clattering, from Mallahide's arms; rats and squirrels ran from his legs in a sudden and seething tide. Now came the people, their faces and bodies forming under the shuddering brown mass, mouths still open in the screams they'd worn when Mallahide had taken them. Released, they floated to earth – shocked, confused, themselves once more. But still Tim continued to exhale.

By now the swarm had shrunk down almost to nothing. Of Mallahide's hulking armoured torso all that was left was a single human silhouette, stranded in the air. Impaled by light, arms outstretched, the figure dissolved, then vanished.

Tim closed his mouth and the light winked out.

Mallahide was gone.

'YES!' roared Ms Plimpton in the bunker, punching the air.

'Yes, ladies and gentlemen,' echoed Fiona Pilkington, 'you saw it here first! With an extraordinary blast of energy from his *breath*, no less, it seems that Tim has come back from nowhere to defeat the Mallahide swarm when we least expected it. The scene below us is one of utter confusion. We're not quite sure what's happened: frankly,' Ms Pilkington added, 'until some facts are established, your guess is as good as ours – but it seems that somehow Tim has *saved the day!*'

'Stand down! Stand down!' From the room in the United Nations the order spread to missile silos and nuclear submarines around the world. The day's secret launch codes remained just that: secret. Fingers retreated gratefully from their red buttons. The world sat back from its screens and breathed a sigh of relief.

Tim and Chris looked at each other.

Tim looked tired: every inch of his tyrannosaur body was banged and bruised and battered. Chris knew how he felt. Chris's legs were shaky, his vision was full of purple splashes, and he was sure he was going to collapse again any second. But Chris smiled.

In answer, Tim let out a deafening bellow of glee and delight that finally blew out any remaining windows in a twelve-kilometre radius. Tim's little blue planet was safe for now, and he was happy. Tim turned. Thrashing his great tail, he stomped off back to the Thames and out to sea – there to heal and wait until he was needed once again.

Chris watched him go. There were (he supposed) worse

fates in the world than playing sidekick to the Defender of the Earth . . .

Then, with a nervous pang in his heart, he looked down.

The streets, the whole world, seemed suddenly to be teeming with people: picking themselves up, helping the injured, and gamely – but with varying amounts of success – trying to figure out what the hell had just happened to them. They were a London crowd, a West End crowd, a *young* crowd for the most part: Chris figured they could look after themselves all right. *But where was the person he wanted?*

Surely the power couldn't have destroyed her too when it destroyed her father . . . could it? Surely Chris's change of heart couldn't have come too late: surely he'd get the chance to make up for what an idiot he'd been! Chris searched the crowd, suddenly frantic.

'Chris?' said a voice.

It was her!

Chris grabbed Anna and wrapped his arms around her. Then, of course, he let go and stepped back, blushing again furiously.

'Sorry,' he said.

'It's all right, Chris,' Anna told him quietly. 'It's over.'

Chris smiled at her. Anna was human again.

Anna was *real* . . .

Anna, Afterwards

London had stood for two thousand years. It had survived the Great Fire, it had survived the Blitz, and being the battle-ground for two giant monsters didn't seem to have cramped its style much either. Everything was slowly getting back to normal. London's sewers crawled with vermin. Pigeons ruled its skies, gleefully marking out their dominion in little grey-white spatters on its remaining buildings. Repairs had begun. People had gone back to work.

Anna Mallahide was sitting on a bench in one of London's parks.

Anna was alone. She had no mother and, now, no father. She had no other family and, apart from Chris, no friends. Anna knew she would soon have to make some powerful decisions about the next part of her life. But just then she wasn't particularly interested in making them. At that moment, Anna was amusing herself with the squirrels.

She shook some nuts out from a packet into her hand. She jiggled the snacks in her palm in what she hoped was an inviting manner – and waited patiently.

Presently, overcome with greed, the American grey squirrel took the bait. With a swipe of one claw it snatched a nut. The squirrel was fully intending to jump back to a safe distance to consume its prize in peace but, much to its surprise, it found it couldn't.

Anna had grabbed it.

She could do things like that now. Among other new skills, Anna was faster than before: she was so fast, in fact, that by the time the squirrel started to react to what Anna was doing, most of it had already happened.

The squirrel had started to change.

Its blood altered in various subtle ways – immunity to the smallpox virus being just one of them. It also shrank slightly and, with a shimmer, its grey fur suddenly turned red.

Anna let go. The squirrel dropped to the tarmac and jumped back, chattering in outrage. When it had reached for Anna's hand, it had been *Sciurus carolinensis*. Now it was *Sciurus vulgaris*. Anna wondered whether the squirrel knew it had just changed species: on balance, Anna thought, probably not. It was probably just annoyed because it had dropped its nut.

Anna sat back. Having made another step in her private effort to redress the imbalance in the squirrel population, she allowed herself a small smile. Then she shook a couple more nuts out of the bag and started waiting for another American grey.

She was her father's daughter: it seemed she'd inherited his talents.

But Anna was not going to make her father's mistakes.

ACKNOWLEDGEMENTS

There's someone I'd like to thank here but sadly can't: the late and much-missed Maggie Noach. It was Maggie gave me this chance to chase my dreams as a writer, and I'll never forget her. One of her last e-mails to me concerned a certain portly British politician and the 'wonderful splatting noise' she suggested he might make if he happened to get caught in the destruction of the Houses of Parliament. I'd love to have heard what she thought of how this story turned out.

A special, giant, *monster* thank-you to the following people:

Penny for taking me on, and Gina and Jill and Josie for continuing to look after me so well. Kelly and Ben for their seamlessly brilliant transatlantic tag-team editorial onslaught – hurrah! Publishers' reps, booksellers and librarians everywhere for the amazing jobs they do. And my brother Jack – once again – for his formidable skills as a test reader ('A scientist would never use that word,' was one of his early-draft notes!).

I'd also like to thank Katie the WebSphinx, who is a genius. My mates for keeping me at least intermittently sane. And, as ever, my wonderful girlfriend Laura, with all my heart.

On with the sinister masterplan!

Very best wishes to you,
Sam
9 May 2007